To my Mom

the Steele Wolf

Chanda Hahn

ISBN: 0615812236
ISBN: 978-0615812236
THE STEELE WOLF
Copyright © 2013 by Chanda Hahn
Cover design by Steve Hahn
www.chandahahn.com

~ I ~

I never expected heaven to be this way. It was my own personal utopia, with rivers of the clearest water and fields of green surrounded by beautiful mountains. Every tree bore plump fruit, and I was able to lie in the soft grass and listen to the song being sung by the river. I never wanted to leave; there was so much light and joy in heaven. I couldn't imagine going back to where I had just left, because here I felt no pain.

So if I were dead, why did I feel as if I were burning from the inside out? Gasping, I clutched my stomach in agony and looked around in horror. My beautiful garden was turning black. The soft grass I was lying on turned to sharp pieces of glass. The once-gorgeous trees turned to ash and blew away in the wind. *"NO! NO! I don't want to go back."*

I tried to sit up to stop the garden from disappearing and sliced my hands on the grass, which had turned razor sharp. The clear river rippled red like blood, and the skies turned dark as night. I cried out again as the burning pain in my stomach increased.

Glancing down, I watched as the blood, my red blood, poured from the gashes on my hands, only to change before my eyes to black. Another stab of pain in my stomach, and I gasped and coughed and felt my body get sucked out of my dying garden as if I were traveling down a narrow tunnel backward to collide with a thud on a cold steel table.

I had died. I knew it. I had tasted heaven, but my soul wasn't ready to give up the fight, and now I was back in hell. Only once again, I couldn't move—I was paralyzed from the drugs they'd given me, strapped once again to the table. I couldn't open my eyes. My lids felt like lead weights, but I could listen and overheard Raven and Crow discussing me.

"What makes you think she's strong enough to survive when the others didn't?" Crow asked.

"Because this one's not like the others. Her blood makes her stronger, more immune. She's the only one of her kind." It was Raven, the leader of the Septori. My hands itched to move against him, to try to fight.

"I hope you're right, because I'm tired of hauling out the failed ones. When will you know?" Crow whined.

"Not for a while. It's going to take weeks of careful injections of the siren serum, plus more sessions on the machine to activate it in her bloodstream. Then we wait. It will slowly change her from the inside out. These things take time." Raven spoke as if to a dimwitted child.

I could imagine the Raven even with my eyes closed, wearing his red hooded robe and his silver mask. He always wore the mask, unlike the rest of his followers, the Septori.

"What about the others?"

I felt the cramping of my stomach as my body tried to fight off the newest experiment.

"We will keep trying the portensi serum on the rest of them. I'm hoping one of them will survive the process," Raven explained.

"None have yet," Crow whined again.

The pain was too much. It was what had reminded my body that I was still alive and brought my soul back. Only now I was burning alive and I couldn't stop it, my body uncontrollably twitching from the pain.

"Wait. Raven, she's coming back."

"I told you this one could survive." The Raven spoke triumphantly as he walked over to my prone form, silver glinting off his mask. My eyes flew open at the touch of his cold skin on my wrist. He pulled a dagger from his robe and brought my wrist up. There were already numerous half-moon puncture wounds along my arms from the machine, but the Raven took the knife and cut along my arm.

I couldn't move; all I could do was blink in pain, but I had to know, I had to see. My eyes followed the Raven's as he and I both looked at my wrist to see which color of blood would flow from my wrist. It was black.

***

Gasping, I woke up. My hair was drenched in sweat. It was a dream...or was it? Each of my dreams had a semblance of truth to it. I pulled up the sleeve of my shirt to look at my arms. The small silver half-moon scars shone in the moonlight, barely discernible, the reminders of my months in prison and the torture machine I called the iron butterfly.

I couldn't wait; I had to know. Reaching under my bedroll, I grabbed my knife and very gently pricked my finger and watched as a beautiful red drop of blood formed on the tip. Sighing in relief, I placed the knife back under my bed. I shivered as I recalled what Raven had said in my dream: that the experiment would change me from the inside out. I saw that the fire had died down to a bare glow and scanned the camp. I saw Hemi's back as he leaned over and added more wood. Quickly, I lay back down and pretended to sleep.

The nightmares were getting worse. We had only been on the road two days, but the closer we got to the Ioden Valley, the more frequent they became. I would wake in the middle of the night, drenched in sweat. Too scared to sleep, I would lie in my bedroll until the sky lightened. For the most part I had been able to hide the nightmares from my traveling companions, but they were becoming suspicious. There was nothing I could do to hide the dark circles under my eyes.

But there was one individual I couldn't hide the nightmares from. My horse, Faraway, was my closest friend and companion. His voice and encouragement kept me sane during these long sleepless nights, but even he couldn't keep the dreams and visions away. No one could. The worst part was that they were real, and the people I saw in them were after me.

The Septori, led by their leader called Raven, were the ones who had kidnapped and imprisoned me, and erased my memories. I was one of only two surviving test subjects. Kael was the other survivor, and he had single-handedly orchestrated our escape.

Joss and his godfather Darren Hamden had found me floating almost dead in a river after my escape from the experimental prison. Joss healed me and took me to the Citadel, which was a school for young Denai. There I worked as a servant until Raven's experiments began to reveal themselves within me. My unholy gift began to surface, and I was forced to pose as a student to learn to control my unnatural abilities.

I was different; I could strip another student of her gifts and use it against her. I had accidentally done it to a young girl who bullied me. Since then I'd learned control and how to pull power from myself and my Guardian, who was a horse. Until Bearen, my father, had come to the Citadel to find me and bring me back to my clan.

There was some joking and laughter, but the men stayed quiet, as if they were always listening for danger. Someone handed me a roasted leg of rabbit and I ate it slowly, studying my clansmen.

Bearen was the largest of the men, with blue eyes that matched mine, and a hawk nose protruding from the black beard. He was the obvious leader of the group. All of the men deferred to him and even served him the first portions of the meat cooking over the fire. Most of the men here wore short-sleeved leather vests that reached to their thighs, with hoods attached. Their upper arms were bare except for intricately designed armbands in varying gold, silver, and bronze. Around his shoulders each man wore a distinct pattern or color of various furs and leather arm bracers. Each warrior had an array of axes, mallets, or swords.

When I had finished eating, I waited until I saw Bearen finish and made first eye contact. He nodded at me to come over, so I threw my bones from dinner into the fire and silently sat next to him. I had been avoiding talking about the Septori and the Denai for the last few days, because the men still felt like strangers. There was no waiting anymore; I needed to confront my father.

"You're safe now," he stated.

"I was safe before at the Citadel," I hinted.

"Bah!" He spat into the fire. "You can't be safe with that kind, — you can't trust them. What they can do is unnatural. They are inbred heathens."

"Is that why you won't participate in the council sessions?" I asked.

"Thalia, you know the reasons why." He looked at me questioningly. "You were my biggest supporter for not going!"

I looked at my feet.

He cleared his throat. "They said something had happened to you."

"Yes, it's time you know the whole truth." I took a deep breath and let it all rush out: the story of my imprisonment, torture, and lack of memories, but I left out going to the Citadel. When I was done, I couldn't even make eye contact, for fear of the disgust I would see in my father's eyes. Instead, I saw indignation, helplessness, and fury, but it wasn't directed toward me. He was directing it toward himself, and I could have sworn I saw tears in his eyes.

My father howled his rage. "WHAT?" He kicked a stump into the fire, which sent ashes flying. He grabbed his sword and motioned toward the closest warrior.

Immediately one of his own clansmen picked up another sword and ran to meet him in challenge. The sound of swords clashing made me jump to my feet and run toward Faraway in fear. Grabbing his mane, I was about to swing myself up bareback and ride away when a hand grabbed hold of mine atop Faraway's mane.

"Wait, Meja Faelan." Stunned, I turned to look at the hand holding mine and saw the one I had nicknamed Fox Fur. "You should know he only fights to vent his anger. When he has bested all of us, he will calm down again." He held out his hand toward the fire, and I followed him back and took up a seat farther away from the fighting. Bearen had beaten one of the clansmen and another had jumped up eagerly to join in the fight.

"I should know all of this, but I don't," I said regretfully to him as he took up a seat next to mine. "I can't remember anything before…"

Fox Fur stiffened next to me and turned to look at me closely. "You don't remember us?" he asked. "You don't remember me?"

Breathing out a frustrated sigh, I turned and looked at Fox Fur a little closer. He was easily the second tallest clansman, next to my father. He had long auburn hair that was tied back with a leather strap. Alert green eyes and an angular jaw complemented his features, making him resemble the animal that he wore on his shoulders, the fox. His boots were well-tended, and his arm circlet was silver in design and wound around a very well-toned arm. Looking away from him quickly and back at the fire, I shook my head.

I heard him swear. "Excuse me — I think it's my turn to join your father." Grabbing a discarded sword, he stepped in the path of Bearen's downward swing and blocked the sword from hitting another clansman. I watched in fascination, as they were both equally matched fighters. Bearen had been fighting for some time, and you could see that he was tiring. About a candle mark later, the fight ended in a draw. Huffing and puffing and with many slaps to the back, both fighters walked away and knelt by the fire. One of the men brought them each something to drink.

An elderly man handed a tankard to me, and I took a swallow before almost choking on the pungent taste. He watched me give it a wary look before pushing it to the side. The grey-haired man sat down next to me, cross-legged.

"Sorry, Thalia, I overheard your earlier conversation. It's hard to believe that someone we've all seen raised from a kittling is unable to remember us." I heard a catch in his throat, and I saw that his grey eyes turned glassy with emotion before he cleared his throat and looked at me kindly.

"I'm Odin, your chosen godfather, and that young one," —he motioned to Fox Fur— "is Fenri." Pointing to the others in the camp, he named them off: Gotte, Forsk, Hemi, Aldo, and Eviir. I tried to place the names with the faces, but I felt a moment of panic as I realized it wasn't sinking in. I started to twirl my hair around my finger as I tried to recall each of their names from memory.

"Ahh." Odin pointed at my finger and hair. "You may have forgotten us, but some things, Thalia, you won't ever forget. You used to do that as a child." He smiled in triumph. "You are still our little Faelan, little wolf." Whereas Joss called me "little fish," my clan called me "little wolf." I couldn't escape the stupid nicknames.

"Odin, what happened to me? What happened to me the night I disappeared?"

Odin's face turned to stone, and he stopped smiling. "You should ask your father, and not bother an old man with heartache in the retelling." He started to shut down.

"Please, Papa Odin?" The name just slipped out.

The old warrior looked at me, and his eyes became glassy once more as he looked into the night and tried to blink away the tears. "See, you called me Papa! You're slowly remembering." Turning his head, he looked to see where Bearen sat before continuing, "It was the night of our Hunter's Moon feast. Amidst all of the rejoicing and celebration, you had disappeared. We don't know exactly when, but your father didn't notice your disappearance until morning, thinking you had stayed the night with your cousin."

"I have a cousin?"

"Two," Odin answered. "When we couldn't find you, your father sent every warrior out on horseback looking for you. For months we've been searching, never giving up hope. We heard of some messengers that were looking for a young girl similar to you, and Bearen decided to investigate. The closer we came to Calandry, the more rumors we heard. Your father had every intention of asking the Council for help in finding you, which is a big step, when you know how against Council affairs he is. It was just our God's favor on us that we found you there."

Looking at the gruff bearded form of my father staring moodily into the fire made me realize that underneath his warrior exterior, there was a kind and loving heart, even if he refused to show it. Getting up, I walked over to Bearen and sat next to him silently.

"It would be best when we get home that you don't speak of those heathen Denai," he said gruffly. "You will go through a cleansing ceremony, and then we will allow some time for you to readjust to being home." Pulling out a sharp knife, he stabbed at another piece of meat that was roasting on the fire and turned it over. "The less you speak of these horrors, the easier it will be for you to resume your old life. I will make excuses to the clan to leave you well enough alone until you are able to remember your old life."

"Father?" I spoke hesitantly, letting the word I had just said sink heavily into the night air. "There's more—we must speak about what happened to me and what led me to being in the training program at the Citadel."

"You are strong and will recover. You are my daughter," he said fiercely.

"No, Father, the Septori…they did something to me when I was captured, and I'm no longer the same. I'm different. I'm twisted. I can do things no Denai—" A quick intake of breath between his teeth and a feral gleam in his eyes made me halt any other words I was about to say.

"No daughter of mine would willingly discuss that which we have forbidden," he growled quietly. "It's against our laws, and you must promise to never do it again. Do you hear me?" I could see a sense of panic start to ride the wave of his emotions.

All I could do was look down at my hands and nod my head, holding back a sense of hopelessness. Bearen commanded me to get some sleep because we would be leaving come first light. Odin brought me a blanket and I curled up by the fire, willing myself to sleep. I lay awake, picturing my return to the village and fearing what would happen when they learned I was no longer the same young innocent girl who left months ago, but something that represented everything they hated. Shivering, I felt Faraway try to soothe me, and then he sent me a thread of power to make me sleep. I prayed for a dreamless sleep.

~2~

The next morning we woke before sunrise and were on the move again. My back and legs were sore from so many hours in the saddle, and I wished for a moment to apply to my muscles the salve that Mara had given me, which was sitting, ever so tempting, in my saddlebag. But my fellow clansmen were in a hurry and spoke little as they packed and readied to leave.

Once again, I found myself in the middle of the group. When the road became too narrow to pass side by side, Bearen and Fenri rode lead and Forsk scouted ahead while Hemi, Eviir, and Aldo rode rear guard. No one was in the mood for talking, so I spent most of the ride silently conversing with Faraway. Odin rode to the side of me whenever the road would allow, and he would shoot me little worried glances.

Finally fed up with his troubled looks, I decided to confront him. "What is it, Odin?" He looked embarrassed that I had caught him.

"You have changed, little one." He paused, thinking. "What has happened has made you grow up too soon." Looking at the road ahead, he went on, "The bad ones have stolen some of your carefree spirit. Instead you look like you are ready to meet the executioner."

"I can't help it, Odin. I'm scared." Reaching down, I began to rub Faraway, more in an effort to comfort myself than him. "I'm going back to where it all started. I'm hoping that by retracing my steps, it will bring back the memories of what happened that night. Somehow I disappeared amidst friends, family, and all of my clansmen, and no one saw anything." Letting out a deep sigh, I looked intently at Odin and let all of the fear and anxiety I was trying to hide show in my face. Lowering my voice, I whispered, "What if it happens again?"

"We will be prepared this time, Thalia." He sat up straighter on his horse, slapping a closed fist against his breast. "No one will steal one of the daughters of the Valdyrstal clan again." His eyes shone bright at the thought of battle. "They will taste our blades and wish for a swift death, but will be granted a long and painful one."

I shuddered at the bloodlust that was evident in Odin's eyes. The clan's ruthlessness and protective spirit were probably the reason why the Septori had not taken any children before me. I wondered what had changed. Thankfully, the path we were traveling on narrowed, and he had to drop back to follow me. I let my mind wander and settle on Joss, his crooked grin, sandy-blond windblown hair and green eyes deep with emotion, and my heart sang with joy before plummeting in shame.

I felt a pang of guilt at leaving the way I did, but I knew that I couldn't fully open up to Joss unless I knew more about myself. I owed Joss more. I knew deep down I wasn't being fair to Joss.

Kael's stern face slowly formed in my mind, and I tried to blink it away, tried to think of anything else. But Kael fighting his way out of the prison flashed through my mind, and then Joss appeared again, bandaging my head. My own mind did a review of all of my encounters with Joss and Kael: Joss holding my hand during my bone setting; Kael fighting off a pack of mad dogs; Joss arguing with Healer Prentiss on my behalf; Kael killing the assassin; Joss stubbornly guarding me while I slept. Back and forth each scene played out, and I felt more conflicted about Kael and Joss.

And then a thought hit me, and I almost pulled Faraway to a standstill as the enormity of what I was doing sank in. I was running away. I was running as far as I could from all of the conflicting emotions.

My hands trembled as I realized, in some crazy way, I had some feelings for Kael as well. Joss was handsome, caring, and safe, while Kael was striking, insensitive, and spiteful.

What was I thinking? I mentally berated myself. I hated Kael. He had done everything he could to make me hate him. Maybe that was why. Maybe my heart knew that he was trying to make me hate him, so instead I pitied him and cared for him. The emotions I felt were only compassion for an uncaring vagrant warrior. Right? As of right now, I would focus on what was good for me. When I discovered more about myself, I would somehow go back to the Citadel and be with Joss.

I must have spent a good hour debating with myself about my feelings; I had completely forgotten where I was. The sun began to go down, and the woods we were traveling through became more sinister. We were traversing a mountain pass. Faraway stopped moving, his withers twitching in nervousness. Glancing around, I opened my mind to him.

What's the matter?

Bad smell all around us.

Not waiting anymore, he opened himself up to me, and I could sense what he smelled. He was right; it was bad.

This was no longer the Citadel's arena; this wasn't a practice game where I couldn't get injured. This was real. I closed my eyes and pushed my senses deep into the forest, searching, something Professor Weston had taught me.

I jumped when I sensed men on all sides slowly pressing in. We were surrounded. My heart started to pump nervously as I looked around. Odin and the others had stopped when Faraway stopped, the trail too thin for them to pass me. Ahead, Bearen and Fenri paused and stared back at me questioningly.

A quick mental command to Faraway, and he began to dance about a bit. Steeling my voice to sound sure and not scared, I called out loudly, "My horse has gone lame. I need help." Bearen carefully turned his horse and rode back to me, leaning down to look at Faraway's flank.

"Bearen, there's no time," I whispered urgently. "There are men in the woods, and we are surrounded."

"Nonsense. You must be imagining things." He looked at me intently. "Forsk would have seen them. He would have warned us."

Quickly, I closed my eyes and scanned ahead past the men, who had stopped and were quietly moving into position around us. I grabbed my head as the sight of bushes and leaves rushed past my vision, making me dizzy, praying and hoping that I was wrong. It took me a second, but my fears were confirmed as I saw Forsk's body in a ditch farther up. He was sixty meters off the path in the woods, lying face down with arrows protruding from his body. His position suggested he'd found the men and had tried to run back to warn us before being shot down.

Tears formed in my eyes as I looked at Bearen, begging him to believe me as I whispered vehemently to him, "Forsk is dead."

Bearen paled. "How do you—?"

I cut him off with a wave of my hand. "Bearen, if you don't do something, we'll all be dead." I glanced over his shoulder to the woods behind him. "Please, you must believe me," I begged. "They're almost here."

Bearen's jaw clenched as he battled inner doubt. If he chose to believe me and armed the men, then he would be affirming his worst fears. If he chose to ignore me, he could go on believing I was still his innocent daughter, but he could lose more lives. He was taking too long.

Jumping off Faraway, I confronted him. "We don't have time. You must decide, but either way I will not sit idle and wait to die." Storming over to Odin, I reached behind him to pull his sword from the sheath strapped to his horse. "Odin, we are about to be attacked — warn the men."

Odin stilled, cocked his head, and listened before giving me a short nod and riding back to warn the men. Walking back to my horse, I knelt and rubbed Faraway's leg as he made a big show of pretending to be lame. I would have smiled if the situation weren't so dire.

Fenri came to me on foot, leading his horse. He stopped and pulled his horse in behind me, and gave a curt command to his horse to stand firm, making a living shield out of horseflesh for me. Sliding his sword and small axe from the saddle pack, he kept it low behind the horse. I watched as the rest of the men slowly moved into defensive positions, acting casually as if we all had stopped to take care of a lame horse. Most cast furtive looks at the woods around them as they silently prepared for battle.

Bearen looked deadly as he walked over to me.

"Most of the group is down wind, and on foot. There are three behind us and two ahead of us," I commented, not looking to see the astonished expression on Fenri's face.

"This terrain is not made for horses. It would be better to meet our foes on foot. Their blood will cover this valley before the night is over for what they have done to Forsk," Bearen growled.

"They have stopped and are waiting to see what we are doing," I said.

"It would be better if we could force them to come out of the forest. I hate not being able to see my enemy," Bearen replied, twisting his fingers around his axe.

"I will force them out and give us the advantage, but you won't like the means by which I do it," I said solemnly, leaving the choice in his hands.

His only answer was a grunt, and the readjustment of his hands on his battle axe. "I hate waiting." He glanced at me and looked away quickly.

Smiling and taking it for the "yes" he would never verbally give, I scanned the forest for help, trying something I wasn't sure if I could actually do. Searching, I found a family of opossums sleeping and a small herd of deer that were moving away from the smell of men. Finally I found something that could be the distraction we needed: a wolf pack.

They were a small pack of five, but they would do the trick. The pack consisted of one white, two brown, one black, and a grey wolf. Gently, I entered the alpha male's mind. I wasn't sure if I was even strong enough to do what I was about to attempt, but I figured if I could speak to Faraway, why not other animals? It was a leap of faith.

Help me? I asked the large brown wolf. He shook his head and snarled at a brown male that had come to close to him, nipping him in the hindquarters.

Frowning a bit in concentration, I realized I was dealing with the alpha, who to lead a pack would need to be very strong-willed. I was about to enter the mind of the female when I felt a tentative touch back. Pulling away, I followed the thread back to a young grey male with a notch in his ear, who stood frozen at the ready in the opposite direction of his pack.

Help? he asked. Following my good fortune, I didn't hesitate to link minds.

Yes, I need help in protecting my pack from these bad men. I sent him the picture of the men, who even now were closing in.

He growled in anticipation, shuffling his feet and snapping his jaws.

I'm strong, fight to death, ja? I almost laughed at hearing a wolf accent through mindspeech.

We will need the rest of the pack's help. Can you get them to come?

Ja, come, I'm strong, pack stronger. Not sure how he was going to do it, I pulled my mind back and came to my father staring at me in obvious horror.

"Get ready," I told him. "They are going to come to you." It was barely two minutes later when we heard snapping, growling, and screams as three men came running from the forest, two wolves chasing them down.

"Ah-ha!" Bearen yelled in triumph, running to meet the first foe head on, swinging his huge axe. The man slid to a halt and fell backward into the dirt as he tried to duck the swinging blade. As all intent of a surprise attack was now gone, armor-clad men from all sides came rushing down the hills to engage us in battle.

My fellow clansmen flew into action, their fighting very basic and strong. Even though they relied more on brute strength over speed and skill, I couldn't help but be proud of my fearless clansmen.

Fenri threw his smaller axe into the shoulder of a large attacker. The injured man kept coming and swinging his own blade. I gasped as the two met in a furious dance of blood and clashing metal.

The wolves chased the rest of the men from hiding and attacked them as they all ran toward us. Looking up, I saw the grey wolf snapping and growling at a tree while desperately trying to climb it. The wolf's large claws raked deep furrows in the bark as he jumped and snarled. I barely had time to ponder his behavior as I heard the familiar *ppffsst* sound of an arrow being loosed.

I heard a grunt and saw Bearen stumble as an arrow lodged in his chest. Screaming, I grabbed my sword and engaged in battle, fighting my way toward my father. Another *pffsst* followed, and tears stung my eyes as a matching arrow protruded from Bearen's chest few inches lower.

Screaming at Fenri, I pointed toward the tree as I desperately looked for a bow and arrow; nothing. None of my clansmen fought with bow and arrows. I had no way of reaching him in time. I was about to take another step toward my father when my whole body was knocked to the ground by a grey blur as an arrow embedded itself in the dirt where I was previously standing.

Rolling over, I saw that the grey wolf had given up on the tree and instead knocked me out of the arrow's path, but not before getting an ugly shoulder graze. I looked to my father, whose chest was covered in deep red. He was wide open for an attack. I knew what I had to do.

Protect my father, I commanded the wolf, who grinned dog-like at me, tongue hanging out of his mouth as he ran toward my father's opponent. With a growl, he jumped up and bit the man's sword arm. I heard a scream and the sound of bone breaking.

Opening my senses, I looked for the archer and found him perched high up in the tree, nocking another arrow. Rage consumed me, and I didn't even blink as I pointed my finger at the arrow embedded in the dirt. Raw power flowed through me as I whipped it around and sent the arrow flying at an impossible speed straight toward the archer.

The arrow didn't lodge in his chest but blasted right through, leaving a gaping hole. I watched dispassionately as he fell from the tree with a thud.

Odin was limping from a bleeding leg wound but was still able to swing his axe with nimble dexterity, beheading his foe. Fenri was fast and deadly as he fought off two attackers. Rushing in, I engaged one of them and saw Fenri's shocked face as I blocked a deadly downward thrust. I showed no mercy as I kicked the man between the legs, and smirked as I wondered what Kael would think of that move.

As the man crouched over and grabbed his groin, I swung the handle of my sword and struck him in the temple as hard as I could. He crumpled to the ground and didn't move. Moving through the battlegrounds toward my father, I wondered if I was now becoming hesitant about killing since I had dispatched the archer so ruthlessly.

Come, I called, and Faraway ran to me. I swung up on his back and raced over to Bearen, who had moved farther and farther away from us and was now kneeling on the ground, clutching his chest. The grey wolf stood in front of him, hackles raised, teeth bared in challenge at the ugly attacker with a short sword, who was trying to dance around the wolf to get to Bearen.

Hold on! Faraway warned me as he ran toward the man and rose up on his hind legs, striking out with deadly hooves. The man was so shocked he dropped his sword and fell on his back as he tried to duck the hooves. The grey wolf lunged for his neck, and I heard snarling and a gurgled scream that quickly ended as his throat was torn out.

I knelt by my father, who had fallen on the ground and was pale as death. Pressing my ear to his bloody chest, I tried to listen for the life-giving rhythm of his heart. Not being able to hear it, I grabbed a leaf and held it to his mouth. The faint flutter of the leaf told me he was alive.

"Oh, what do I do? What do I do?" I cried, the tears freely falling, as I heard a bloodcurdling cough erupt from his large chest. "I don't know how to do this!" I fervently wished that I had taken a healing course.

"Bearen, I don't think I can take the pain and heal you at the same time. In fact, I'm not even sure I can heal you."

Odin came over and leaned down to look at Bearen's wounds. "It's pierced a lung, Thalia." He looked at me gravely. "There's nothing we can do now but pray that his spirit finds peace."

"No! I just got him back." I glared at Odin. "I won't let him die." Reaching forward, I gritted my teeth and pulled out the arrow that was piercing his lung.

"THALIA! What are you doing? You are just killing him faster!"

Placing my hands over the wound, I tried to open my senses and follow the instructions Healer Prentiss had given to the students when they healed my leg. I could see the hole in his lung and the blood flowing in, filling it up. I reached deep inside myself for the power to heal it and found none. What?

"NO, NO, NO, NO!" I chanted.

FARAWAY! HELP! I mentally called. I felt a rush of power, his, and I sent it toward the hole, siphoning the blood out and at the same time encouraging his lungs to keep breathing. Faraway was giving me his strength. I focused the energy into the surrounding tissues and encouraged them to reknit and grow. A grunt and cough erupted from my father as sweat beaded off his forehead. He gritted his teeth in pain.

I tried to reassure him. "I'm so sorry, Father." The tissue was healing, but very slowly. I didn't think my father had that much time, and I felt myself beginning to panic when another wave of power washed over me and I felt a cold nose press into my shoulder. Without looking, I knew it was the wolf. I was drained from vision searching and my arrow stunt from earlier, and I was using all of Faraway's strength to do the healing, so I took what the wolf was willing to give, pulling that power into the healing process. The lung reknit itself faster, and I was able to quickly heal any other damage. Before moving on to the second arrow, I released his lungs and watched him breathe on his own for a minute or so.

Odin's eyes had gone wide, and his face turned grey when he saw what I was doing. My hands trembling in exhaustion, I reached for the second arrow, but he stopped me.

"Thalia, I wouldn't have believed it if I didn't see it for myself. I will do it." His strong hands pulled out the arrow from Bearen's shoulder. He grunted in pain. Desperately wishing that I had Joss's abilities, I did what I could to heal the shoulder wound, albeit more slowly this time.

When I was done, my father was breathing on his own and seemed fine except for the pain. I leaned down and rested my head on his large chest and cried.

I cried for what I had almost lost, realizing that my heart remembered my father even if my mind didn't. My tears made my father's vest damp with their wetness, and the smell of dried blood tickled my nose, but neither one of us moved. I knew he was well because I could, in this position, listen to the beating of his heart, and I uttered a prayer of protection over him. When I felt a light touch on my head, I almost moved, but the touch began to stroke the back of my hair, and I sighed in relief as my father tried to comfort me as I comforted him.

~ B ~

We stayed the night. My skin crawled as I tried to help with the cleanup. Odin and Fenri kept shooing me away and telling me to watch over Bearen, who was on the mend but just tired and sore. After all, the healing process was painful. I wasn't talented at taking away pain, and I myself felt drained and sluggish. So after numerous requests, I collapsed on the ground and stared at the bonfire that lit up the night sky.

The smell of the dead burning made me want to retch, so I pulled out a spare piece of cloth and tied it around my face. Odin had counted thirteen bodies, and saw the tracks of at least two who had escaped back into the forest.

"Well, Thalia, my girl," he had said to me earlier. "It didn't look good for us. Fifteen to six were not good odds."

"Seven. Fifteen to seven," I countered, raising my eyebrow at him, daring him to dispute me.

"Aye, girl," he chuckled. "Fifteen to seven, and they had the high-ground advantage and an archer. We would have been hard put to come out on top without more casualties." Odin solemnly looked past the bonfire to the wrapped body of Forsk, which was slung over one of the horses.

Aldo had gone on ahead and brought him back to camp. He would be returned to the village and his body given to his family.

A sad howl filled the night, making Odin jump and curse. "Darn wolves," he swore. "They are what tipped the scale in our favor, and I'm grateful, for if it weren't for them we wouldn't have made it. But why do they continue to hang around?" He walked away and picked up a stick and threw it into the woods, screaming.

The wolves spooked Odin and many of my clansmen. They wouldn't understand that they were there because I had asked them to stay and guard us. I was already getting strange looks from Eviir, Gotte, and Hemi, who were kept in the dark about what I had done to heal Bearen. They knew something had happened because they saw him go down, but no one wanted to voice aloud any speculation. Because what I had done, no matter how good, or how right it was, went against everything they believed in. I knew deep down that it was too soon to tell them about the wolves.

Bearen was propped up against a stump and was staring into the large bonfire. He hadn't spoken since I healed him, and I wasn't yet ready to address the situation, either. I was a coward. I also hadn't seen to the other small injuries of my clansmen. They set to bandaging and stitching up each other's wounds with practiced ease. Thankfully, they all had only light flesh wounds.

The men had stripped down anything of value from the dead bodies and found nothing to signify who they were or what clan they were from. They could have just been a band of mountain bandits, but Fenri didn't think so.

"We came this way four days ago and saw no sign of bandits. We don't tolerate them on our lands. Most people know better than to trespass. This was something else."

He was right. I had to agree. But that was hours ago, and now all I wanted to do was sleep. My eyes had started to droop when I felt another touch in my mind.

Nothing's out here but rabbits. Want to chase rabbits. Rabbit is good.

I felt my mouth start to drool at the thought of eating rabbit, but the flavor that came to my mind and mouth was not cooked rabbit, but raw and bloody. I coughed to try to clear the taste out of my mouth. That was weird. I could usually see through Faraway's eyes if I wanted to, and we could sense each other's feelings, but this was the first time I had shared taste. And with the wolf, no less.

Ughhh. I grimaced. *Ummm, that's all right, you don't have to share with me.*

My answer was a panting laugh. But since the wolves were still here and hadn't run off, I decided to ask him how he was able to get the pack to come and stand guard if he wasn't the alpha male.

I did not give them a choice. I made them come.

A confused set of images flooded my head.

I don't understand?

Vorl is good alpha for the pack. A mental image of the brown wolf I had originally tried to ask for help popped in my head. *He is strong and fierce. When I leave here, Vorl will be leader again.*

You took over the pack, just to help us. How could you do that?

You needed me. You needed us. I'm strong.

Where are you going?

Another panted laugh filled my mind.

I'm searching.

For what? He didn't answer. *Will you be able to control the wolves to guard us until we leave? You're not leaving before then, are you?*

Yes, we guard as long as you are here.

Thank you.

Ja, burning humans make us hungry. We hunt rabbits but still guard.

And then he was gone from my mind. I was still confused as to what exactly the wolf was, when Faraway decided to interject.

Don't worry about him. He knows his duty.

What duty? I don't understand.

He's a guardian. He's on a journey to find his chosen one. Though I think he was a little disappointed to find out that you already had me. I am, after all, the finest guardian.

You mean there are more like you?

Faraway snorted. *Of course there's no one like me. I'm—*

How many more? I interrupted.

My horse became silent and refused to speak further on the subject, but it was the most he had ever disclosed about guardians. And knowing that the grey wolf was a guardian and was watching over us eased my mind.

Odin had said we would reach Valdyrstal's clan home in another two days, depending on how slowly we took our pace for Bearen. But I, too, needed sleep, because I was exhausted, and I knew that Faraway was equally tired.

~ 4 ~

Three more very slow days of rocky travel brought us to the home of the Valdyrstal Clan. Cresting a hill, I had my first view of my home, and my heart flip-flopped in anticipation. The village, which lay amidst the Shadow Mountains in the Iodin Valley, consisted of many large wooden buildings that could easily hold multiple families apiece. Each was decorated with beautiful carvings of animal designs on the columns. High pointed roofs sported multiple fireplaces per building to fight off the obvious cold winters the people faced each year. Each home had painted wood shutters over its windows and large doors. On rare occasions when the winter was too harsh, the people would bring the horses and cows into their homes to help increase the body heat.

I could see the fires of about fifty dwellings within the valley. Odin explained that there were branches of our clan that lived farther up in the mountains and preferred to spend the winters up there trapping, bringing in the sought-after furs. Breathing in the smell of cold air and stew cooking, I had a feeling of completeness — of being home.

Fenri took out a silver-tipped horn and blew three short blasts into the chilled air, the sound echoing through the valley. A light was lit in a watchtower, and the returning sound of another horn announced our arrival. Torches were lit and doors opened as men, women, and children poured out of their homes to greet the returning clansmen.

I had lost feeling in my toes late yesterday, and Fenri had wrapped my boots with fur that he turned inside out. Many of the men were used to the cold weather and barely blinked at the drop in temperature, and they still wore their arms bare.

Fenri, noticing my chattering lips, shook out a soft white fur cloak, and I gratefully accepted it as I wrapped it around my shivering body.

"We came prepared in case we found you," was all he said.

I could tell the fur was of the highest quality, and I felt a brief flash of heat in my cheeks as I rode past all of my clanswomen. Many gasped in surprise, and whispers followed us. I saw cold expressions, and many of the women wouldn't meet my gaze. I wondered what I had done in the past to receive such a welcome. We rode past them and up to the largest wooden dwelling with a giant wolf carved into the highest peak of the roof.

Aldo took Faraway, and Odin stood next to Bearen protectively in case he needed help getting down from his horse. Bearen made only a small groan as his feet touched the ground; I kept my distance and waited until he entered our house first.

The room was large, with a fireplace on one end, wooden benches, chairs covered in fur, and a large table and bench for meals. The kitchen was on the other end of the room and had another fireplace, which was burning already. Stairs by the kitchen led to more bedrooms upstairs.

Bearen crashed into a large chair by the fireplace and buried his hawk-like face into his hand. A small, tired groan escaped him. I went to the kitchen and started water boiling for some kava. When it was done and I brought him a cup, he looked at me in surprise before taking it. He gave me a look before taking a small hesitant sip and drinking the rest of it down in a greedy gulp.

"It seems that someone taught you to make kava."

Surprised, I asked him, "Did I not know how to before?"

Turning his large form in his chair, he looked at me carefully before speaking. "Thalia, you would never touch the stove or the wash. But here you are, cooking, tending to your father, fighting in a battle — which you have no business doing — and caring for a bewitched horse."

"I don't understand."

Shaking his head, Bearen sighed. "Siobhan does all of that. As the Clan Leader's daughter, you are given a level of status that is second only to mine. You don't have to do any of it. We have others who cook and clean for us." He stared off into the distance, and his words started to slur together.

His words shocked me a bit. I had become so self-reliant over the past months that I didn't know if I could go back to being waited on by others. I saw my old self in a different light, and I didn't like what I was learning. "Did I have any friends?"

"You were the closest to Siobhan, my brother Rayneld's daughter. But, Thalia, you didn't make a lot of friends among our people. You understood that a strong leader is more important than a friend. If something should happen to me before you're lifebonded, then Rayneld would be the head of our Clan. "

"What?" I felt myself go weak-kneed at the sudden talk of marriage.

Looking at his tired and aged face, I could see that Bearen, despite a gruff appearance that would ordinarily instill fear in a man's heart, was lined with worry.

"It is why we mustn't speak of what you did in the past, because by our own laws, you would be banished into the mountains, without food, water, or horse." His knuckles popped as he clenched his fist tightly. "I have just gotten you back, and I don't want to lose you again. And I definitely don't want my brother to know what happened. So keep quiet around Siobhan. If he learns what you did, he'll try to have you banished."

"Can't you change the law? You're the Clan Leader, surely you could." I broke off as Bearen shook his head sadly.

"The law is what we hold most holy here. It is why we have survived for so long in a wilderness that no one else wants to inhabit; it is our lifestyle. Our children are taught the laws from birth, and we pride ourselves on being pure, unlike the Denai. It's only the land border that says we must be a part of the Denai-infested Calandry."

My eyes began to widen as I started to take in what he was saying. "Do you mean that..." I couldn't finish.

"Valdyrstal is, always has been, and always will be a vassal to Sinnendor."

~5~

"Then why pretend? Why pretend to be loyal to Calandry?" I shouted, frustrated and secretly torn.

"Bah! We have never pretended to be loyal to those heathen pigs." Bearen lunged forward and spat into the fire. "It is why we don't go to the Council meetings, and why we deny their heathen ambassadors entry to our land. We are the direct descendants of the banished king of Sinnendor, King Branccynal II, who was sent to the Shadow Mountains."

My mouth dropped in confusion and shock. It finally made sense. The protectiveness my family had over pure bloodlines…but I wasn't sure how it was possible. "How? How can that be?" I blurted out in confusion.

Bearen leaned back in his chair and grabbed his pipe before going on. "You know the story of the war between Avellgard, which is now Calandry, and Sinnendor. When Sinnendor's King Branccynal II was defeated by the Denai, he couldn't return home. His army was destroyed, and his younger brother forcefully took the throne of Sinnendor. So the king and what was left of his loyal followers sought refuge in the cold, undesirable Ioden Valley to live a quiet life in disgrace."

Neither one of us spoke for a minute, as I let his words sink in.

"Look at our crest." He pointed above the fireplace to a barely discernable worn-out tapestry. On closer inspection I saw that it wasn't actually a tapestry but an old and faded black war standard with a silver wolf. "We kept our family crest and renamed ourselves Valdyrstal."

"Valdyrstal means 'wolf of steel,'" Bearen chuckled. "The crest is the same as that of King Branccynal II, who was my forefather. Therefore, you have royal blood in your veins — you are his direct descendant. And I will fight for the right for you to rule our clan of Valdyrstal over my brother any day. King Tieren of Sinnendor doesn't have anything of your heritage. If Branccynal had never been banished, then you would be the heir to Sinnendor. Alas, that is not the path chosen for us. And it is why we live up here in the mountains and seclude ourselves from the Denai way of life and detest them so."

"Does King Tieren know about us? Does he know that the line of Branccynal still lives?" I asked.

"Of course," Bearen growled angrily. "It's the reason we can't go home to Sinnendor. They have made it very clear to us that they would kill us if we ever went back. They won't attack us because no one dares set foot in Calandry for fear of the Denai. But he keeps a careful eye on the Valdyrstal clan. Don't be fooled, Thalia — Tieren knows all about us. He has his spies." Bearen coughed. I was worried about his healing lungs, but everything looked healthy.

"If only he knew that we have become content with our way of life. Thalia, we may still be vassals to Sinnendor, and live in Calandry, but we are our own people and have been for years. We are now just Valdyrstal clan," Bearen said sadly.

I couldn't believe it. The Denai must know that the Valdyrstal clan was from Sinnendor, yet they still acknowledged them as a part of Calandry and had even tried to give them a vote on the Council. This changed everything. I was about to say so to my father when he interrupted my thoughts.

"I hope you regain your memories quickly, because I've been doing my best to distract the men from asking too many questions about you." Turning his beady blue eyes toward me, he held me frozen in his gaze. "They know that something's different about you. Because no matter how much I try to deny it, you are not my daughter who went missing from here months ago. You look the same, but you're different."

Pulling my hand from the arm of his chair into my lap, I looked at my fingers, head down. "Is different bad?" I asked quietly.

Leaning forward, he rested his large hand on my head. "Oh, Thalia, what am I to do with you?"

Those words rang over and over in my head throughout the night and most of the morning. I got up at the first ray of light that peeked through my green shutters and went downstairs to start breakfast. I was very grateful that Tearsa had put me to work in the kitchen and had been hard on me. I turned over the ham on the fire and pulled out a fresh batch of sweet corn cakes from the oven. *The old Thalia would never do this*, I thought. But I didn't care; I wanted to do this for my father.

The sound of the door opening and closing with a thud made me almost drop the bread as I turned in surprise to see a girl about my age, dressed in blue with a red fur cloak. Pulling the hood back revealed dark braids pulled up intricately and secured with ribbons, and the darkest brown eyes.

"I'm so sorry that I'm late, Thalia. I wasn't feeling well last night, and I just heard the news you came home this morning. I won't do it again," she stammered, rushing over to me, stopping when she saw the bread in my hands.

The heat was soaking through my towel, and I needed to turn and drop it quickly on the oven before I burned myself. Turning back I saw her mouth quickly close, and she smoothed her skirts down. "Why, umm," she went on.

"It's okay, Siobhan. I can handle breakfast for Father." I smiled at her, and I saw one petite eyebrow raise in question.

"No, really, I've learned how to cook over the last few months," I said reassuringly. Her eyebrow rose even higher, and I felt myself burst out laughing in response. She was shocked by my outburst and had slowly let herself start to laugh with me when my father's voice boomed out from above.

"What's going on down there? Can't a man get any well-deserved sleep?"

"Not if you want any cooked ham, fried eggs, and fresh-baked corn cakes!" I yelled back.

"CORN CAKES!" was the only retort I could hear, followed by a loud scuffling upstairs. What followed could only be described as the sound of two bears fighting, followed by a loud thump, before a door was thrown open and Bearen lumbered downstairs in a slow and somber manner.

"Well, ahem, if you made corn cakes, then we shouldn't let them get cold," he said in his most nonchalant voice. "How about I, uh, help you put them on the table?" Reaching for a hot cake, he jumped back and put his large fingers in his mouth. "MFFFHOT!"

"Of course they are hot. I just pulled them out of the oven." Rolling my eyes, I caught Siobhan looking at me as if I had sprouted horns. *Oh, dear*, I thought. *I failed again.* Sighing, I brought everything to the large table and set it out for everyone to eat. Siobhan stayed to eat at my insistence, but she seemed ready to bolt at the first chance.

She asked me if I would need her today and I couldn't think of a reason to have her stay, but I decided to invite her to stop over tomorrow. She left, looking confused and relieved at the same time.

"Well, so much for taking this slow and not scaring everyone off," Bearen grumbled, the evidence of corn still apparent in his black beard. "Keep cooking like this, and soon everyone in the village will know that you are not the same girl, I guarantee it."

"Father, I don't know how to be that girl again."

He just grunted in affirmation. "I have business to attend to with the elders."

"Should I come? Do you need me?"

"No, this is business that would be better handled by your absence." Bobbing my head in understanding, I watched Bearen leave.

After cleaning up the mess I had made, I looked around the house to find something to occupy my time. Since nothing fit that category, I went upstairs to my room to change into warmer clothes. I found a blue wool short-sleeved jerkin with hood, trimmed in white rabbit fur, and white doeskin boots, also lined with fur, in my armoire. At the bottom on the floor was an intricate wooden box carved with flowers and birds. The box contained elaborate armbands. Some were silver with aquamarine stones, and others were gold with rubies.

Feeling like I was treading on someone else's life and not mine, I gently fingered them before selecting a silver armband that had a unique design and sliding it up my arm. I was shocked when I looked at myself in the mirror. Granted, I was wearing my own clothes, but the person staring back at me was a stranger. A cunning, strong-hearted woman who lived by clan laws. I swallowed nervously as that image disappeared and I saw myself. A fraud.

~6~

I had been cooped up for three more days, hiding from the world, from my clan, and from my father. I grabbed the fur cloak before heading to the central stables. Going around back, I let myself into the stable and found Faraway.

Run fast? he asked.

Yes!

After I saddled him, we headed out to a field, and I let him have his run. It wasn't long before the sound of pounding hooves could be heard from behind me. Drawing back, I looked over my shoulder and saw another rider riding hell bent toward me.

Faster! To the woods, Faraway.

Faraway ran like the wind and headed into the woods. As soon as we had disappeared a ways, I had Faraway slow, and I carefully stood on his saddle and latched onto a tree branch that overhung the path we traveled on. Quickly shimmying up to a higher branch, I sat and waited as Faraway waited farther up the path, getting ready to run as soon as the rider drew closer.

I heard the sound of the horse panting and the man curse as he came into view.

Go! I commanded Faraway, who took off, making a lot of noise but never going so far that I couldn't draw on him for power. We hadn't fully tested the distance of our bond. When the rider and his horse came into the woods and saw Faraway farther up, the man cursed again and changed direction, heading toward Faraway and me. When he came near my tree, I concentrated and pushed a branch farther underneath me into his path at the last minute, and he hit it with a thud and flew backward off his horse. The horse panicked and dashed farther into the woods.

"OHH, stars!" the man cried as he slowly lifted himself off the ground. His hood fell back to reveal familiar auburn hair and pain-filled green eyes.

"Fenri?" I called down from the tree. "What are you doing?"

"Thalia?" Fenri looked around the forest floor in confusion before looking up. "What are you doing in the tree?"

"Bird watching," I teased.

"Can't you see birds just as easily from the ground?" he asked, oblivious to my joke.

I sighed. "I didn't know who was chasing me, and I thought this was the easiest way to find out." I lay along the huge branch on my stomach, not moving an inch closer to the ground.

Looking up at me with newfound respect, he continued, "That is smart." Confusion filled his eyes. "How did I fall from my horse?"

"I think you must have hit something," I said as truthfully as I could while trying not to break eye contact or betray any hint of a smile. "Why were you chasing me?" I asked sternly, sitting up on my branch, comfortable in the fact that I was still high enough to be out of his reach.

He gazed down at his feet before he looked up at me. "I thought you were running away."

"Why would I run away? I just got home."

"Has your father spoken to you yet?"

"About what?" I asked, feeling myself start to get angry. He was dancing around the subject as if I were a two-year-old.

"Thalia, if you can't remember, then maybe it is for the best."

"Oh, spit it out, Fenri!" I snapped. "I'm not a child that is going to run away."

"You may have already done so."

"What?"

"I won't say anything else until you come down from the tree. I promise that I mean you no harm, but this is ridiculous."

Sliding back along the branch until my rear hit the tree, I turned and lowered myself down and had a moment of panic as I realized that to get into the tree, I had stood on top of Faraway. There was still a good five-foot drop. Gritting my teeth, I let go and felt warm hands encompass my thighs and squeeze as I was caught midair and lowered gently to the ground.

Fenri made sure my footing was good and then backed up, giving me space. Taking a deep breath, he went on, "Your father just revealed your future lifemate to the elders."

"I don't understand."

"Thalia, you've been different since coming back. Your father is worried about the clan succession and about you. You need a strong lifemate who will help you lead the clan after your father."

"How could he do this to me?" I blurted out, turning my back on Fenri, while I mentally called to Faraway, who was around the bend.

Fenri went on, speaking quickly, trying to convince me, "Bearen and Rayneld don't see eye to eye. They've had an intense rivalry since childhood. He's worried that you'll be banished if you don't have a husband. He did what he had to do."

"No! He didn't. He could have asked me, given me more time," I shouted, frustrated at my inability to do anything.

"No, he couldn't. If your father didn't take these necessary steps, your uncle would have and still could petition the council for clan rights and clan leadership as the strongest candidate. Your uncle would be the clan leader, followed by his son, Bvork."

Biting my lip, I kept myself from commenting in anger as I listened to everything that Fenri said. After he quit speaking, I slowly turned toward him. "Who did my father choose as my lifemate?"

Fenri stood back about six feet from me, and he looked nervous as my horse slowly walked back to me.

"He needed someone who knew what happened to you when you were captured, and the experimenting and about your gifts. After all, we all saw some unusual things in the pass. What we saw was enough to make us question some of our beliefs. We all took a blood oath to keep your secret."

"That would mean one of my clansmen who fought in the battle at the pass." My mind worked quickly as I thought about being bonded to each of them. "Who?" I asked quietly, too quietly, because Fenri didn't respond at first.

"Who?" I said again, louder, my fingers curled into a fist of fury and fright.

Fenri slowly met my eyes.

"Me."

~ 7 ~

My heart dropped. I grabbed Faraway's mane and pulled myself up. Faraway felt my agitation and danced back and forth.

"Thalia, don't run away again." Fenri spoke firmly, beginning to show some of his warrior spirit.

Turning Faraway back, I said, "What do you mean, 'run again'?"

"The night you disappeared was the night I had planned to ask your father to consider me for your lifemate." He spoke roughly. "You disappeared before I asked him."

Looking Fenri over, I thought about the bravery he had shown at the pass. He would make a good clan leader.

"Fenri, I can't say what I thought back then. But today— right now, I have to decline."

"Why?" he said stubbornly.

"Because I've already lost my past, and I can't let my future slip through my hands without a fight."

His mouth pressed into a firm line of understanding, and he nodded his head in acceptance.

I rode hard for home, letting Fenri chase after his horse, which, according to Faraway, was stopped by a stream a quarter mile away. Riding up to the door, I left Faraway and strode into the house, yelling for my father.

"What?" the great voice rumbled back, as he was sitting barely four feet from me in his favorite chair.

"You chose my lifemate without consulting me? How could you?" I yelled at him.

"I had to. Rayneld was acting too pleased this morning, and I heard rumors of him going before the council." Even though Bearen ran the clan, the council of elders was used to decide on any discrepancy of the laws, for someone had to make sure the clan leader didn't betray them.

"Well, I refuse," I firmly stated. A feral gleam of challenge rose up in Bearen's eye, and I knew that I looked just as menacing. After all, this was the man I got my famous temper from.

"You choose to willingly disobey your father?" he growled.

"Yes—a thousand times, yes!"

Bearen threw his hands up in the air in disgust. "What in heaven's name, girl, do you want me to do?"

"Why do I have to have to be married? Why now? I'm too young to have my future decided."

"It's not your future I'm worried about. It's the clan's future. If you don't have a man by your side soon, then Rayneld may try to press the ongoing witchcraft rumors and have you banished. I may even be banished, and he'll take over the clan. And you know that he won't stop trying until I'm in the grave. I can't imagine what will happen if he takes over."

His words hit me like a slap in the face. It wasn't about me — it was about our clan and the struggles they would endure under my ruthless uncle.

"Well, if you don't want me to choose a husband for you, than I have one option left. It's one that even Rayneld and the elders can't argue against. I'll call a Kragh Aru."

My mind struggled to recall the words, but finally an old memory started to surface. It was Odin telling me stories of warriors competing in an elimination contest for money, land, and even a bride. For some reason, this idea didn't bother me as much as the idea of an arranged marriage, because I saw a chance to get the upper hand. It wasn't the best idea, but I could enter. I could win the prize and buy myself time, because I wasn't ready to get married. It was a gamble, and I knew my father was hoping I would say no and wed Fenri. Instead, I did the opposite.

"Yes, I you're right. We need to have a Kragh Aru."

Bearen stuttered in surprise at my announcement, proof that I had caught him off guard. "Was there something wrong with Fenri?" he asked.

"No, I actually hope he wins," I lied, knowing full well that I wanted to win, but if I didn't, then I hoped Fenri would. I knew Joss would never be allowed to be my lifemate since he was a Denai, and the reason I myself could face banishment.

"Are you willing to live with the outcome?" he asked slowly.

Lifting my chin in defiance, I felt my knees go slightly weak before answering, "Yes, Father."

My father's dark eyes squinted in thought. "I will go and make the announcement. We will have a Kragh Aru, and the prize will be you, Thalia, as the winner's lifemate." Bearen's huge form rumbled as he walked across the wood floor. When he disappeared out the door, I waited until he turned the corner and then ran to Odin's home. I could barely contain myself when he opened the door and I rushed into a house very similar to ours.

"Odin, you have to help me," I blurted as soon as the door was closed behind us.

"Ah, little wolf. What did you do now?" His wrinkled forehead became more wrinkled in worry as he looked at me. He was sitting in front of his warm fire, whittling a piece of wood.

"I've agreed to a Kragh Aru, and I'm the prize!" I stated, my hands itching in excitement.

"Why would you do that? I heard your father planned to announce that you would be bonded to Fenri! You are going to make people think you've gone mad."

"Papa Odin, I may be when you hear what I have to say."

~8~

Weeks passed. As the news of the Kragh Aru spread, distant members from other clans arrived from far and wide to compete. After all, the chance to become bonded with the clan leader's daughter and help govern the whole clan was something they couldn't pass up. Especially since the Valdyrstals were the largest and the wealthiest of the remaining clans.

The week before the competition, my father became sullen and angered easily. I had thought it had something to do with the influx of clan members, who seemed to be appearing daily. Family members greeted many of their distant relatives, while others brought tents of their own to set up along the outskirts of the fields. On more than one occasion I had gone to the gathering hall, where many chose to eat and drink, and found my father passed out drunk.

But the next morning, Bearen was back to himself again. He even wore his finest leathers and furs, and spent the morning looking to the mountains as if he were waiting for something or someone.

I was spending the morning avoiding the new faces and the odd stares by hiding in the stable with Faraway. I crawled up into the hayloft to bring another bale down to the stalls.

Throw some of that hay my way!

Instead of throwing Faraway a handful of hay to munch on, I dumped a whole loose bale on him. I laughed out loud as he shook his head and flicked his tale comically to get the offending hay out of his mane.

Oops. I guess you should have said how much hay.

I don't think you brought down enough.

I threw down plenty, you pig.

Never underestimate my stomach, Faraway taunted back, and began to munch happily on his snack.

I heard the pounding of racing horses before I saw men hurry past the stable and barrel down the road toward the mountains. Normally I wouldn't have cared, except that I recognized two of the riders as my father and Odin. Quickly, I jumped down the ladder and ran out of the large double doors and into the road, trying to see where they were heading. I went back inside to grab Faraway, with the full intention of riding after them.

"I wouldn't do that, Meja Faelan." It was Fenri. He had sneaked up behind me and gently laid his hand across Faraway's stall.

"Do what?" I answered.

"Follow them. It is your father's business, and if he wanted you to come, he would have asked you."

"Is he in danger?" I couldn't help but let the worry show.

"No, he's not the one you should worry about. Besides, he has Odin with him. I guarantee you they will both be back by nightfall in time for the feast. After all, how often does our clan get together, and we have such a glorious occasion to celebrate." Fenri made a show of waving his hands in the air, but I could tell that he was somewhat disappointed.

"Look, Fenri, about the Kragh Aru." I stepped closer and looked up at his clean-shaven face, and couldn't help but reach out and touch his cheek. "I'm sorry—"

44

He closed his eyes and gently pressed his cheek into my palm before pulling away abruptly. "No, you have the right to make me fight for your hand and your honor. There is no need to feel shame." He moved toward the stable doors and turned back with a half smile on his face. "Unless you don't dance with me. After all, I am the best at the Tipturo." He left.

I felt a quick pang in my heart and felt a soft nuzzle against my shoulder. I turned to pat Faraway's warm cheek.

You're filled with sadness for the red-haired one.

Yes, I can't give him what he wants or probably deserves.

Which is?

My heart.

Why not?

An image of Joss flashed through my mind and then it flickered away.

I don't know.

Well, maybe it's not your love you need to give him.

What else is there?

Your loyalty.

He had me there. It is what I was doing anyway if my plan failed. I was going to marry whoever won the competition. So why didn't I just accept Fenri's offer or agree to my father's choice? What did I hope to achieve if it didn't work? I finished my work in the hayloft, and grabbed a currycomb and brushed Faraway as I went over my problems. I kept glancing out the doors to the mountains, waiting for my father and Odin to return. It was nearing dark, and I had to change for the celebration soon. As I was about to leave, Hemi led three latecomers into the stable. He looked surprised to see me and quickly stepped in front of me, hiding me behind his large body.

"Oi, since you have no family ties, and you didn't bring your own tents, you get what's left," Hemi said gruffly, gesturing to the hayloft above me. "Which would be the loft."

Taking the cue from Hemi, I kept my head low and pulled up the hood on my vest, hiding my face. I grabbed a pitchfork and pretended to muck out the stall. I studied each one, trying to see if I recognized any of them. I didn't.

One was in his fifties, with long grey hair and a nose that looked like it had been broken on numerous occasions. The second was completely bald, medium build, muscular, and was the loudest of the three. The third man was slightly taller than the bald one. He wore a furred cap that covered most of his head and was apparently drunk. He collapsed onto my fresh pile of hay and immediately began snoring. The other two kicked him and made some crude gesture. I heard their words and had problems understanding. Their dialect was different — harsher.

I backed up and whispered to Hemi. "Who are they?"

Hemi stroked his long red beard and eyed them warily. "The news spread quickly, and you gained attention from the Stahler clan. I didn't think any from that clan would show themselves, but the prize must have been too much for them to pass up."

The grey-haired Stahler made a lewd comment about hoping to get ahold of some ladies tonight for some entertainment.

Hemi's face turned bright red, and he made a curt reprimand before grabbing my elbow and physically removing me from the stable and out of their line of sight. Thankfully, the men never paid me any attention.

"Whatever you do," he warned me, "stay away from them, and don't go anywhere near the stable." I nodded and quickened my steps to match his as we put as much distance between the Stahlers and me as possible. Something about them made my skin crawl.

Faraway, can you keep an eye on them?

How about my nose? Can't miss that stench.

Hemi walked me to my house and paused. He shuffled his feet back and forth before looking up at me with pride in his eyes and something that could have been tears.

"It doesn't matter to me, what happened to you. I've seen it with my eyes — you're special. You are worth a hundred of us warriors, and you shouldn't hide who you are. You have my axe if ever you need it." He put his giant hand on the handle to the axe that he always wore on his back and lumbered down into a bow.

I felt myself begin to tear up as well. Somehow I had earned the loyalty of one of my father's trusted friends. Now if only the rest of my clan felt the same way.

"Thank you, Hemi. You are indeed a loyal warrior, and one that I would like to call my friend."

His large face beamed with happiness, and he stood up and ambled away, but not before I caught his quick look to the mountains. I knew he knew where my father went, and if Hemi was worried, then I knew I had to worry.

***

"Is it true that you turned down Fenri in favor of a Kragh Aru?" Siobhan asked. Her hands deftly parted my hair and began to braid and arrange it. She reached for another pin and gently tucked a stray piece of hair in place. I looked up in the mirror, then met her amazed look and shrugged.

She had come over to help me get ready for the ceremony and had been very careful to avoid the topic of marriage for the first hour, but not anymore. Her questions flowed as swiftly as the Kirakura Falls.

"I'm so envious. Did you see how many people showed up to compete for your hand? I can't imagine what it must be like to have that many people wanting to marry you."

"Well...I never thought this many people would come."

"Of course they would come. But I have to ask you — did you not like any of the men in our own clan? Or are you just trying to make Fenri jealous?"

I was at a loss for words. "Fenri is striking, but I'm not sure if we are right for each other."

"Not right for you, Thalia! He is the most attractive man here! You should just be happy that your father chose someone for you who was your age. I happen to think he is..." Her comments dropped off, and I could see a faint rose color appear in her cheeks.

My eyes opened wide as I realized my cousin had a fondness for Fenri. How could I have been so dense? Maybe that was why she was being friendlier to me, because I chose the tourney instead of Fenri.

She dropped her hands into her lap and swallowed. "Well, who am I to say what you should do? You've already made up your mind...but do you think you can go through with it? I mean, marry the winner? What if it's a total stranger?"

I sighed and looked at myself in the mirror. My eyes sparkled with the slightest bit of fear and excitement. I stood up and smoothed out any wrinkles in my dark blue wool dress. White fur lined the high collar and short sleeves. My hair, arranged in twists and braids upon my head and paired with my mother's silver wolf armbands, made me look exotic, powerful, and regal. The only hint of my worry was my slightly swollen lip, which I had been biting for the last hour.

"I keep my word, cousin. I will marry whoever wins the tourney tomorrow," I said with false bravado. "Let us worry about tomorrow, tomorrow. Tonight is for celebrations and dancing." I grabbed her hand and pulled her to my armoire, where I pulled out a pair of beautiful gold bracelets. I put them on Siobhan's arms and gave her a quick hug. "Let's enjoy tonight."

We left my home to walk the streets, heading toward the main square. I experienced a pang of loneliness as I realized how similar this felt. Did I not just walk like this a few months ago with my friend Avina? Could I really cast my friends aside that easily? What about Joss? I would be forced to wed someone else. Was I really ready to gamble so much, to try to prove myself? My nerves got the better of me, and I stumbled. Siobhan caught me.

"Are you okay, cousin?"

"No. Yes…. I don't know. Maybe I should speak with my father." I raised my head and scanned the crowd, looking for him.

"He's over there." Siobhan pointed to the main hall, and, sure enough, I saw my father duck into the building.

The main square was alight with colorful paper lanterns, music, and dancing. Women walked around with trays on their hips, selling food. Children ran between them, playing games. Men were in smaller groups off to the side, sparring and wrestling with each other, testing out the competition before tomorrow. Everyone was happy, excited, and drunk. Everyone but me.

We made our way through the crowded streets, and I felt someone press in close to my side. I looked up and saw Hemi. His face was stern as he gently touched my elbow and led me into the main hall.

Inside the hall a giant silver shield hung from the rafters, and a hammer lay next to it. It was tradition that whoever wanted to enter the competition would do so by striking the mighty shield. A line had already begun to form before the shield. The warrior would step up, hit the shield, and then come and speak an oath to the woman whose hand they hoped to win.

My lips felt dry, and I kept trying to wet them as Hemi led me to the front of the hall. My palms were sweating, and I found myself digging my nails into Hemi's arm. I saw my father standing in front of the large stone fireplace, with two high-backed chairs next to it. Bearen somehow had come back to the village without my knowledge and found time to change for the festivities.

His large sword leaned against the chair, and I counted at least two other blades on his belt. A glance behind the chair showed me another axe hidden within a few feet. His eyes darted warily between the clansmen, and I felt myself tense up. He was worried, and I wasn't sure why.

Slowly, I turned to sit down on the high-backed wooden chair, like a queen, as my father came over to address the room. All of the warriors, women, and children gathered as close as they could in the room. Others waited outside the windows and in the square to hear my father's announcement.

Bearen stood tall and proud. He turned his piercing eyes upon the men in the crowd and spoke loudly. "Tonight is a night for many celebrations. Many of you have heard how my daughter was kidnapped in the dark of night, and we thought we had lost her. Someone tried to steal that which is most precious to me. But, by sky above, we got her back, and I can't bear the thought of losing her again. So I have called the strongest warriors from our clan together to issue a challenge. A challenge that goes back hundreds of years. The warrior's test. The Kragh Aruuuu!" He raised his fist into the air and howled the last word. The room erupted into howls of encouragement, mimicking the Aruuuu call.

Bearen continued, "This is also a test to find the fiercest and boldest among you who will be worthy to protect my daughter from all that hunts her, and so the prize for the winner will be…my daughter as your lifemate. So, without further delay, because we all want to get to the mead as soon as possible, let the challengers come forth."

The men began to stomp their feet on the wooden floor. The stomping was fast and matched the pace of my wildly beating heart. There was more howling, and I scanned the men's faces, trying to read their expressions when they looked at my father and me.

The first warrior, a young man with curly hair, stood up and used the mallet to strike the shield.

Clang! Roars of approval moved through the hall. He came forward and knelt in front of my chair to pledge his oath to me.

I was taken aback by how young he was; he had to be younger than me. His green eyes twinkled with excitement and hope. I just prayed that my stupid plan wouldn't get him killed.

"I'm Arthur, and I choose to fight for you." He grinned and pounded his chest playfully. "*Min hjart en sterkur*," he recited. (My heart is strong.)

I was proud that I remembered the correct reply. "*En meja min sver vera sterkur.*" (But may your sword be stronger.)

He bowed low, and I could feel the heat rush to my cheeks. The room erupted into whistles. I spared a look toward my father, and he shook his head in disappointment. He knew and I knew that the boy wouldn't win.

Clang! The shield rang again, and another warrior came forward to declare his intentions. Some of the men looked me over appraisingly, while others winked at me. A few were old enough to be my father; some were missing teeth, and more than a few needed baths.

I was quite shocked when a familiar face rang the shield and knelt before me. His long black hair draped past his shoulders, and his eyes looked black by the firelight. My cousin Bvork smirked at me and made a deliberate show of reaching for my hand to plaster a kiss on it. I quickly pulled it away and wiped it on the front of my dress, hearing a few laughs follow as he sauntered away. I leaned over to Odin, who had moved to stand next to me.

"How can he enter?" I whispered furiously. "He's my cousin."

"I did what you asked. I looked into the rules, and nowhere does it state who can and can't compete in the Kragh Aru. It's what you were personally counting on."

Sighing, I mentally wished that I were back in Calandry and taking classes again. My troubles there seemed so much easier than the trouble I was causing here. I was actually beginning to miss Syrani and her awful barbs.

The next clansman who was presented had a slight accent as he pledged his vow. Actually, I had heard quite a few variations on the pledge. I smiled widely when Fenri stepped forward and kneeled and grasped my hand. "My heart is strong."

"But may your sword be stronger." I smiled back and reached for his hand, delaying him. I leaned forward and whispered urgently, "Do you think you can still win?"

"Are you changing your mind? You could have had me without the tournament."

"No, I'm not changing my mind," I answered.

"Then what choice do you give me? I have to win." He pulled his hand roughly out of mine and moved away.

I felt a little guilty at what I was putting Fenri through. A slight cough made me realize that it was time to move on.

The grey-haired and the bald Stahler men came, rang the shield, and pledged, followed by another clansmen whose furs were dirty and whose helm covered his head and most of his face. He slurred through the vow as if he was drunk and then looked at me with a sneer in his voice. "This is what I traveled all this way for? This is the prize?" He hiccupped and started to fall over. "What a waste."

I felt my hand pull back to slap him, but Odin caught me and sternly told him to move on. I watched him out of the corner of my eye as he made his way back to a corner by the other two men. I realized I recognized him as the drunk Stahler, and I decided I needed to keep a closer eye on those three.

The shield rang over and over. Sometime during the procession, someone started playing the drums. I took a deep breath and closed my eyes, trying to hide from the rhythm and the rush of feelings and emotions that were rolling over me. I could feel them: excitement, joy, hope. But then others came, darker ones: lust, hate, revulsion.

I opened my eyes and saw the piercing gaze of the Stahler men, and I almost choked. I scanned the crowd again and met more angry eyes, but these were coming from my own family members: my Uncle Rayneld and my cousin Bvork. Fear boiled up from within me, and I tried to push it away. I desperately needed the noise to stop.

My nails gripped the armrests of my chairs, and I felt myself start to lose control. My head began to throb, and I just wanted the noise and pain to cease. Someone was laughing at me. Or they could have been laughing at someone else, but it felt like it was directed at me. Another warrior rang the shield.

How many more could there possibly be? I barely made it through reciting my line before the buzzing in my head got louder. It was finally over and I could breathe, but barely. It was time to go outside and do the last thing I felt like doing. Celebrate.

~ 9 ~

I felt odd. I was swimming in a sea of faces. Many of them called to me, wishing me well. Others were warriors looking to get my blessing or a token to wear tomorrow. But they were all strangers. My face was stiff from pretending to smile, and my heart was weary with grief. I could feel the pressure build in my mind, and I needed to escape. Thankfully, Fenri appeared and pulled me into a dance.

"It seems that you needed rescuing from yourself. You look like the earth is about to swallow you whole." Fenri smiled and took my hand, guiding me alongside him. I watched his feet carefully and mirrored him.

"You have no idea how close you are to the truth."

He winked at me, and I smiled. I felt the load on my soul lighten. Fenri spun me and gripped his hand around my waist to steady me when I overturned. I threw my head back and laughed.

"You looked beautiful tonight, in the main hall."

I felt my cheeks redden. "Thank you."

"No, I mean it. It will be an honor to fight for your hand tomorrow. I just wish… No, what I mean is…"

"What?" I asked him. Coming to a halt in our dancing, I pulled him to the side so we could focus on each other. We began to walk away from the center of town and down a rarely used trail that led into the forest.

Fenri seemed frustrated. "I'm sorry for what happened to you. I feel like it was my fault. Maybe if I hadn't been distracted that day, you wouldn't have been kidnapped. I feel responsible because I should have been watching over you like I have since we were kids. You disappeared and ended up in Haven in the midst of all of those Denai. We were prepared to take you back by force, but you came willingly. Only you came back different. To protect your secret your father arranges a great lifemate for you…who you rejected, and now this… The Kragh Aru. Out of the blue you are willing to give yourself away to the winner." His words slowly slipped from playful to ice cold.

"Fenri?"

"No… Don't say my name like that." He dropped his fists to his sides and looked at me like he was the one who'd had his soul ripped out. "I'm tired of pretending everything's fine when it's not. Tell me. What is wrong with me?"

"I don't understand."

"Why won't you become my lifemate? We could have been good together. We were friends growing up, or at least I like to think we were friends. I know you came back different. I saw how you saved your father and whisked arrows in the air without bows. You see I'm worthy to keep your secret." He turned and began to pace back and forth.

"Yes, you are." I reached out to touch his shoulder, but he shrugged me off. Embarrassed, I gripped my skirt and waited.

"Thalia, people know that your father chose me for you. We both thought you would accept. And since you didn't, it makes me look bad. It makes me look weak in the eyes of the clan."

"So this is a pride thing. You're upset because of how this makes you look in the eyes of others." I wasn't expecting this from him, and it was making me angry. My temper was something one didn't mess with.

"Yes!"

"Well, that's not a good enough reason. I want someone strong, someone who can defend my clan."

"Thalia, I'm one of the strongest men here and worthy to lead the Valdyrstals. I thought that's what you wanted, to keep the leadership out of your uncle's hands. Well, you had the answer. You had everything you could have wanted, but you threw it away…and for what?" He pointed to the crowd of warriors to the side, who were sparring and setting up their tents in the field behind. "For this?"

"No, for a chance to be free," I answered, knowing he wouldn't understand.

"That's not freedom, Thalia. That is responsibility. Leading a clan is a lot of work. In our province, in our clan, we rule."

"No, Fenri. My father rules with the elders. And the way you're acting makes me think that you aren't ready for that responsibility."

"And some stranger is?" he argued. "I love this clan. I would die for any of them. I would die for you, so why don't you want me?"

"It's not like that." I tried to console him, and I could feel my answers were breaking his heart in two. How could I tell him that there was someone else? That I dreamed of another?

"Then tell me what it is like. Tell me so I won't go into tomorrow knowing that the person I love, the person I would give everything for, will reject me in the end." He turned suddenly and grasped me by the shoulders. I could feel his warm breath brush across my cheeks.

My heart started pounding in my chest, and I felt dizzy and weak. Fenri had just admitted to loving me. My mouth felt dry, and I tried to speak. He looked into my eyes, and I felt my cheeks burn with embarrassment. He saw my reaction and mistook it for favor.

He leaned in to kiss me. It caught me by surprise. The kiss was firm, aggressive, demanding. I expected it to be earth-shattering or to feel something. But there was nothing. I let him kiss me, hoping that maybe if my mind didn't remember him, my soul and heart would. After another moment, I knew that Fenri, memories or not, wasn't my soulmate.

The sound of branches snapping made us jump apart, and I looked around guiltily, as if I had been caught doing something wrong. Well, maybe I had. I used the back of my hand to wipe at my mouth, and Fenri turned to stand in front of me.

"Who's there?" he called out.

"I am, numbskull," a man called out of the bushes and half fell, half stumbled as he came into view. "You'd think a guy could find a place to relieve himself in quiet without being interrupted none." It was the drunk Stahler. I felt my chin rise in disgust. When he saw me, he perked up and ambled over.

"I never got my dance with da girl. I think she owes me a dance. Don't you, sweetie?" He gripped my wrist roughly and pulled me after him.

"Don't touch her!" Fenri roared, and knocked his hand away from me.

"Ay, that's not nice. You out here sneakin' kisses in the dark, and all I want is a dance. Seems kinda unfair to me, since she could be mine come tomorrow. Unless she is giving everyone free kisses." I was surprised when he didn't back down from Fenri.

"I'm warning you, move away," Fenri threatened.

"Not without me kiss. Seems like maybe I should be tell'n her father about this. Could cause quite a stir among the men. Might even cause a fight between neighboring clans." He patted his vest and glared between Fenri and me.

"I'm not kissing you!" I spat out.

"If it's a fight between clans you want, then you've got one." Fenri pulled his sword from his side trying, to intimidate the man into backing down.

"Stop it!" I yelled. "Save it for the tourney."

Fenri started to lower his weapon, but a knife appeared out of the drunk's sleeve, and in an instant he had it at Fenri's throat.

"Tsk-tsk. Seems the warrior got distracted by his lover and let his guard down. Not a smart move."

I was at an impasse with the knife at Fenri's throat. The drunk had surprised us both, but that just showed us what a smart adversary he was. Before I had a chance to act and try to save Fenri, the Stahler pulled his knife away from Fenri's throat and backed away. He tucked his knives back into his furs and turned his back on us in a gesture of goodwill…or as an insult to us.

"Slow, both of you are slow. I was expecting more. I don't know why I keep expecting more from the Valdyrstal, but I'm a bit let down. Tomorrow should be an easy win." He turned and pointed a hand at Fenri. "If you're not going to share her, then get her home. Don't want my prize ruined. And as for you," he pointed to me and smiled crookedly, "It's okay, love, I'll just claim my kiss tomorrow after I win the tourney." He stepped backward into the darkness of the forest and was gone.

~IO~

The next morning we headed over to the meadow. Various fighting rings were set up around the field, with a rope circle hammered to the ground. Tents were spread throughout for the clansmen who traveled here and didn't have any family in town. Other tents held varying aromas of stews and meats that were cooking. A medical tent had been centrally set up close to the fighting rings. I ducked into the small tent that was farthest from the fighting arena, the one I had asked Odin to set up for me.

"Thalia, my girl, this is the daftest plan I have ever heard of," Odin said as he greeted me inside the tent. I quickly stripped out of my ceremonial outfit into my pants and shirt as Odin began to buckle me into light-fitting leather armor.

"Do you have a better one?" I called back to him cattily.

"Nah, it's just so crazy it might work."

I already felt hot as the leather covered me. I was aiming for light. Some fighters had dressed themselves with so much armor trying to impress or look intimidating that it would be their downfall. It would also slow them down and bake them in the sun. I was actually counting on it. Once I was outfitted from head to toe, I tucked up my hair and put on my helm, and then began to have serious doubts. I had never fought while wearing armor.

"What's your plan?" Odin asked me, his face serious as he grabbed my shoulder to stop me from leaving the tent.

"Truthfully?"

"Yes, truthfully, how do you expect to win?" he asked again as he handed me a sword, one that I had become familiar with since I had spent the last week practicing with it whenever Bearen was absent.

"I plan to cheat!" I grinned and then ducked into the crowd. I felt a small pool of sweat begin to drip down my back at the thought of being caught using magic among hundreds of my clan members. It was worth the risk. I was planning to enter the competition and try to win. If I could win, then I could declare myself the Kragh Aru winner and choose to stay single. I would have proven my strength, and no one could deny my right to lead or wed when I wanted to. If I somehow couldn't win, then I would hope that Fenri would.

Making my way toward the fighting arenas, I hung back so I could get a good view of my competition. There were over forty fighters that had shown up to compete for the title of Kragh Aru.

Various shields, swords, axes, and bows were displayed on wooden stands, and the fighters were grouped into three groups. Each group would be pitted against each other, with the loser being eliminated and the winner moving on to the next round. The winner would need to achieve three points in any combination: one point for disarming the opponent, one point for breaking a shield, and one point if the opponent stepped across the rope. I positioned myself so that I wouldn't be in the same group as Fenri. I didn't want to be the one to fight him in the first round, or even the second. I hoped I would never have to. I was counting on someone else taking him out; I didn't know what I would do if I was actually pitted against him.

We were paired off, and I watched as the first set of paired fighters entered my group's ring. Two very large clan members faced off against each other. One giant of a man with long, braided red hair and beard, with a two-handed sword, was paired against an equally sized blond clansman with an oversized battle-axe.

The earth shook as they ran toward each other, screaming, weapons clashing, and the sounds echoing through valley. I did everything I could to not give in and place my hands over my ears at the noise they made. Teeth gritted in determination, spit flying, the two were equally matched. My heart pounded as I realized I couldn't possibly hope to match them for strength. My rounds would have to be won through speed and agility.

My eyes caught a flash of red fur, and I moved so I could watch Fenri's fight in the other ring. Fenri fought a much larger opponent, and danced around him and used quick maneuvers. I saw him feint high and turn and bring the handle of his sword into the gut of the man. The man doubled over in pain, and his sword dropped.

Fenri kicked him, and the man stumbled backward over the rope. A roar went up from the crowd. Pieces of a broken shield on the ground indicated that Fenri had already scored one point earlier, and it was two more for the win. Another roar went up as the red-haired barbarian broke the wooden shield of the blond fighter in the other ring.

What was I thinking? I couldn't do this. Faraway had positioned himself with a few other stock horses as close as he could to my arena. I had made sure that he was pampered, well-fed, and rested before this day came. He deserved it for participating in my crazy plan. And when the day was over, we both would be sore and tired.

When my arena emptied, I was paired with a fighter who actually was shorter and stockier compared to the previous two fighters. It was the one bald-headed Stahler. Today his head glimmered with sweat in the sun, and he chose to forgo a helm.

I bit my lip in trepidation as I saw the bald one's weapon of choice. It was a large battle-axe. My sword was half the size of the axe, and I stilled in fear. How was I to evade that edge? I hadn't fought against an axe that size even in training. I almost turned and ran. I now regretted not staying and practicing that day at the Citadel when I refused to fight with a battle-axe. I was sure Kael would be laughing now.

My opponent grinned at me and began to bark challengingly. Walking to the stand, I picked up a heavy wooden shield and prayed that I would survive my foolish plan. I tried to calm the beating of my heart and concentrate on reaching for power as I stepped into the ring. The Dømari, or game master, started the games and kept score. When he yelled out the "begin" command, my opponent rushed me, swinging his heavy axe.

Jumping to the side, I rolled to my knees and brought up my wooden shield just in time to block the downward blow at my head. I grunted in pain as the weight of the blow reverberated through my arm, and I could hear the first crack of my wooden shield. I almost dropped my sword to use two hands on my shield. *Stupid, stupid, stupid*, I chanted to myself.

Pushing up with both hands against the shield, I tried to shove my opponent back a foot or so. I had barely won that ground when he came at me again. This time I used the shield to deflect the axe blow to the side of me, and I swiped my sword downward, intent on trying to break the handle of the axe. The sound of wood being hit was the only satisfaction I got, as the handle was far thicker than I had anticipated, and I didn't have enough strength to break through it. I pulled back on the sword, only to feel it stick in the long handle of the axe. I heard a bark of laughter, and I looked up to see him land a kick on my stomach. I flew, releasing the handle of my sword as it stuck fast into the wooden axe handle.

"*EIN!*" the Dømari called and pointed to the bald Stahler.

He grinned and strutted around the arena like a rooster. Walking over to the weapons rack, I glanced over the selections before choosing a different weapon. My eyes fastened upon a mace and chain. Grasping my shield and mace, I reentered the arena as a small plan began formulating in my brain. I swung the mace experimentally. I was down one point already. I would have to take him out, and fast.

The Dømari shouted to begin, and I had to hand it to him — the Stahler didn't try anything new; he rushed me, same as before. Moving backward, I got myself as close to the rope as I felt comfortable being. Focusing power, I waited and quickly sidestepped him and turned my back toward him in a graceful arc as I swung the mace as hard as I could toward the shield. At the same time, I focused more power behind it. The mace hit the wooden shield, and I heard a grunt from the Stahler as the shield split into three pieces.

"*EIN!*" the Dømari called out in my favor.

Surprised, my bald opponent stumbled, and this time I advanced, swinging the mace forward as I closed in.

He grinned in triumph as he brought up his axe to catch the mace and wind it around the handle. He knew with one good tug he could disarm me. But that is what I was counting on. With the mace chain wrapped around the axe, he started to pull backward on it, and I held on and ran toward him. I jumped forward at the same time he yanked. Leaping onto his bent knee, I kicked him as hard as I could in his chest, using his own momentum to pull me into him, which caused him to stumble backward over the rope and drop his hold on the axe handle.

"*Tvier, Prir, and Svegari!*" Which meant two, three, and winner. I thanked God that these early rounds went quickly. Walking over to a stand, I grabbed a tankard of water and drank it down, making sure to stay hydrated and to not drink any mead. Sitting in the shadows of a huge tree, I waited and watched the opponents.

How's Fenri doing? I asked Faraway.

He's won all of his matches, Faraway answered. *So have Bvork and a few others.*

My next match, I waited to see what the other opponent was bringing into the ring before selecting my weapon. Luckily, he was using was a sword. Feeling more confident, I followed a similar procedure of fighting, only this time I made attempts to draw out the fighting a little longer and added more hard strikes to the shield before using power to crack it in two. I didn't have to use power to work on disarming him of his sword. I used the basic training I learned from Garit and Kael.

I grinned as I thought about Kael accusing me of not engaging in combat. I did get disarmed once again, but the score was tied one-one. It came down to sword skill and stamina. I got pushed over the rope once, and then the score was two-one and I was able to push him over the rope. Finally, I was able to disarm him and take the win. I watched tiredly as his sword hit the dirt. I heard cursing and kicking as he walked out of the ring.

Odin slowly walked over to me and handed me more water, being careful to not show me too much attention. "You're slowing down, lass, but not as much as the larger brutes. If you keep your focus, maybe you can do this."

Nodding my head, I took another swallow, refusing to say a word lest someone hear me. I was physically exhausted and losing control. I was drawing on more and more of Faraway's strength. More cries of disappointment and shouts of congratulations were heard as another match ended.

"I think it's gonna be close," Odin whispered as he covered his mouth and stroked his beard to hide his words. "I think it will be between Bvork, Fenri, and that one." Odin tilted his head towards the far arena, and I felt my face turn into a disgusted frown. It was the Stahler clansmen with the dirty furs and helms who had assaulted me the night before.

Oh, great, I thought, *just what I needed.* When my turn came again to fight, I noticed we were now being paired against the winners from the other arenas.

Fenri was pitted against Bvork, and they were equally matched in strength and swordsmanship. I could tell from the way they taunted each other that there was an intense dislike between the two men. They weren't fighting for a simple win; they were fighting for something else—pride. And they were ruthless in their pursuit. They were tied two each, and I prayed that Fenri would come out on top, when Bvork took a handful of dirt and threw it into Fenri's green eyes, blinding him. Taking full advantage, Bvork swung his sword and sliced into Fenri's leg, bringing him down to the ground. Blood spilled from the leg wound, and dirt covered his face. Fenri tried to scrabble away, holding his sword while desperately trying to wipe the dirt from his eyes.

Bvork came up from behind and grabbed Fenri's head, and smacked it into the ground with a loud thud. Blood poured from a fresh wound coating Fenri's forehead. The onlookers booed Bvork's unsportsmanlike conduct. Without pausing, Bvork stepped on Fenri's hand that gripped the sword, and I heard a sickening crunch and a muffled scream from Fenri.

I turned my head so I wouldn't see, and tears started to come to my eyes unbidden. What had I done? Because of me,

Fenri was injured. An ugly laugh came from Bvork, and I turned back to see him kick Fenri's sword away from his prone body. The crowd turned silent; there was no joy in winning this way. So far very little blood had been spilled today, which was rare, but none that was done with such obvious intent and hatred. Even in the heat of the games, a warrior's battle rage took over, and there were always a few in-the-moment casualties. But our clan was a clan of warriors, and they readily accepted any loss as normal.

I slid to my knees and stared into the arena to see if Fenri was all right. He was flat on his back. Slowly he turned his dirt-and bloodstained face toward the crowd, blinked the last of the dirt from his eyes, and stared at his crushed hand.

His eyes then followed the path of his hand past the arena to meet up with my wide tear-stained ones. It took Fenri only a few heartbeats before his eyes widened in surprise as he recognized me in my warrior disguise. As he sat up and cradled his injured hand, I could see that his expression went from astonishment to anger to a blank mask. With all of the dignity he could muster, he pulled himself off the ground.

Fenri walked toward me and stopped, leaning in to me to whisper angrily, "Is this what you wanted?" Glaring at the people around us, who backed away in fear, he went on, "I could have made you happy. I thought you wanted me to prove to you that I was strong enough to be your lifemate. I had no idea that this is what you had in mind. What were you thinking?"

Holding still, I shook my head and raised my shoulders in answer.

"Well, I hope you win, or that you are ready to live with the consequences," he said, nodding toward my cousin, who was speaking with my uncle Rayneld, a great bear of a man. As that last warning still rang in my ears, Fenri pushed past me roughly and headed away from the crowds, steering clear of the medical tent.

Dropping my head in shame, I looked at my scuffed boot. I felt defeated. My only hope now was to win the competition and maybe try to convince him of what I was trying to do later. I gripped my sword in anger and waited until it was my turn to enter the ring.

The crowd parted for Bvork. Raising his hands to the crowds, he saluted them and then strutted in carrying a two-handed broadsword and no shield. He'd fought with a shield with Fenri. He must be changing his tactics after talking to his father.

Looking at Rayneld, I saw that his black beady eyes narrowed as he studied me and then nodded to his son. Sweat started to pool down my back as I looked at his son, too. He must be extremely confident in his blocking abilities if he chose to fight without a shield.

There went my plan. He must have heard that I'd won most of my fights by breaking the shield. Now I would have to win by disarming him or pushing him out of the ring. Licking my lips nervously, I waited in the center for him to approach me.

"Ah, what's this? How did a young boy like you make it this far in the competition without getting skewered alive?" Bvork said, his crooked bottom teeth showing. "How do you plan to win the Kragh Aru, eh? You're barely a man. I don't think you're man enough for our clan leader's daughter!" Loud, raucous laughter rose up from the crowd around him.

I gritted my teeth in anger and watched him carefully. Making a quick decision, I went to the sidelines and handed off my shield as well. I was tiring quickly, and I needed to lighten the load.

Bvork's eyebrow rose disbelievingly, and then he chuckled as I came back and gripped my sword. When the match started, I decided to attack instead of waiting for him to. Rushing forward, I swung as he stepped to the side, bringing his sword up to block. Then he swung, and I parried.

We continued to dance around the ring, and sweat dripped freely down my back and face and into my eyes. It wasn't until I saw him grin in triumph that I realized he was purposely trying to drag me along and wear me down. He wasn't using his full strength to fight me; he was toying with me, and it was working.

The next swing, I blocked. Gritting my teeth, I felt the vibrations ring, and I lost hold of my sword. I watched as it hit the ground. A puff of dirt surrounded it.

"*Ein!*"

Quickly, I opened myself up to Faraway.

Help! I need you. And immediately warmth encompassed me, and I felt renewed. This time it was my turn to grin in triumph as my footwork and sword work became faster, and I paraded him around the ring. His grin turned down as he went on the defense. With a large sword it was hard to disarm him, so I quickly pushed him back and kept attacking until he stepped on the rope.

"*Ein*" was called. I grinned, and Bvork's face turned downright ugly, which wiped my smile right off. Bvork walked over to the weapons rack, and picked up a second sword and quickly entered the ring and engaged me in combat before I could even think of picking up a shield.

I marveled at his strength as he maneuvered both swords easily. That marvel turned to fear as I was quickly put on the defense. I felt the sting of the sword rip through the flesh of my upper arm, and I blanched in surprise. Backing up, I felt the boundary rope hit the heel of my boot and I ducked as both swords swung at my head in an effort to take it off. Rolling, I turned and barely got up before another sword came at my midsection. Jumping back, I felt the sword nick my stomach. If this kept up, I would bleed out through numerous wounds.

Gasping for breath, I tried to focus my powers, but Bvork came at me like a madman, crisscrossing his swords in a complicated maneuver. I watched and counted, as the weight of the heavier sword made the pattern a little off. Feinting to the right, I dodged left and thrust my sword sideways into the swirling vortex near his hands and gritted my teeth as both swords came to a halt, and my blade made contact and nicked his hands. Bvork yelled and dropped one sword. I had hoped for two.

"*Tvier!*"

Looking at my cousin, I could see the rage building as he let the heavy two-handed sword lie on the ground and continued with his shorter, lighter sword. He made me pay for that second point as he pounded me with his sheer strength.

Another cut mirrored my other arm, and I felt myself begin to tire again. I had no idea where he got all of his energy. Missing a feint, I was too slow as he swung his sword level at my head again. I barely turned my head sideways in time. I felt the blade slice the side of my neck. It caught on the edge of my helm and ripped it off. I watched in horror as it flew, spinning in slow motion, across the arena to land at the feet of the drunk Stahler.

Grabbing my neck to staunch the flow of blood, I turned to see my cousin's eyes widen in recognition and then turned dark with fury.

"Is this some sort of joke?" he growled. "Are you just trying to humiliate me and our clan?" He approached me menacingly.

"No, it's a chance to win my freedom from having to marry because of someone else's whim," I called back. "It's a chance to prove myself strong enough to lead our clan without a mate."

He grimaced and came at me again. "Don't think because you're my cousin and the prize for the Kragh Aru that I'm going to take it easy on you." Lowering his voice so only I could hear, he went on, "I couldn't care less if you are male or female. All I care about is becoming the clan leader, with or without you."

Screaming, he attacked me, and I had problems holding onto my sword, which was slick with blood. He swung his sword downward, and caught my sword and pinned it to the ground.

Glancing up, I saw his fist swing, and I saw stars as he punched me in the eye. I heard the crack and I tried to draw power, but he punched me again in the face, and this time I fell. As I fell, I felt my sword, bloody, slip from my fingers and hit the dirt. I landed on a large, round, rough bump, and I realized sadly right then that I had landed on the rope. I had lost.

The Dømari was too stunned to even call the count and winner. The whole crowd had gone deathly silent as soon as my identity had been revealed. I choked in pain and felt a hand touch my face, and I looked into the angry, stormy eyes of the drunken clansman. How did I not notice his eyes before now? Was I that distracted by his smell and perverse acts that I didn't notice how much they reminded me of Kael's?

~ II ~

"What were you thinking?" A familiar voice echoed, or at least seemed to echo, as my head continued to ring.

"Stop shouting," I murmured.

"I'm not shouting, and you should explain yourself," Bearen grumbled.

Opening only one eye because the other was swollen shut, I gasped as Odin leaned over me and applied a poultice to my numerous wounds. Reaching for the side of my throat, I felt the length of the already stitched wound that reached from my neck up the side of my jaw to my ear. Odin quickly slapped my hand away.

"Don't touch the stitches. You are going to have a scar to remind you of this day."

I grimaced at his tone of voice. I wished that I had the ability to heal myself, but I wasn't that strong. My own recklessness had gotten me here, and I would have this reminder for the rest of my life. Odin put something on my neck, and I immediately took a quick intake of breath.

"That stings. What is it?"

"Harrumph, you don't want to know. But it will keep any infection from setting in," Odin answered. I believed I already knew what he was applying because the familiar smell of cat urine invaded my nose.

"Did you know about this?" Bearen rumbled at Odin. "Were you a part of this from the beginning?"

Odin continued to minister to my wounds and spoke without making eye contact. "Aye! She told me of her plan."

"How could you? She could have been killed, and then Rayneld's son would appeal to the clan council for leadership."

"And you!" Turning back to me. "You have a lot to answer for. Do you realize that Fenri is out of the running, and that some stranger and your deceitful cousin Bvork are the last two standing to win the Kragh Aru?"

When he said deceitful cousin it made me wonder what he could have done to anger my father so. But then, I also had deceived people, as I entered the competition in disguise. So maybe the apple didn't fall too far from the tree on both sides of our family. Sighing in regret, I asked about Fenri's injuries.

"He'll be lucky if he can ever get the use of his hand back. I doubt he'll be able to hold a sword again. Bvork crushed it," Bearen gritted out angrily and his eyes shone with anger as he looked at me.

Odin quickly interrupted, "Well, maybe it's not as bad as all of that, hmmm? Maybe Thalia should take a look at it, considering it was her fault that he was injured."

"What? My fau...?" I stopped as I caught Odin's pointed stare. "Yes, I will look at it."

"NOOOO! You won't!" Bearen roared loudly. Quieting down, he came over to me and spoke slowly. "Do you understand what the consequences are of being found out? If someone sees his hand ruined now and then sees it later and it's fine, questions will arise, and you will be banished." Turning, he ran his hands through his dark hair. "If I was a good clan leader, I would have already banished you. But I can't do that to my Thelonia. You are her spitting image, except for the black hair." I wanted to speak up and interject on the topic, but he shushed me with his hand. "You will obey me, Thalia. I still can and will punish you if you disobey me again. Right now, having to be bonded to the winner of the Kragh Aru is punishment enough for this crime."

My face paled at the possibility of having to marry my cousin. "Please, I need to leave the tent." I began to panic. "I have to know what's going on."

"Relax!" Odin said encouragingly. "You've caused quite a stir by entering. The clan is in an uproar! For one, Bvork injuring you the way he did after he found out it was you. Two, that you entered the competition at all. And three, that you were able to do so well." He smiled. "The final match has been delayed for a few days."

Breathing a sigh of relief, I lay back and tried to contact Faraway. But I was still in a lot of pain, and it seemed to be blocking my abilities. I heard a commotion of people outside the tent, asking various questions. Looking to Odin, I asked him if he could get me home. Nodding, Odin wrapped his arms around me, picked me up, and went out the back of the tent, while Bearen went out the front to distract the crowd. I couldn't ask for a better distraction than Bearen. His fierceness and size would deter anyone from coming near me.

Taking a back path, Odin and I cut through the forest and wound our way through the trees, heading toward home. There was nothing wrong with my legs, but I was weak. My head was still spinning, and I didn't want to fall and cause a scene, so I let Odin quickly and quietly carry me.

Leaning my head against his shoulder, I tried to keep my good eye closed against the fast-moving trees. I still couldn't open my other eye. A quick shadow caught my attention, and I motioned Odin to slow and stop. Seeing my alert expression and the tensing of my body made him tense and turn in response. Scanning the forest, he listened and sniffed the air for any sign of intruders.

"It must have been my imagination," I said meekly.

"Nah, Thalia, my girl," he whispered back. "I would trust your instincts any day." Stepping with more care, we continued on. When we reached a turn, we took the path back into the open. I glanced again into the woods, and I saw very distinctly the bushes move and heard a twig snap. Odin heard it, too, and stepped back into the direct sunlight and quickened his step. He started to head to my home, but I pointed at his. Looking at me in confusion, he nodded and went to his. Once inside, I curled up on a long wooden bench with a high back covered with furs.

"Quickly." I motioned back to the door. "Bring Fenri, don't tell him I'm here, and try to not let anyone see him."

Giving me a hard look, Odin bit the side of his mouth and left without a sound. After I collapsed on the bench, exhaustion overtook me, and I slept until I heard the creak of the back door and the sound of two pairs of boots.

"I told you, there's nothing you can do." The unmistakable sound of Fenri's angry voice reached my ears.

"Nah, don't you go yelling at an old man. I may have a few trade secrets that no one knows about. So you sit down and shut up."

Fenri walked into the main room and stomped loudly over to the single stool by the fire. I could see that he had tried to bandage his hand, by the evidence of wood bracers. I grimaced in guilt and empathy at his pain. Sitting down abruptly, he jumped just as fast when he came face to face with me lying down on the long wooden bench.

"I refuse to stay here." He moved across the room as far from me as possible.

"No, you'll sit down and be quiet." Odin challenged, pushing him back toward me. Odin, though older, was still a large clan warrior, and he demanded respect. Forcefully grabbing Fenri's shoulder, he pushed him down on the chair.

"If it weren't for her hare-brained ideas, I wouldn't be crippled," he breathed angrily through his teeth.

"Nonsense, this could have happened during any hunting trip. And it's not Thalia's fault. Why are you blaming Thalia, when it's Bvork who chose to play dirty? Listen to me, young warrior. It doesn't matter how it happened. What matters is what you are going to do about it." He spoke slowly and with meaning.

"Do? Are you kidding me?" Fenri spoke with such anger and despair that spit flew from his mouth. "There's nothing I can do. I can't use my hand, old man. I'm crippled." Standing up, he paced the room. "What honor is there when I can't hunt game or protect and provide for a future wife?" Stopping to stare at me, he went on. "I'm useless."

I could see that Odin was quite pleased with the fact that he was wearing down Fenri. Watching silently, I listened as the old wise warrior talked down and calmed the injured young man. When Fenri was tired and out of options, Odin went and grabbed a small knife and cut his own palm, letting a small flow of blood ebb onto his hand. Fenri opened his eyes wide in confusion.

"I know that you already made a blood oath about what happened in the pass, and you swore to protect Thalia. But I'm surprised that after all you saw, you didn't give her a chance to try to help you." Fenri's shoulders dropped in shame.

"I didn't think she would want to help me after the way I talked to her after my fight." He looked away from me and stared at a far wall.

I spoke up for the first time. "I do, Fenri. Or I would like to try, if you will let me."

A small glimmer of hope shone in his eyes. "You would still help me?" he asked disbelievingly.

Smiling, I nodded.

"But," interrupted Odin, "you will swear a new blood oath about anything you hear and everything you see happen tonight. Your hand being healed is not worth my goddaughter's life. You hear me?" Odin threatened, pointing the already bloody knife at Fenri's throat. Fenri swallowed and shook his head.

"Good. Now hurry up before I have to cut my hand open again," he complained. Fenri eagerly took the knife and made an identical slice on his palm, and the two swore an oath in the old language.

When they were done, Odin unwrapped Fenri's hand, and I almost vomited at what I saw. His whole hand had turned purple and swollen to twice its normal size. His fingers were bent in unnatural positions. I knew that the human hand consisted of numerous bones, nerves, and muscles, and that usually an injury like this would make a warrior lame. I could tell that Faraway and I were both to the point of exhaustion, but we needed to work fast before anyone saw this.

"How many people have seen your hand like this?" I asked quickly, feeling myself start to second-guess what I was about to do.

"No one. I was afraid that if I went to the healer tent and someone told me that I would never regain the use of it, I would believe them, but it was already obvious I would. I went into the woods and tried to wrap it myself."

Throwing me a look of relief, Odin nodded encouragingly for me to continue.

"Fenri, I can't take away your pain while I'm doing this. But I will do the best I can to make it like it was before. You have to make sure that you keep it wrapped for the weeks to come. You have to pretend it's healing slowly. Do you understand?"

He nodded. "I think I have some dye that I can use to color my hand and make it looked bruised."

"We are talking weeks of pretending to not use your hand at all, Fenri. If you mess up, I could be in serious trouble."

Fenri came and knelt before me, and, taking my hands with his good one, he spoke. "Thalia, if you can heal my hand or even heal it to where it can then heal itself on its own, then that is worth not being able to use it for a few months. I would be eternally grateful to you." I could see tears of hope form in his eyes.

"Papa Odin, if you have any ale or medicine for pain, please give it to him now. He's gonna need it."

Odin had both, and we gave Fenri pain medicine and got him near drunk. We switched spots on the bench so that he was lying down on it and I was kneeling. I let myself relax as much as possible before reaching for Faraway. It was starting to come easier to me the more I reached for it. Now that I was calm and numb from the pain, it came almost eagerly.

Closing my eyes and opening my sight, I saw the mangled mess of bones and muscles and nerves, and I began to doubt myself.

Don't doubt. We are here.

We?

I heard it first and then felt a familiar breathy laugh touch my consciousness.

Wolf?

Ja, it seems small one needed my help again. Four feet called me back, the laughing retort came back.

My heart soared with delight. And I could visually see the grey wolf snapping his jaws in wolfish laughter.

I tentatively reached out toward the wolf and felt them both in the woods outside the house. I plucked at their energy and pulled it back to me, and all sense of nervousness fled.

Grasping Fenri's hand gently with a newfound confidence, I carefully worked on maneuvering each bone and set them to reknitting, then restored the nerve endings. I had to take frequent breaks, and I stopped when Fenri's pain became too intense. I was so proud of him. He grunted and held in all of the agony, and made very little sound. When my hands started to shake and my sight became blurry, I had to quit for the night.

"I'm sorry, Fenri, I can't do any more." A terrible guilt washed over me. I felt like I had failed him. I tried to stand and immediately came to my knees. Even with the help of my friends, my body was physically drained.

If borrowing power from one being was doubly draining on me, pulling from two was three times more exhausting. I was just glad I didn't throw up. I was unable to heal myself, and my own injuries were making it hard to help him.

"I've set the bones and sped along their reknitting. I've also healed all of the damaged nerves, and your muscles are starting the healing process. I've taken some of the swelling down, and your body will heal itself, although faster. So wear the splint and check it in a few days. But everything looks normal. Maybe in a few days, I can try again," I said, feeling my eyelids start to droop with weariness.

"No, Thalia, thank you for what you have done. It's better this way. If people ask about it and look, it still looks like it's injured. You've prevented me from being a cripple." Sitting up and biting his lip through the pain, he held up his hand and slowly moved each of his fingers. "Everything's, set and now Mother Nature will run her course."

Sitting down on the floor, I leaned on the bench and laid my head on my arms. "I'm glad. I truly am glad, Fenri." As I closed my eyes, I felt a slight touch on my face, and I opened my eyes in shock.

"You can't do anything for yourself?" he said, gesturing to my bruised face and stitches.

Smiling, I shook my head. "That's not how the gift works. We were taught to use the gift for others, not ourselves. I wouldn't, even if I could," I whispered tiredly. Fenri nodded to Odin, who came and gently picked me up. I felt the cold night air brush my skin as I was brought back to my own home and room. My body felt numb and tingly, and I instantly fell asleep, only to dream terrifying dreams.

Again, I dreamed I was back in the iron butterfly and being tortured. The pain felt real as the clamps buried themselves deep in the pressure points along my body. I felt weak and drained.

Even though I knew I could access power now, the mere thought of the iron butterfly made me freeze in panic. I started to whimper and cry out, and then I felt like I was suffocating. My eyes flew open as my mind came awake, and I struggled to breathe. Someone was in my room, trying to smother me.

~12~

"MMMFFFFF" I screamed into the hand that covered my mouth and nose. As I opened my eyes, fear shot straight to my heart as a dark figure leaned over me and had one hand pressed on my chest and the other over my mouth, keeping me from moving or screaming.

"Shhhhh! Quiet!" the deep voice rumbled.

I tried to kick my legs, but I was too tired and weak from my exertion earlier. All I managed was a pathetic twitching of my knees.

"Darn it. Thalia, be quiet and stop moving," the figure growled out quietly.

I knew that voice. I stilled and tried to think through all of the possibilities of how he could be here, but none of them made sense.

"That's a good girl." As he sat back on the bed, the moonlight from the open window illuminated him. I stiffened when I saw the drunk Stahler. Only this time, his voice didn't match his body. He didn't have an accent.

What I saw was the same drunk, smelly, fur-wearing Stahler. What I heard was Kael's voice. I dissected his costume with my eyes, stripping away the many layers of fur, leathers, and dark makeup. If I had paid attention to the eyes, Kael's dark stormy eyes, I would have noticed sooner.

"You were having a nightmare," he said, interrupting my revelation.

I nodded, unable to speak, as the tremors from my dream rocked my body, making me shake.

"Brush it off," he demanded. "You're awake now. Whatever it was, it can't hurt you."

Sitting there quietly, I let myself adjust from waking up from a nightmare and almost being smothered to realizing that Kael was in my room. The shock of it made me stare at him in confusion.

"What are you do—" I started to ask, and then jumped to a different train of thought as I began to piece things together. "It was you fighting in the tournament today, wasn't it?" I found the strength to sit up in bed. "I wasn't imagining things. It's been you the whole time. You saw me in the stable. You insulted me in the main hall. I hardly believe it."

Backing away from me, he sat on the edge of my bed. "Yes. And you were fighting as well."

"You stink!" I spoke without thinking.

He looked at me and raised his eyebrow in question. "Well, so would you if you had to wear so many animal furs and were trying to impersonate one of your Stahler clansmen. I take it you haven't gotten close to many of them, because truthfully I did too good of a job; I fit right in. I infiltrated their party the day before they got to your village. Pretty easy; they aren't that bright. All I had to do was listen and pretend to be drunk until I learned their heavy accent." He grinned.

This was a side of Kael that I hadn't seen before, and I wasn't sure what to make of this nonchalant attitude. Maybe it was because we weren't at the Citadel, or maybe it was because Joss wasn't here.

I gave him a look of pure disgust as I got up and moved to my small fireplace and lit a fire. I had begun to get goosebumps from the night air let in by the window. But I refused to close it, because then I would be enclosed in the room with him. When the small fire was roaring away, I looked at him intently.

"Why are you here?" I asked, tilting my head to the side.

"I'm here because I don't take orders from you."

"No. I mean, why did you come to Valdyrstal? After we escaped the iron butterfly and prison, you could have gone home, but you didn't. You showed up in Calandry and now here."

"I had to."

"What do you mean, you had to? From what I've read about your clan, no one can make you do anything if you don't want to do it."

"From what you've read?" He smirked, shaking his head as he walked past me to the bench by the window. He sat in my favorite spot and pulled one knee up, while the other lay extended. He stared out into the darkness, and the moon illuminated his face. Looking at me, he crossed his arms and raised one eyebrow.

"So you think that if you read some book that is probably full of lies, by the way, it would explain everything there is to know about a person? About me?" He rolled his eyes. "The things in whatever book you're reading don't apply to me anymore." He looked across the village, and his voice deepened to a whisper. "I can hardly call myself a SwordBrother."

"Of course you are."

"How would you know? You're not a SwordBrother, now, are you?" he said sarcastically. "A SwordBrother wouldn't have let himself get captured and drugged. A SwordBrother vows to protect the weak, which I was unable to do until it was too late." He looked at me pointedly. "Listen, I didn't forget my past like you so conveniently did. Now I wish I could."

"You think losing yourself, losing your memories, is convenient? You're wrong."

"I know what happened down there. You think I'm some hero when I'm not. I couldn't even save the boy, Tym. I found his body outside the stable in the dark. He had been stabbed in the back."

Sitting on a small wooden chair by the fire, I looked across the room to him. He was angry, his jaw clenching and unclenching in his familiar way. His left hand flexed in anxiousness as if he longed to clutch a knife that I knew he had hidden somewhere on his body. My heart lurched at the reminder that Tym had only tasted freedom for a few minutes, but at least he was free now from the Septori.

"But you saved me. That should count for something."

"Yeah, you would think so, huh? But it doesn't. I have to save you."

"What do you mean, you have to save me? And you never answered the question. Why did you come here to Valdyrstal?"

"Because of you." He spat the words out and glared at me. Here was the side of Kael that I was used to—the angry side.

Those words spoken from Joss would have melted my heart, and if Kael had said them in any other way, I probably would have smiled. But the animosity behind those words made me sit up, legs extended as if I was going to bolt.

"You didn't have to come here. I was fine. I still am. You can leave anytime—the door is right there. In fact, I will help you out." I moved to the door.

"No!" Kael jumped up and then slowly sat down. After a few minutes, he continued, "I tried to go home after we escaped. I did. I made it out of the barn and looked around and saw that the horses were gone, so I figured you were gone and took off on foot toward home. I began to feel an intense pain, and there was a strong pull on me toward the river and not home. I tried to fight it, but the pain overcame me and wouldn't leave until I followed this strange pull."

He started to pick at a splinter on the windowsill, and I waited patiently until he was ready to go on.

"So I followed the river until I came to signs of a camp."

"But Darren and Joss hid any signs that we had camped there."

"They were hidden, and only a SwordBrother would have noticed the signs. Your friend, this Darren, did very well."

Smiling in relief, I began to relax. "Good."

"I tried everything. All of my clan's herbal remedies and pain medicines, and nothing worked. I was covered with sweat and started to shake, and it didn't release my body until I took off in the direction that you three had gone. I followed you to the Inn, and I was fine again. The next day I waited until all three of you left, and again the agonizing pain came back. I had no choice but to follow you three to Calandry."

Kael stood up and walked over to me by the fire. Putting his hands on the back of the chair, he leaned down and whispered to me, "It's you."

I paled at his words; my mouth tried to form a rebuttal, but I couldn't.

"I can't be more than a few miles from you without being brought down in agonizing pain." His fingers dug into the wood of the chair in anger. I jumped up and moved to the fireplace, putting as much distance as I could between us.

He grabbed a vase of roses off the end table and threw it into the fire, the vase exploding into pieces and the water causing the fire to pop and boil. I watched as the roses caught fire and turned brown, and then withered up into nothingness.

"I'm so sorry, Kael." Tears started to form in my eyes, and I tried to turn away from him so he wouldn't see me cry. "They must have done something to us in the prison."

"They did. The Septori blood-bonded us."

"Blood-bonded?" It took me a moment as I tried to process what Kael had said. It came down to the book I borrowed from Adept Kambel. There was a chapter in the book that explained how SwordBrothers were the bodyguards of the Kings and Queens. The bravest SwordBrothers could choose to be blood-sworn to their charge through a process called blood-bonding. It would tie the people's souls together. Sometimes, a royal would have up to three sworn SwordBrothers. Then, the SwordBrother would always be able to track their charge wherever they went. But if something happened and their charge died, the SwordBrother would inevitably die, too.

"But I thought SwordBrothers don't do that anymore."

"Of course we don't!" Kael huffed. "Not since one paranoid king many years ago, in a maddening fit, had hundreds of SwordBrothers blood-sworn to him. You can imagine what happened next. He kept sending us into battle for him, using us as his personal assassins to kill the children of his enemies. The horror stories are true, Thalia. The ones you heard about SwordBrothers being evil. It's because the king forced us to be that way."

"That is horrible! I can't believe someone would do that to the SwordBrothers."

"It's one thing to choose to be blood-sworn of someone. It's quite another to have that choice taken away from you."

"What happened?"

"The SwordBrothers' code of honor was broken, and they couldn't live with themselves. Finally, one of the king's own blood-sworn, a man named Lake, was able to free the hundreds of SwordBrothers bonded to the king."

"He did? That's fantastic—how did he do it?" I was getting excited. I hadn't read this part in the book. I didn't know there was a way to undo the blood-bonding.

"He killed the King of Sinnendor."

My mouth dropped open in shock. When Lake killed the king, he also simultaneously killed the blood-sworn and himself, and that meant the SwordBrothers were originally from Sinnendor, like my family.

"He freed hundreds of souls and prevented more wars. And because of that one king, the few remaining unsworn SwordBrothers and their families disappeared. They went into hiding, refusing to be blood-sworn again."

"And that is why your clan is in hiding to this day. And you think that is what the Septori did to us?"

"I'm not sure. Everything between us feels like I'm blood-sworn to you, but I don't know how they would have gotten the knowledge to do it. We destroyed all of the books and history when Lake killed the king."

"I'm sorry," I whispered.

"Do you understand now? I'm free from the Septori, but now I'm tied to someone who seems to have some sort of death wish." He chuckled sardonically.

"Is that why you wanted to kill me?" I asked, and understanding finally dawned on me.

"Yes." He grabbed his head in frustration and stormed around the room, and then stopped, dropping his hands in defeat. "And no. I want to go home to my family and friends."

The word "family" made me wonder if Kael had a wife back home. He was certainly old enough to marry. A sour feeling hit the bottom of my stomach at the thought of Kael bonded to someone.

"But then I'm scared, because I don't know what would happen to me if you died. Would I die? If I am truly blood-sworn to you, then I would. But I don't know if it is the same kind. It feels like it, which makes me wonder. SwordBrothers don't feel fear. We are taught that to fear is to hesitate, and to hesitate is to die."

"Maybe there is a way to reverse it," I said, trying hard to not cry.

"If there were a way to do it, we would have done it hundreds of years ago instead of committing mass suicide. But I don't know. I had hoped to find the answers with the adepts. So I presented myself to Adept Pax, and he thought of ways to pay me for my services so I could stay close to you and test our boundaries. And then you told me quite emphatically to get lost and that you never wanted to see me again." He rubbed the back of his head to remind me of our parting ways.

"Yes, I did, didn't I?" I chewed on the bottom of my lip, feeling terrible.

"Well, you can see how that's going to be a problem. Not to mention that you decided to go run off to the Shadow Mountains. I didn't even know that you had left the Citadel until the blood-bond kicked in, sending me reeling in pain. I took a horse from the stable, and I left the next day. I followed the pull until I found you, knowing that you would somehow get yourself into trouble again." He snorted and rolled his eyes. "Only this time, it was some sort of contest in which you were giving yourself away."

"That reminds me," I interrupted. "If it was such a stupid contest, why did you enter it?"

"To stop you from having to marry the winner, of course." He raised his hands palm up, and the look on his face bespoke truth. "Why else? If you had to marry the winner, then you would be forced to stay here and get married. I can't let that happen."

"What do you mean, you can't let that happen?" I argued, feeling my famous temper start to rise at his nonchalant attitude. "What gives you the right to decide my future?"

"Everything!" he yelled. "Because I am tied to you until we reverse this. So right now, your future includes me. I need you free and not tied down so you can travel and find a way to break this curse. And once the blood-bond is broken, you can then be free to make whatever stupid mistakes you want to with your own life."

"What if I don't want to help you?" I said in anger, because I hated that he was deciding my future without even asking me. "What if I want to stay and marry and rule my clan?"

"You want to marry the brute who did this to you?" he said in disbelief, pointing to my face.

My chin jutted out in defiance, and without thinking I blurted out, "It's better than the alternative."

He snickered. "Ha! I'm not that bad. I'm not even going to marry you. So what if I win—I just delay your plan a little bit. You can have another stupid Kragh Aru tournament in a year, after you've helped me."

That wasn't the point; he didn't understand my feelings of trying to prove to my family that I was strong enough to run the clan by myself. He didn't even ask me why I had entered the competition. I was too tired to fight with him, and I was getting more annoyed with him every minute; besides, I was feeling overwhelmed.

"Well, your plan will only work if you win tomorrow," I said slowly, trying not to betray my feelings in my voice. He looked at my change in mood with confusion and started walking toward me.

He lifted my chin and saw the tears that I wasn't able to hide from him. As he brushed them away with his thumb, I felt a small jolt of electricity at his touch.

"I don't like to be tied down." He then copied the same movement that Joss did weeks ago and ran his roughened thumb over my lips. The spark was undeniable, even if it was obviously only one-sided. His eyes narrowed and were void of emotion.

"Please…leave." My voice had become husky with warring emotions.

"And go where? You've imprisoned me," he whispered.

I turned my face away, and he dropped his hand as if I had stung him. Kael walked to the door and let himself out. The door closed with a soft click.

My legs felt like rubber, and I slowly collapsed to the floor in front of the fire. I realized that his stealth abilities would let him sneak by anyone downstairs without being caught. In fact, he probably liked the challenge. Lying with my cheek pressed against the soft rug, my fingers grasped hold of it. I stared at the flickering fire and let the tears flow.

I cried silently for the pain that I had seen in Kael's eyes at his inability to be free of me. I cried the tears that I knew Kael himself would never shed.

~13~

The scream of a horse woke me a few hours after Kael left. This night was bound and determined to never end. I rolled over on the rug by the fire and noticed that it had died down to a mere burning ember. So if my fire had burned out, why was my room still alit with a glow? Then the scent of burning hay reached my nose, and the sound of another horse screaming made me jump up in panic. Something was on fire.

Quickly donning my clothes, I looked outside and could see flames in the distance through the trees, dancing on the rooftop of Aldo's house and barn. My first concern was my horse.

Faraway?

I'm okay, I'm in the field, he responded. *I wanted to be near our new friend.*

Breathing a sigh of relief that he was safe, I rushed into the hall and half slid, half fell down the steps and caught myself at the last moment, but not before spraining my ankle.

"Father!" I yelled through the house.

"He's not here," a soft feminine voice echoed from downstairs. "He's already outside helping the others." The voice became louder as it got closer, and Siobhan turned the corner and came into view. Her eyes were red-rimmed and puffy, as if she had been crying. "I've come to help you."

"Are you okay, cousin?" I asked in concern.

Shaking her head, she came closer. "I'm sorry," she said. "Aldo's dead."

"What? I don't understand."

"It was the fire," she cried, starting to hiccup. "He died while trying to save the stupid horses. Now the fire has spread to the next house, and everyone is trying to contain it. We must leave, cousin, because if they can't, then your house is next. Your father wants you safely away." She came over to me, and I tried to stand but cried out as I put weight on my ankle.

Stupid, stupid stupid, I thought angrily at myself. "I'm gonna need help."

Siobhan quickly wrapped her arm around my shoulder and helped me stand and walk toward the back door. It was when she was standing shoulder to shoulder to me that I noticed a fresh bruise on her face, but I didn't comment on it as she deftly led me out.

The noise, light, and heat from the fire were definitely weaker at the back of the house. I let Siobhan lead me away from the fire and into the dark. I could hear the sounds of people and animals crying out.

"How much farther?" I asked as I limped along.

"I'm sorry, Thalia. Not much farther," she went on.

"Siobhan, I never got a chance to apologize for how I treated you over the years. I really don't remember it too much, but Father says I was downright horrible."

She froze mid-step and listened. I quickly went on. "I was told I did it to prove my place as the next clan leader, but I don't know, and really I don't care. I've had time to think it over and I was wrong—no matter what the reasons, no one should treat another poorly."

Siobhan continued walking, although this time more slowly. I wished she would take faster steps so we could get to wherever we were going and I could sit.

"A lot of things have happened to me over the last few months, and I've tried, I really have, to be the old Thalia that Father wants me to be." I took a quick intake of breath as I stumbled again, before finishing, "But I can't be her. I don't know her. I only know who I am now. And frankly, I don't want to go back to the way I was."

Nodding her head in understanding, Siobhan spoke up. "You've changed. You are not the same power-hungry, mean-spirited cousin of before. You have grown. It's as if when you disappeared for months, you grew and have emerged into a better person. Like a butterfly."

I shivered at the comparison.

"Yes, Cousin, we do many things, good and bad, to try to please our fathers." With her free hand she unconsciously touched her bruised cheek. "Thalia, you must understand…the need to make your father proud."

"Unfortunately, I do, Siobhan. So will you forgive me for how I treated you in the past?" We had finally quit walking and were at the edge of the village under a stand of trees.

"I...I can't." She pulled her arm from around my shoulders. "I can't accept your forgiveness, knowing that in return you won't forgive me." Two large figures stepped out of the shadows of the trees and came toward me. I tried to balance on one leg as my support walked farther away from me and turned back.

"I'm so sorry, Thalia. I had to. He made me."

The "he" in question stepped forward out of the woods.

It was my Uncle Rayneld. The similarities in the looks between my father and his brother once again made me freeze in confusion. But I couldn't mistake the undertone of hidden contempt in Rayneld's voice.

"Well, hello, Niece."

"Hello, Uncle."

"I'm so glad that you are safe."

I stared at Uncle Rayneld and had a moment of déjà vu. I looked around the dark forest in confusion.

"I'm surprised, really, that you don't remember. I thought for sure when you showed up again that you would have called for my execution. I was surprised when you didn't," he said, taking another step forward. He paused and cocked his head, as if to study me. "Well, I guess that works to my advantage."

"Enlighten me. What exactly should I remember?" I asked. I couldn't ignore the hidden meaning and aggressive body language of my uncle. But at the same time, I wanted to give him the benefit of the doubt. He was family, after all.

"They said it would work, and obviously it did. I never would have expected the effects to last this long. Otherwise, I would have waited a bit longer. But Siobhan says you're starting to remember things." He stopped walking toward me and turned to the side, walking slightly away from me.

I hobbled on one foot and tried to keep him in view as he spoke. "What are you talking about?"

"You have to understand, Niece—it was just a simple error in birth order. I should have been born first, not second, and rightly be the clan leader, not your father. I can uphold the laws just as well as Bearen. I'm an even more ruthless fighter than he is, and I would never have married your outcast of a mother." He spat out those last words, and his eyes lit up with revulsion.

"She may have fooled your father, but I refuse to take that chance. Her bloodline must end. And I can never allow you to rule as the clan leader. I won't allow you to infect the clan."

Turning on me in anger, he pointed one large ugly finger at me. "No more lies." His upper lip curled and showed his teeth in a feral gleam. "Is it true?"

Looking at him square in the eye, I raised my shoulder and chin and firmly stated, "Yes."

"How much of it?" he declared angrily.

"All of it." I wasn't about to back down from him. He didn't need to know that I wasn't really a Denai; the alternative, I thought, would be worse if he knew I was something else entirely.

I saw his shoulders bunch up and fingers curl as the look he gave me was filled with hate. "I knew it." He smiled cruelly. "I was right to drown the mother. I only wish I would have drowned the pup with her."

"What?" The news staggered me, and I fell to my knees and grasped the dirt as images and memories flooded my mind.

Memories of a loving, beautiful woman with long gold tresses, holding me in the air, laughing and spinning in circles. Pictures of us rolling and playing in the grassy meadow and swimming in the lake. I remembered sitting on a blanket, playing with a toy, while my mother sat at the edge of the lake with her feet dangling in the water. My father called to her, and she rose and walked out of sight while motioning me to stay where I was. I remember waiting patiently for her to come back, but she didn't.

Hours later, Odin came to find me still playing on the same blanket, and he asked where Thelonia was. I pointed to the water and told him she was swimming. Sure enough, he looked and saw her golden tresses floating in the water.

My mind blanked and then skipped ahead a few years, to Bvork teasing me, throwing dung at me, and calling me a pig among many other names. There were rumors about my mother, and where she had come from. Some said she was a goddess, others a ghost, because she appeared out of the morning mist, walking cold and barefoot out of the mountain pass. No one knew who she was, and she refused to speak of her past. My father found her, fell in love with her, and married her, refusing to believe the things the people said about her.

They were secretly relieved when she died, and I remember my father telling me that I was teased because of her. He told me that I would have to be strong and prove that I was different.

It was then that I became the strong, uncaring Thalia. I had to prove myself to everyone and close off any emotion. I became the strongest advocate against the Denai and impure bloodlines, even though deep down there was always the fear that I would always be different, mistreated like my mother.

The memories, one by one, flew back as if I was reliving my life from childhood to adulthood in slow motion. I felt myself gag as I was overwhelmed with the knowledge of how much self-loathing I had for the Denai and myself. The hatred was strong and deep. My eyes couldn't focus, and I grabbed my head and waited for it all to stop.

Breathing in a deep breath, I looked at my uncle. "It was you at the river that day, not my father," I stated, feeling myself go nauseous at the thought that I was there when my own mother was murdered. "You killed her."

Rayneld's eyes opened in disbelief, and then he chuckled in pleasure. "Ah, so you do remember." He turned back toward me. "Yes, I killed her, and I tried to get rid of you. But you came back." My neck hairs went on end as he talked, and I let him, because I needed to know everything he knew. "They promised me you would experience great pain and wouldn't live through the process. They lied, because here you are, back to plague me again."

"Who?" I asked him. "Who was it that you gave me to?"

It was coming back; I remembered everything from the night I disappeared months ago, or almost everything. Bvork had refilled my tankard of honey mead for me during our feast. An act that made me raise my eyebrows in question, but one that made him throw his head back in laughter.

"Relax, Cousin." He gestured to his own in an offertory salute. "A toast to the future clan leader. I heard Fenri talking to your father. Your future looks secure."

Warily, I clanked mugs with him and drank down my drink. A few minutes later, I began to feel light-headed and fuzzy.

Something was wrong with my drink, and I stumbled out of the main hall and tried to make my way home. Bvork met me and led me into the woods, where Rayneld was waiting. Slowly, my limbs felt like lead, and my body began to go numb. Even my consciousness began to fade in and out.

There were more men in the forest, and I remember seeing red robes and horses. A gag was placed in my mouth, and a bag that smelled faintly of flour was placed over my head and tied around my neck. I could still hear, and I heard the sound of a moneybag exchanging hands, and Rayneld and another talking.

"She won't remember anything," a low voice interjected. "As long as she drank all of the serum."

"Are you sure she's what you're looking for?" Rayneld asked.

"If she's from the bloodline you think she is from, and she carries any of their blood, then she will do," the low voice replied, too low to determine actual gender.

"That's fine. Just as long as you promise that she will never show up here again."

"That would be inconvenient for your plans, wouldn't it?" The gender-neutral voice chuckled. "Few rarely survive our...how can I put this, um… delicate process."

Deftly, with my hands tied and feeling weighted down from the drugs, I was hefted over someone's lap on a horse, and the saddle pommel dug painfully into my rib cage. I gasped for breath as the horses took off into the woods, and my head slammed against the side of the horse and everything went black.

I awoke a good deal later; it could have been hours or days, because I was still in a drug-filled haze. But I opened my eyes to the putrid-smelling laboratory as I was being strapped into the iron butterfly for the first time, and had my first glimpse of the Raven wearing the silver mask. All of the hated and suppressed memories came flooding back.

Tears burned my eyes and dripped onto the ground, and I screamed in rage at my Uncle Rayneld. "How could you?"

"It was easy. I did what I had to do to guarantee the succession of our clan to be untainted. With you gone, that only leaves my bloodline left to rule. There were rumors that you had been found, and when Bearen went to bring you back, I couldn't let that happen. The men I hired at the pass were supposed to kill all of you, but you survived. Imagine my surprise at learning you didn't remember anything. Siobhan noticed it first, so we changed tactics. Bvork would have been willing to marry you if he won the Kragh Aru and rule in your stead. It would have been such a simple solution. Of course, no children would be allowed from the union. And if you ever regained your memories, an unfortunate accident would have to occur." He sighed dramatically and shook his head. "But your antics at the arena, by fighting in disguise… How stupid. You've disgraced yourself and us. Now he refuses to marry you, the fool."

Rayneld came forward and pulled a knife from a sheath. The moonlight glinted off the sharp blade, and I stared, mesmerized by the beauty of a weapon so deadly. Shaking my head from the trance, I glanced up from the blade. Standing up and precariously balancing myself, I squared off for battle.

"Did it hurt, Thalia? Were you in pain?"

"No," I lied.

"You know if your father really knew what you have become, he would kill you."

"You lie. My father wouldn't."

"That's why he is weak and will be killed next," Rayneld promised.

"Who was it that took me?" It was my turn to change the subject and surprise him.

"What?"

"I want a name. Who approached you to kidnap me? How did you get involved with the Septori?"

"What good would a name do you now?"

"I need to know."

"It's not who you think it is, and there are more than one. The master always has an apprentice. If you cut off the head, the snake can still bite."

Quickly I started to pull power to me so I could try to attack him. But I needed to keep him thinking and distracted. This was the last bit of information I needed from him.

Casting a quick glance over my shoulder, he looked at me hesitantly before answering. "Yes, I think I will tell you. The leader is one of your precious Denai."

I looked at him in confusion, but I had no time, as he lunged forward with his blade. I grasped for power to defend myself and felt Faraway jerk awake at my onslaught for power, but I was too weak and too slow. Too slow to realize that the whole time he was talking he was moving in a circle to make my back face the forest. I had forgotten about the second person. I was too slow to realize the glance over my shoulder was to signal Bvork to attack from behind.

I saw my power connect and send Rayneld flying backward into a tree with a loud crack; his huge form fell forward onto the ground with a thud. It was the same time a club hit me in the side of my face, and I heard more than felt the cracking of my jaw. Only one thought consumed me before I fainted.

"Again?"

~ 14 ~

I was in a wagon being pulled by horses. My jaw hurt, and the bouncing of the wagon over the trail jostled it. Gritting my teeth from the pain only made more pain shoot through the whole side of my face. I desperately wished for unconsciousness again so I could escape it. My good eye was blurry, and I had problems getting it to focus. But I could see the body of a man lying in the back of the wagon with me, covered with a tarp.

Another jostling of the wagon, and the tarp slipped slowly from the man. I could see the still, deathly white form of my father. I tried to grunt out a cry, and I alerted whoever was driving that I was awake. The wagon came to an abrupt stop, and the sound of feet hitting dirt told me that the driver had gotten out. A moment later the wagon bed dipped with the extra weight as he then stepped into the back with me.

Roughly, I was grabbed, and a canteen was pressed against my swollen jaw and teeth, but the pain was too much, and I started to sputter and choke as liquid poured down my throat. I tried to turn my head away. I wasn't really surprised that it was Bvork who was holding the canteen. I tried to spit out the liquid.

"Swallow it!" Bvork ordered and pressed a rough hand on my windpipe.

I had no choice; it was either swallow or die. The liquid had a bitter aftertaste, and a familiar sense of heaviness overcame me.

"Good thing I still had plenty left over from that night months ago." He gave me the same disgusted look that I had seen earlier on his father. "I saw what you did to my father. And I'm not taking any chances." He glanced over his shoulder at the still form.

I breathed a sigh of relief as I realized it wasn't my father lying in the back of the wagon, but Rayneld. In my fuzzy, drug-induced state, I hadn't looked at the length of the beard, and the eyes were closed.

"And I'm gonna make sure you pay." He glared at me and gave me a swift kick in the stomach before nimbly jumping down from the wagon bed.

"Ah didna nean to," I answered as best as my swollen jaw would allow. He must have hit the tree and fallen forward onto his own knife. I closed my eyes in disappointment at what I had accidentally done.

"It will all work out," he chuckled from the side of the wagon. "Siobhan will stay behind and has agreed to say that you ran away again, only this time in shame, and that my father and I have gone after you to convince you to stay. But something awful happened and Rayneld tried to save you, but you both died."

I was left to wonder in silence what that something awful could possibly be. He was right about me not having access to any kind of power as long as he kept me drugged. I tried to reach for it, and I couldn't touch anything—it was gone, or I was numb to it. Whatever this drug was, it also kept me from speaking to Faraway and the wolf. It humanized me. Bvork must have gotten the drug from the Septori. I tried to organize my thoughts over the last few hours, but the fuzziness in my mind kept distracting me.

My cousin or uncle must have set Aldo's house on fire to be a distraction for the clan as they once again tried to arrange my death and disappearance. I applauded their tenacity in trying to keep the clan bloodlines pure. After all, it wasn't very long ago that I was just as cold-hearted and strict. My father was right; we had cast out anyone with any hint of Denai gifts into the mountains.

The sun was directly overhead, and I tried to turn my head and shield my eyes from the glare, but that left me staring at the dead form of my uncle. So I settled for closing my eyes against the brightness on my lids as the drug made me sleep. We stopped two more times as Bvork made me take more sips from the drugged canteen. Soon the sun was starting to set, and the wagon started to climb uphill. Racking my brain, I tried to imagine what was up this way, and I couldn't form any coherent thought. It wasn't until I heard the sound of rushing water that I realized where he had taken me. It was Kirakura Falls.

"Kirakura" actually meant "silent death" in our old language. No one ever came up this way except for trappers. And they would forge the river farther upstream with their wagons. If you crossed at the wrong time of day or season, you could easily be swept downstream in the swiftly running currents and over Kirakura Falls, the steepest waterfall in the Shadow Mountains, with wicked-looking rocks on the bottom. I remembered looking over it as a child and seeing various wagon wheels and small boat pieces littering the embankments on either side of the falls.

My mouth went dry in fear. My mother was drowned in the river, and he planned to send me over the falls, where the rushing river or rocks would very possibly crush me to death, even if I survived the fall. I tried to rock myself back and forth in desperation to free my hands, which were tied behind my back, but only succeeded in twitching my fingers. My body was still numbingly paralyzed.

Bvork unhitched two horses I hadn't even noticed were tied to the back of the wagon. "A horse for my father and one for me," he explained as he caught my surprised look. "We had to come after you on horseback, or we would have never caught up to you. I'm not dumb; I won't underestimate you like my father." Leading the horses away, he tied them to a tree and then proceeded to step into the wagon. He pulled off the tarp that covered his father and wrapped it around his arm. He placed next to me a bag of food and my cloak.

As he reached down with his knife, I blanched, expecting to feel the sting of the blade cutting me, but instead I felt a small jerk as my hands were cut free. Throwing the rope to the side, he again poured more drugs down my throat. Jumping out, he went to the horse and began to lead the horse and wagon down to the water's edge.

Leading the horse in a full circle, he made the wagon enter first and was making the horse back into the rushing current. I could tell from the roaring sound of the waterfall that we were really close to the drop-off, and if the rushing water caught the weighted wagon, it would pull it into the river. All of us would be swept away over the falls. I cringed that he was going to unnecessarily kill the horse.

Bvork was having trouble getting the horse to back into the current. The horse was fighting him. I felt the splash of water as the wheels dropped off the small embankment and hit the water. But it wasn't far enough in. The horse was refusing to enter the river and was desperately trying to turn to the side.

I grunted out in frustration as I tried to move my body, but I was a prisoner in my own mind. I felt my hands twitch in response again, and I focused all of my attention on moving my feet. The curling of my big toe gave me hope as I prayed that the horse was stubborn enough to delay getting any deeper in the water.

"Darn it, horse," I heard Bvork yell out, as an angry snap of a whip accompanied his curses. The horse whinnied in protest and snorted and stamped against the oncoming lashes. My life was being spared by the stubbornness of a horse. I heard another whinny, this time in pain, and the horse stumbled backward into the wagon, which made the wheels sink into the riverbed and start to slip on the rocks, farther and farther into the river. *This is it*, I thought as more water splashed into the bed and began to pool around my feet.

Another tug, and the wagon stopped. Furiously the horse fought and pulled against the current and strained toward the shore.

"Bvork! Stop!" a feminine voice yelled out, riding to the river's edge.

"Siobhan! What in the world are you doing here?" The sound of the whip stopped as I assumed Bvork turned to deal with his sister.

The cold water made my limbs tingle and burn with feeling. *Come on, come on*, I silently urged as my legs started to spasm and twitch. *Almost. PLEASE!* I prayed. I didn't want to die.

"I can't let you do this!" she begged.

"You have no right to be here," he yelled back. "You should be back in the village telling them that she ran away. It will look suspicious if our whole family has disappeared."

"I won't do it," she snapped back firmly. "I won't live under your rules anymore. You can't make me."

Yay, Cousin, I thought in amusement. I could really get to like her, if I lived past today. The grunting of the horse as he continued to try to pull the weight up the embankment stopped as he slipped and fell into the water.

More water filled the wagon bed and weighed it down. The horse gave up on the embankment because it was too steep and tried to turn upstream to find another way out. The wagon lurched, and water sloshed into my mouth and face. I spit it out as the wagon bed evened out. We were in trouble; there was five inches of water in the bed, and it was covering and stinging my whole body. But at least it was taking the numbness away as pins and needles of cold encompassed me.

Grunting in pain, I was able to reach up my hand, which felt like dead weight, grasp the wagon side, and slowly pull myself into a sitting position. I could see that my ankle was swollen and black and blue. I didn't want to even look at my face, knowing that I had one swollen eye and a swollen jaw.

I saw Siobhan pull out a sword that was too large for her and challenge her brother. Bvork laughed and pulled out his sword from his pack.

This was a very uneven fight, and unfair knowing firsthand how devious a fighter he was. She charged first, and I was surprised at how determined Siobhan was. She attacked and parried and fought her brother with the intent to kill. But I could see where it was going. She wasn't as strong as her brother, and her heavy sword was tiring her. Bvork blocked her sword thrust and then backhanded her across the face. She fell into a heap on the ground and didn't move.

An undertow caught the wagon and started to pull us into the middle of the river, and the horse screamed in fury. He dug in his hooves and desperately tried to get out. I had to hand it to the horse, he wasn't going to give up. My uncle's heavy body rolled against me and pinned me to the side.

"Aahhh," I grunted as I struggled to move his body off me.

Another scream of the horse, and I turned to look at a very familiar white back. Faraway! Somehow, Faraway was the horse that was attached to the wagon. Of course he would have to be here. No one would believe I had run away without my horse. I smiled in delight as I realized why this particular horse was fighting so hard. I couldn't speak to him, and I tried to encourage him with prayer. But my smile turned to fear as I realized he was losing the battle. By turning upstream, he was fighting the weight of the wagon and the rushing current.

Bvork stood on the side, arms crossed, and watched silently as we were slowly being pulled farther out into the river. Any farther, and Faraway wouldn't be able to touch bottom. I felt around Rayneld's body until my hands found a knife on his belt. Turning my body as much as I could, I pulled myself over the back onto the driver's bench.

The bench dug into my stomach as I slashed at the tethers that bound Faraway to the wagon. I cut one tether off, and the wagon slid sideways and Faraway screamed. It was too late. We were pushed into the middle of the current.

Movement on land caught my eye, and I watched as four men on horses charged out of the woods, led by a giant grey wolf. Fenri, Odin, Kael, and what looked like Joss were leading a thunderous charge to Bvork, who turned in surprise and raised his hands as he was almost run over by the horse; unfortunately, he rolled away at the last minute.

Dismounting at a run, Kael ran at Bvork, engaging him in a fight for his life. Fenri stopped to check on Siobhan, while Odin and Joss ran to the water's edge.

Odin hollered and ran down the side of the embankment, following us as we were flowing at the river's mercy, Joss running as fast as he could ahead of him. Reaching for Faraway's reins, I wrapped them around my forearm and then desperately slashed at the remaining tether. Once the tether was cut away, the wagon flew from under me. I was dunked head first into the water. My arm burned in pain; it took the brunt of my whole weight.

Faraway moved more easily without the wagon, but by now we had floated too close to the waterfall. I tried to shift and move to one side of my horse so I wouldn't be in the way of his dangerous, kicking hooves.

Gasping for air, I was repeatedly dunked underwater. There was nothing I could do, as I had wrapped the reins around my arm and I didn't have the strength to grab them higher up. At least my body didn't hurt so much in the water.

Faraway made me proud as he fought and kicked to get to the edge. He foamed at the mouth with effort. Odin was yelling and pointing, but it was no use. I couldn't hear him over sound of the roaring waterfall. I heard the unmistakable sound of the wagon being smashed against the rocks. I turned and watched it get bashed to pieces before heading over the falls.

Faraway was getting closer to the shore, but he was tiring fast. I was too heavy, and he hadn't recovered from the ordeal yesterday. I looked and saw Joss perched on a large rock that protruded into the river. He was lying on his stomach, but the current slowly pulled us out of his reach. He caught my eye as I floated past him, and he must have known what I was thinking, because I saw him mouth the words. *NO! Don't!*

It was too late; we both couldn't make it out alive. I fumbled and unwound Faraway's reins from around my arm and sent, with all the effort that I could, one last mental thought to my horse, praying he would get it.

Farewell.

I released my grip on his reins and swallowed a mouthful of water as my head dunked underwater before I rose to the surface and bobbed precariously through the waves. I watched

Faraway, load lightened, touch the embankment and struggle slowly out of the water.

Joss' horrified face was the last thing I saw as the thunderous roar became deafening. I felt like I was falling and flying at the same time as I went over the falls. My body was still too numb to feel the crushing waves pound me, and I truly felt a freedom and peace, as if I were being embraced by God even in death.

God must truly be a loving and forgiving God if he was willing to save a twisted monster like me. All of a sudden, a bright warm light surrounded me, and I was floating in the air. It was ethereal—until I was dumped, wet and cold, on the rocky embankment back at the top of the falls.

My eyes flew open, and I spit up what must have accounted for half of the river. Choking and wheezing, I tried to calm the frenzied beating of my heart.

Joss was next to me, pale and gasping for breath as he leaned his sweat-stained forehead against the ground. This was something I was very familiar with, a sure sign that he had overtaxed his Denai abilities pulling me from the water.

Odin collapsed next to me, and the large warrior broke down into sobs. "I thought you were gone. I saw you go over." He sniffled. "It's a miracle." And then he looked at me and gasped in horror. "What did they do to you?"

Silent and ashamed, I looked away and saw Kael slowly walk toward me, his shirt torn and bloody. When Kael saw my injuries, he paused and stiffened, and his eyes turned stormy in anger. I looked to Kael and flicked my eyes to where I had last seen Bvork, and Kael nodded slowly. It was all the affirmation that I needed; the SwordBrother had already avenged me.

Joss looked at me with joy in his eyes, and then sorrow.

"Are you okay?"

"Yes, I'm fine."

"Thalia, don't you ever do that again," he admonished me. "I wasn't even sure if I could."

"You could have burned yourself out doing what you did," I challenged him.

"I was going to try to slow the water and bring you closer, but you let go. You left me no choice. I had to try."

"Have you ever tried to stop a raging river?" I asked.

"Uh, no. I've never tried that, either." He looked sheepishly at me.

"Then don't get mad at me for a decision I had to make. You would have done the same thing in my shoes." I smirked at him and then felt the pain flare up in my jaw.

He touched it, and I felt a slight tingling go through my jaw. "It's not broken, just fractured. But I don't have the strength to heal you. I'm sorry." He looked angry with himself.

I reached up and grabbed his hand. "Joss, don't be sorry. You saved my life... Again. As long as you get me back on the road toward home, I'll be fine. The sooner I get home, the better. How's Faraway and Siobhan?"

"Both are good." This came from Fenri, who walked Faraway over to me. The horse leaned down and nuzzled me.

I felt a warm flicker of emotion touch me and then another thought.

In the words of the human, "Don't ever do that again!"

The human must be Joss. I painfully grinned at Faraway.

I won't do that again. I promise.

We are bonded—we go together. Okay?

All right.

"Where's Father?" I asked, looking around.

Odin answered. "Thalia, he was injured in the fire, and we wouldn't let him come after you."

"Then what are we waiting around here for? Let's get home."

~15~

The trip home took longer than the trip up to the falls, mostly because we had two injured people and a very tired horse, and night had fallen. We chose to stay the night at a halfway point and make camp using supplies that survived the falls. Joss was strong enough by then to heal me of the worst of my injuries, but I asked him to leave the bruises and my stitches alone.

"Let Mother Nature take her course on that," I joked. "Save your strength for my father. Believe me—you'll need all the help you can get with that one, because I'm bound and determined to have you look at him when we are done. You are a much better healer than I am." Joss chuckled and then headed to get some food.

Odin came and sat near me, and I asked him for more details.

Apparently Bearen had rushed into the burning house to try to save Aldo's child, and the roof collapsed on him. The men were able to get him and the child out, but he was burned quite badly. Bearen had protected the child from the flames by shielding him with his own body.

"How did you know I was gone?" I asked him.

Odin was chewing on a stick thoughtfully and pointed at Kael with the chewed end of the stick.

"That one came running up to me, swearing to no end that you were gone. I tried to ask him how he knew, and he said he just did. I thought he must be crazy, but we searched for you, and sure enough we couldn't find you. We did find a note from Siobhan saying that her father and brother had taken you."

Odin looked across the fire to where Fenri was leaning down, giving Siobhan a bowl of soup. Fenri was really a caring man, and he was hovering over Siobhan protectively.

"She's had to live under their thumb for her whole life, and she found the strength to finally stand up to her brother. She could have died today, Odin," I said.

"Well, what she should have done was come get us instead of leaving a crummy note. Or better yet, left us a map," he complained gruffly. "We had to follow that one." Again Odin pointed to Kael. "Back and forth around the village until he took off toward the mountains. I'm not sure what kind of compass he's following, but I'm pretty sure it's broken."

I couldn't help it; I snorted and almost spit out the soup I was eating. Kael, Joss, and the others looked at me in surprise. I muffled my laughter with my hand.

"So, then," Odin went on, "we are following the crazy wannabe clansman. Oh, by the way, we figured out he's not from the Stahler clan. We take off toward the mountains, and he starts to head in the wrong direction again, and that huge wolf from the pass shows up, and starts dancing and spinning and acting all wild." Odin did a sign to ward off evil spirits. "So here I am, a crazy old warrior following a crazy young man and a crazy grey wolf into the middle of nowhere in the mountains, on a hunt for you." Odin waved his hands dramatically, and I could see Kael leaning against a tree, listening in with a comical smile on his face.

I knew that Odin was having a little too much fun in retelling the story, but I knew that he did it for me, to make his goddaughter laugh. I glanced around the camp, looking for the grey wolf, and saw glowing eyes in the woods.

Wolf? I called him mind to mind.

Ja?

Thank you.

Then I realized how lame a thank-you it sounded, but before I could say anything else, I felt a growl of appreciation from him and felt him melt into the forest and take off running. I chuckled.

"What about Joss?" I asked Odin, settling down.

"Lass, you will have to ask him yourself. That one came riding into town as if ghosts were chasing him, looking for you. When he heard you were gone, he demanded to ride with us in search of you."

I nodded in understanding and then caught Joss' eye over the fire. He stood and made his way over to me. Odin politely stood up and gave him his seat.

He looked at the ground, then back up at me. "Are you strong enough to walk?" To show him that I still could, I stood up without help, and we walked slowly around the camp. Joss led me into woods and pulled me into a close embrace, resting his chin on my head.

"I was so worried about you."

Turning toward Joss, I looked at him curiously.

"Joss, why did you come here?"

"A messenger arrived from my family. My sister is missing, and we believe it has something to do with the Septori. I selfishly implored the Council to send me after you, in hopes that you would help me find her. You are the only one who has made it out from the prison, and you may know more clues about how to find them."

Shocked, I froze and felt my knees started to shake at the thought of hunting the Septori on purpose.

"No…um, not the only one," I whispered nervously.

"What do you mean, you're not the only one?" He clutched my shoulders desperately. "You mean there's someone else who can help us as well?"

"Well, if you can get him to agree to."

"Who?" he demanded urgently.

I pointed with my chin over in the direction of Kael kneeling by the fire.

"How come you never said anything before?" he asked accusingly.

"It wasn't my place to tell his story," I explained quietly. "Not everyone wants to the world to know what happened to them down there."

I saw Joss' eyes fill with pity as he looked at Kael.

"No," I snapped. "Don't pity him. He would hate that. None of us want that. We are all stronger than that. We may be different now and changed, but please don't ever feel pity for us." I didn't realize it, but that look he'd given Kael cut me deeply.

"I'm sorry, Thalia," he whispered as he cupped my cheek in his hand. "I won't feel sorry for either of you, even though I know what you went through." He leaned forward and kissed each of my closed eyelids. His lips pressed lightly against them before giving me a light and reassuring peck on my nose. I was too shocked with emotions to do anything, and I let him give me a soft, slow kiss on my lips.

It was warm and comforting; when he pulled back, I saw a soft, caring look in Joss' eyes—but not before looking over his shoulder and seeing the exact opposite emotions displayed in Kael's eyes. I stiffened at the hard, uncaring glance he shot

Joss as he turned away and silently stepped into the darkness. The dark cloud followed him.

Joss felt me stiffen and turned to see Kael's back. He let out a discouraged sigh. "Well, there went my chances of convincing Kael to help me. He's been very blunt in his feelings toward me."

"It's okay, Joss. I will help you find your sister," I said good-naturedly. I hated what I was about to do, but we needed to find Joss' sister, and time was of the essence;. Afterward I would help break the curse on Kael. Who knew, maybe the answer lay in hunting the Septori.

"What about Kael?" he asked. A sliver of hope came through in his voice. "I'm pretty sure he won't want to help find my sister."

"Don't worry. If I'm with you, he will surely be close by. He can't help it." I grinned reassuringly at Joss but felt my gaze search the darkness for Kael's form.

Sadness overcame me, as I knew my decision to help Joss first and not Kael would hurt the stoic SwordBrother and drive an even deeper wedge of hatred between us, one that I didn't think could be repaired.

~16~

"Absolutely not! By all that is holy, I refuse to allow you to travel with this heathen." Bearen breathed in deeply, as if he were trying to make himself look more intimidating. At six foot four, he was a bear of a man with his black beard and hawk-like nose, and his blue eyes were intense with anger. But he was only scary until he started to cough great heaving coughs that shook the whole house, which were the aftereffects of breathing in smoke as he saved Aldo's child from a fire. Then the clan leader was reduced to being tended to like a sick child as my cousin Siobhan rushed in with water and a handkerchief.

Odin, Fenri, Joss, and I didn't tell him that when he was sick with fever and passed out from pain, I had Joss sneak into his house and heal him of the worst of the burns and blisters from the fire. I thought it prudent to have Joss heal him this time, so if he awoke he couldn't accuse me of disobeying him. Except that when he awoke, he didn't notice how much better he felt. I think the great warrior was trying to play up being sick to get as much sympathy as he could, except for the cough. We didn't touch his lungs because that would draw too many unwanted questions.

But he wouldn't let a little cough burden him when he was about to lose his only daughter whom he'd just found again. He wasn't about to let her leave with his greatest enemy. When his cough had settled, he once again turned those angry eyes on me. "You are still underage, and must obey my rules. That is, until you become clan leader."

I had been, up until that point, sitting on a short three-legged stool next to my father's bed, but I sent the stool flying as I jumped up in anger and pointed to him. "Father, you have to listen to me. You've ignored me every time I've tried to tell you about what happened. But you can't ignore it. Not anymore, especially when it was Rayneld who had a hand in my kidnapping. It was your brother who sold me to the Septori to be used as an experiment. It's his entire fault that this happened to me."

Siobhan, who had only a few days ago betrayed me and handed me over to my uncle and cousin to be killed, stilled at my words. I didn't believe she would have done it if they hadn't beaten her into submission. She had redeemed herself in my eyes when she rushed to the waterfall, sword in hand, and tried to save me from her brother. I glanced at her quickly to see if I had offended her by bringing up her father's involvement. But she seemed unaffected by my words and went on changing the bandages on Bearen's almost healed wounds. It was as if, in her grief at losing her father and brother, she had sought comfort in caring for her uncle.

"You will listen because it involves your family," I spat out. Bearen's eyes widened in shock. "Your brother was trying to kill you at the pass. He was the one who hired those mercenaries to ambush us so he could become clan leader. Bvork was the one who, months ago, drugged my drink and led me outside, where your brother handed me over to the Septori."

My anger started to get the best of me, and I could feel myself grasping for Faraway's energy, something I tended to do when I got mad. But I quickly gained control of myself and released it. "Do you even know what they did to me?"

"Thalia, I told you that we would never speak of this, and you agreed to the Kragh Aru so you could find a strong lifemate and become clan leader." Bearen was sounding desperate from hearing the words, as if, by my speaking them, he could ignore what happened. And I could still be the clan leader, still be a perfect example of a Sinnendor vassal, still be his little girl.

"No, Father!" I interrupted him. "You agreed that I would never speak of this, not me. And I let my love for you keep me from speaking, but no longer." I walked to the shuttered windows and threw them open, knowing that I would need the cool wind to blow on my face to remind me that I was free and no longer a prisoner.

"They took me to an underground prison where I and other children, human and Denai alike, were kept to be used as test subjects. They were cruel. They starved and beat us if we disobeyed or spoke. The overdose of serum that Bvork gave me erased my memories, and every night I prayed that my family would find me." I turned from the window to watch my father's reaction. His eyes had closed and his face had turned pale; the only movement was the bobbing of his Adam's apple as he turned his head away so he wouldn't hear what I said next. But even though he was my father, I knew it was time he heard it; he couldn't ignore it, and because I loved my father, I would have to hurt him with the truth.

"I prayed that you would find me." My anger started to disappear when I looked at my father's stricken face. I knew he had searched desperately for me. "But no one came for any of us. Each night I would be hauled away to the Raven's experimental lab and tortured, pricked, probed, and subjected to a terrible machine. The Septori used their power and this machine to change me. I didn't know what they were trying to do. I had no clue it had worked until after I escaped. Father,

I'm no more a Denai than you are, but I'm definitely not human anymore. I can do things similar to a Denai, but the way I do it is wrong, twisted, inhuman. I steal where the Denai borrow. So if you think the Denai are inhuman beasts, then I can only speculate on what you think I must be." The tears that I had been holding back started to burn at the corner of my eyes and run down my face.

"I had no idea," Bearen whispered, his voice breaking and choking on the words. "I'm ashamed of myself and my clan for not being able to save you. But I had no idea what they did to you. I was too scared to know, for fear of hearing these very words. I thought maybe if I ignored it, we could pretend that nothing happened. Pretend that I didn't fail at saving my daughter, being there for her when she needed me most." Bearen's voice tapered off into nothingness, and I heard soft sobs coming from behind me. Turning, I saw that Siobhan had righted my stool and was crying softly into her apron.

"Father, I survived, but my cell mate Cammie didn't. She died in that prison, along with countless other children who didn't have to. And more are going to die, because the Raven and the Septori are still out there. One of the prisoners, Tym, was murdered during our escape."

"Then let the Denai hunt for the Septori and this Raven. If he is a rogue Denai, then he is their problem, not ours," Bearen protested. It was always hard to win an argument with Bearen because he was so stubborn, but so was I.

"It's not their problem—it's everyone's problem. Human and Denai alike were kidnapped. It was specifically because of my Sinnendor blood that the Raven wanted me." I grasped my head to cease the sudden pounding that had started again, though it happened less often. Usually it was a sign when Kael was near, a side effect of our shared bond. Sure enough, a knock came at my father's bedroom door, and I wasn't in the least bit surprised to see that it was Kael.

When Kael stepped through the door, Siobhan quietly let herself out. I had not forgotten that Kael had killed her brother at the waterfall; the fearsome Swordbrother intimidated her.

Kael met Bearen's steely stare without flinching. The two warriors engaged in a silent battle of wills. Kael was the first to move as he conceded with a nod of his head. He took out a small dagger and unsheathed it. Silently he placed it between both palms and bowed stiffly to my father, offering him the knife. I was stunned. He had given my father one of the highest honors a SwordBrother could give by acknowledging my father as a fellow warrior. Bearen grunted, and a small smile crept over his weathered face.

After my father took the knife from him, Kael turned and addressed me. "Has a decision been made when we will depart?"

"No, she will not be allowed to leave and chase after those men without protection and with a heathen Denai, unescorted, no less. I forbid it," Bearen growled. I was sure that Odin and Joss could hear my father from downstairs.

"Father, I told you, we need to travel fast and light. We can't afford to take a battalion of clansmen with us."

"It doesn't matter—you won't be allowed to go. I am not above putting you under guard and locking you away." He glared at me. "Especially after what you just told me, that the Septori were very interested in your bloodline. I will not allow them the chance to take you again. I will not be lax in my duty."

"We are wasting time. Joss' sister needs help!" I raised my voice to match my father's. A clearing of a throat made me spin in anger toward Kael.

"WHAT?" I snarled.

"Do you mind if I speak with your father?" he asked politely.

"What?" I was floored that he had actually asked permission. "Fine, be my guest," I said as I waved my arm dramatically in front of me so he could feel free to address my father.

"Alone," he said.

"What? NO!" I said indignantly. "You can speak in front of me."

"THALIA!" Bearen spoke my name in the one tone I knew I couldn't disobey.

"What could Kael possibly wish to discuss that he can't say in front of me?" Bearen just glared. My voice rose in pitch like a child's; I didn't care. "But he's not even clan. And pretending to be a clanmember to fight in the Kragh Aru does not make him clan." I was furious. I knew I was losing the fight, but why not make my opinion known and go down fighting?

Another cold stare from my father, and I was reduced to the tantrum of an only child not getting her way.

"FINE!" I sniffed, and made sure to slam the door on my way out. I stomped downstairs to fling myself theatrically on a chair. The sound of barely contained laughter drew my attention to Joss and my godfather Odin, who were both covering their mouths and making awful faces. I glared at both of them and then threw the first thing I could get my hands on: a half-eaten dinner roll. Odin ducked, and it smacked Joss in the face, which only led to another round of laughter.

"Well, you two are no help at all. Joss, this is serious. I may not be allowed to leave. You will have to look for your sister, Tenya, without me. I'm very sorry." I felt horrible; I personally knew what she was going through and knew that

121

time was of the essence. The trail could go cold if we didn't leave soon.

Joss' demeanor changed instantly. "I know, Thalia. Even now it could be too late, but I didn't know where else to turn. My family is looking for her, the Adepts have sent Graduates and Guards out looking, and no one has come up with any clues on where to find the Septori. You and Kael are the only ones who have firsthand experience with them."

"Well, Kael destroyed the prison and lab we escaped from, so if they are still kidnapping people, then they must have moved to a new one. It could be anywhere in Calandry." I was making myself depressed, and the longer it took for us to leave, the more I seemed to lose hope at ever finding her.

Odin picked up the half-eaten dinner roll I had thrown at Joss from the floor and was tearing it apart in frustration. "I'm sorry, Thalia, my girl," he said. "I've known your father his whole life, and I can't see anything or anyone changing his mind on this. It would be best if the boy left on his own and returned to the city to seek help."

"I could run away!" I said desperately. "I will leave my father a note. Odin, you could explain everything after we have left."

"I will not," Odin said sternly. "You will not take the coward's way out. You will obey your father's decision, no matter what. I will not be privy to helping you deceive him again by helping you run away."

"She won't have to." Kael spoke from the stairs. "Even though I know she would take the coward's way at her first opportunity. That won't be the case this time."

Joss spoke up. "What do you mean, Kael?" Kael, slowly taking his time, walked the remaining steps down and didn't speak a word until he came up to me.

Kael's lip went up in the slightest hint of a smile. "Because we leave in an hour."

~ 17 ~

"How? What did you say to him?" I gasped. "He is still alive, right? You didn't kill my father so that I could go, did you?" I wouldn't put it past Kael. In fact, he would and could. "Odin, go check on my father," I blurted out worriedly.

Kael looked at me, and he actually looked smug. "Relax, Thalia, your father is fine. We just spoke warrior to warrior and have come to an understanding. If you don't believe me, go speak to him, but make it quick. I want to be on the road as soon as possible."

I did just that; I ran up to my father's room and burst through the door. Bearen was no longer lying in bed but was pulling a box out of his closet. He looked tired and worn, but his eyes had a glint in them. The same glint I saw when he was about to go into battle. He turned to me and opened the box to pull out a small handkerchief. He handed it to me, and I could feel a small weight in the middle. Opening it, I saw a man's ring with an onyx stone and a silver wolf's head on it.

Clearing his throat, Bearen spoke. "Take it, Thalia. It's your heritage. It's King Branccynal's signet ring. They may take our land, but they can't take our heritage."

"Thank you, Father."

"Go—the SwordBrother has agreed to go with you, and I put my trust in him. So come back soon, my daughter."

"How?" I demanded. "Why him? Why are you all of a sudden letting me go when you refused before? Did he threaten you?"

Bearen chuckled. "A warrior knows how to battle with things other than weapons. He battled with words, strong enough to make me see the light."

"No. That doesn't sound like Kael at all. I know you, Father. There is more that you are not telling me," I said accusingly. "What about the contest?"

"That hardly seems necessary now, does it, since the SwordBrother already killed Bvork."

"Wait, does that mean...that he is considered the winner? What are the elders going to say about it, he's not of our clan? What about—"

"Thalia, I have a huge mess to clean up with the fire, your cousin's and uncle's deaths, and the Kragh Aru. Kael suggested to me that it might be best if you weren't here for a while. Until things cool down."

"But how come you trust him...and not—"

Bearen interrupted me, "He also made an oath. He would bring you back safely, or he would come and forfeit his life to me."

"Why would he do that?"

"You will have to ask him, not me. Now go before I change my mind." He was firm. But he was letting me go. I'd heard it with my own ears. Bearen turned, and I ran into his arms and hugged him, knowing that this could be the last time I ever saw him.

"But you will take Hemi with you. I know this Kael is a strong warrior, but I will also send one of mine." He stared me down as if daring me to argue. I did the only thing I could think of doing—rolled my eyes and hugged him again.

***

We'd been on the road for over a fortnight. I was surprised how far Skyfell was from the Ioden Valley. We had been delayed by days of cold rain that made the roads muddy and hard to travel. We weren't making the speed that we needed to, and this added one more thing to worry about. Closing my eyes, I grasped my family ring on the chain around my neck and sent a quick prayer to the heavens to grant us speedy travel and fair weather the rest of the way. Kael rode us at a hard speed but argued with Joss more than necessary over directions. Kael was trying to lead, but Joss was the one who knew how to reach Skyfell.

"I'm telling you, we need to keep going. We've got another hour of daylight." Kael was like a hound on the scent, frantic to chase after the prey. In his case, the closer we came to finding the Septori, the closer we would come to breaking the bond between us, and he would then be free to return home.

"And I'm telling you that you aren't going to find a better place to camp. There's shelter off the trail a bit. Another storm is coming in, and we have better coverage there. If we keep going, we are going to be caught in the middle of it with no place to seek shelter." Joss threw his pack on the ground and stood firm, his blond hair blowing in the wind, green eyes blazing.

Kael's muscle in his cheek twitched, a sign that he was holding his temper in check. His eyes flicked to me briefly and then back to Joss before nodding in consent. He pulled his pack off his horse and grabbed the reins, and started to lead his horse into the woods toward a dense stand of trees.

Joss cleared his throat. "Um, it's that way." He pointed left across the road in the other direction. Kael froze midstep and waited ten whole seconds before turning his horse around and charging in the other direction, showing the bushes and twigs no mercy as he stomped them to pieces.

Hemi, the ever-quiet one, just gave me a look, shrugged his large shoulders, and followed Kael into the woods. Joss walked up to me, irritated. "What's his problem? He's been acting weird since we left the Ioden Valley."

I hadn't told Joss about Kael's unfortunate bond, and how much Kael resented being tied to me. But they were both irritating me this trip. They'd been snapping and challenging each other's authority. I was so glad that my father had sent my clansman Hemi with us. His solid, quiet presence was a relief, and I would oftentimes sit with him and let the peacefulness that surrounded him calm my nerves.

"What's your problem, Joss? You keep goading him on! He is the one who's risking his neck to help find your sister. I thought you would be pleased to have a SwordBrother on our side." I needed to remind Joss how important Kael was to our quest. Having Kael was like having an extra ten fighting men.

"I am pleased to have a SwordBrother helping me locate my sister," he said loudly, before dropping his voice to vent under his breath, "I just wish it were a different SwordBrother."

"And what is the likelihood of that ever happening? How many SwordBrothers do you know?" I challenged Joss playfully as I dismounted Faraway in preparation to lead him down the same path Kael had gone.

"Well, let's see." Joss pondered for a moment. "Excluding Kael, that would be… none." He smiled at me, and reached for my hand and placed a kiss on it, rubbing the back of my hand with his thumb where he had just kissed it. My heart soared at the gesture and beat even louder when Joss leaned in to follow his peck on my hand with a full kiss. I wanted to prolong the kiss, but a crack of thunder made us jump and grab our horses and start to head toward camp. I went to move away, but Joss held firmly onto my hand, and that's how we approached the shelter.

Kael was unsaddling the horses and moving them into the stable that was built into the side of the small but cozy shelter. It looked like an old way station that hadn't been used in a while. Kael covered his horse with a blanket and stepped out of the stable, and froze as he stared at our hands clasped together. He paused for three heartbeats, glancing between Joss and me before continuing on into the shelter, the door slamming loudly behind him.

My cheeks burned in embarrassment, even though I knew that Kael knew that Joss and I had feelings for each other. It was obvious that Kael disapproved of Joss and me being together. And so did my father, because Joss was a Denai. Maybe it was because I felt like Kael was the eyes and ears of my father now. The two had become fast friends, whereas I had thought that my father would be angry at Kael for entering the Kragh Aru tournament and happy that Joss had saved me from going over the waterfall. But it was the opposite. My father liked and even respected Kael, and had an intense and ingrained dislike of Joss. So maybe I was feeling guilty that I was letting myself start to have feelings for a Denai against my father's wishes.

Sighing, I dropped Joss' hand and followed him into the stable to get Faraway settled against the storm.

Are you going to be okay with the storm coming? I mentally asked my horse.

Of course. I'm well sheltered and have fine company. He snickered good-naturedly.

My horse happened to be very vain and found himself in the company of two mares on this trip. So he would pride himself on being the strong, courageous stallion if they were frightened.

Why did I even bother asking? I thought at him sarcastically as I ran my fingers through his mane, pressing my forehead against his.

Because you care for me and worry about me. It's all right, I worry about you, too.

I know. Turning away from Faraway, I saw Joss watching me quietly. I had told him that my horse and I could speak to each other, and it never fazed him; he was very observant and never interrupted when he saw me withdraw and become still, a sign, he said, of when I was speaking to Faraway.

"You ready to go in?" he asked politely.

"No." I walked over to Joss and wrapped my arms around him, and leaned my head into his chest. He smelled wonderful, of earth, spice, and faint horse. "Joss, I'm scared. I want to help find your sister, but I'm terrified."

"Thalia, you're only human. I expect you to be scared. I would be worried about you if you weren't. After all, you have a reason to be scared." He hugged me tighter and kissed the top of my head. Another crack of thunder hit, and we both jumped as a torrential downpour started. Even though the stable was next to the way-station shelter, we still had to run outside to get to the front door. It didn't matter; a few seconds in the rain, and our clothes were soaked clean through.

Entering the one-room way station, I realized what my delay in coming inside had cost me. There was no place to change. Joss and I took off our soaked boots and placed them by the fire. He stripped off his wet shirt and hung it to dry. My eyes were drawn to his abs, and I felt myself blush and look away, only to find Kael's stormy blue eyes, and my blush deepened. Refusing to take off any clothes, I just scooted closer to the fire and did my best to wring them out, pulling the wet material away from my body.

Hemi handed me a plate of food, and I did my best to eat it. But every mouthful felt like it was about to make a hasty exodus. It had been this way our whole journey. Every time I ate, I felt sick, and I wasn't sleeping. I could feel the concerned looks from Hemi as he watched me eat. I tried, but I couldn't keep it down. Sighing, I pushed my plate dejectedly away and stared at the fire until my eyes drew heavy. Moments later I felt myself being lifted off the ground by strong arms and laid gently on one of the two bunks in the room. My eyes fluttered open briefly to make out the red hair and trimmed beard of Hemi. Covering me with a blanket, he turned. I could hear a heated whispered debate going on between him and Kael.

"This is not protecting her!" he argued. "You must be blind if you haven't noticed. She is not eating, not sleeping, and is losing weight. She weighs nothing more than a small child now. She's having nightmares. She is obviously terrified."

"I'm not blind. I've seen it before. In even the bravest of warriors. It is to be expected. She knows what we are going up against."

"She's just a child. I should turn around and take her back to our valley, back to her father, since you seem to be lax in the duty that you were charged with. It would be the right thing to do."

I couldn't hear Kael's quiet answer, even though I strained to hear it against the rumble of thunder. When the thunder faded, they had obviously quit talking and had gone to make up their beds. The storm sounded like it was about to get worse.

***

A crack of thunder made me jump, and I felt a pulse of lighting soar painfully through my body. It was the iron butterfly, and I was once again trapped within the machine. The iron bands wrapped around me and pierced the different pressure points along my arms and body. The Raven peered at me closely through the silver mask, his eyes black and sinister. He raised his hands and called down another bolt of lightning and sent its currents through the bands, and I jerked upright as the spasm wracked painfully through my body. Tears of pain poured uncontrollably down my face, and I started to sob.

But my sobs were muffled as I awoke to strong arms holding me and my face buried into a masculine chest. The thunder from the storm made me sob and shiver uncontrollably in terror. Strong hands held me and comforted me as I tried to get a hold of my fear. The fire had gone out, and darkness enclosed the shelter.

A low voice whispered comfort to me "Shhh, Thalia. You're okay—it's just a dream. It can't hurt you anymore." Another crack of thunder, and my body jerked in memory of the pain; the sound of thunder would forevermore be linked to torture. The whispered voice continued to hold me throughout the storm, never letting up, never releasing me. I was safe; the voice kept the terror away as I snuggled into the deep chest and fell asleep, barely realizing that the scent was not the familiar scent of earth and spice but of leather and musk. It was the first time in weeks I was able to sleep through the night without fear of being plagued by my real-life nightmares.

***

The next morning I awoke alone, cold and a little disoriented. Glancing over my shoulder, I saw that I was the only one left in the way station. Sounds from outside attested to the whereabouts of Hemi, Joss, and Kael. I was glad for the moment's reprieve, as I had the privacy to get dressed and ponder over last night. I was originally under the assumption that it was Joss comforting me during the storm, but now that I was awake, I wasn't so sure.

Rushing to change into fresh clothes, I packed up and ran outside to find Joss, who was clearing the path to the way station of broken tree limbs. It was an unmentioned code to users to leave the station as you found it. Clearing the path of debris and restocking the wood was expected.

I sneaked up behind Joss, and sat on a stump and waited until he saw me before speaking. "That was quite a storm last night, wasn't it?" I quipped more cheerfully than I actually felt.

Joss turned and grinned at me. "I love thunderstorms! It always reminds me of home. You will see why shortly."

I pasted a fake smile on my face as I asked him as carelessly as I could, "So how did you sleep?"

"Like a baby. Nothing could wake me during a thunderstorm. How about you? Did you sleep okay?" he asked, handing me a long branch to haul to the side of the path without sparing me a second glance.

My smile wilted in confirmation that Joss was definitely not the one who had chased away the terror last night. Otherwise, he wouldn't be acting so carefree this morning. "Um, fine," was all I was able to spit out, as my stomach churned with unanswered questions. I flung the branch to the side of the road and went to find Faraway so we could get on the road and leave this way station as far behind as possible.

I had no sooner stepped into the stable than I felt Kael's presence behind me. Turning to him, I looked at him hard with questions in my eyes. His blues eyes were calm this morning, with no hint of hardness; the dark shadow that I could sometimes see following him when he was angry was gone. I couldn't figure him out. It was as if he was hiding behind a mask. One moment he was hard, uncaring, and acted like he hated me, while the next, he would be polite, soft-spoken, and nice. He confused my senses. I was about to open my mouth and ask him about last night, but I saw in his eyes a slight fear, as if he knew what I was going to say. He spoke first.

"I've brought you breakfast. We are eating a cold meal today so that we can be on the road." Kael handed me biscuits and a slice of jerky.

My stomach quelled at the thought of food, and I took it without words and put it in Faraway's saddlebag.

"No, Thalia. You will eat it now," he ordered firmly. I whirled on him, my mouth open wide in shock.

"I'll eat it later, when I'm hungry," I stated, refusing to back down. Too late, I could see the darkness start to form around him. He was getting angry.

"No, I'm going to watch you eat every bite, or I'm turning you around and marching you straight back to your father." Gone was the kindness I had seen earlier, and back was the stubborn hardheaded SwordBrother I was used to. Kael was the only other person I knew who could be as stubborn as my father. "Hemi was right to take me to task. I promised your father I would look after you, and I'm doing a poor job. You are wasting away. I will not have you die on the road because you can't take care of yourself and eat properly."

"I'm taking care of myself—" I shot out, but Kael interrupted me again.

"No, you're not. I've noticed it and let it go on long enough. I should have said something sooner. Remember, it's my life on the line if I don't bring you back safe. I will not be lax in my duty again! So you will eat now, or I'm taking you home!" he roared at me, and I felt chastised.

Gone were any lingering feelings of gratitude I might have held toward Kael as they were replaced by anger and resentment. He was only being nice to me out of duty, out of preservation of his own life; how typical, how selfish, how just like Kael. Flipping open Faraway's pouch, I grabbed the jerky and bit a hunk off it. I chewed furiously on the meat, but the sweet and salty juices hit my empty stomach, and I paled and headed for the nearest unoccupied stall and spit it up. I had been stupid. I should have started with the biscuit, something gentler on my queasy stomach.

"Here, chew on this first." Kael gently touched my elbow and handed me a small green leaf. "It will calm your nerves and stomach. I think that's what making it hard for you to eat—your nerves."

I took the leaf and chewed on it, and felt a moment of refreshment as a mellow mint flavor enveloped my mouth. I sucked on the leaf as long as I could and then spit it out. I took another bite of the jerky, and sure enough it stayed down. Kael watched me like a hawk as he made sure I ate every bite before handing me a cup of water. When he was finally satisfied, he turned and left.

When we were on the road again, the trees soon became larger and greener, and the valleys turned into mountains. The scenery was slowly changing before my eyes; the roads became steeper, rockier, and harder to find.

We stopped at midday to feed ourselves and water the horses. Kael came over to me and handed me lunch. I looked at it despairingly, but Kael's stern gaze left no room for argument.

"Do you happen to have that magic leaf again?" I sounded pathetic, and I knew it. Kael pulled out the leaf out of his pocket, and I followed the same routine as breakfast. He made sure I ate every bite, and then he brought me a second plate.

When we stopped for the night and dinnertime came, it was again the same routine. Joss and Hemi noticed the change in routine as Kael made sure to bring me dinner and once again babysat me while I ate it. My stomach was growling, and for once I was actually hungry for dinner. I asked for the stupid leaf anyway just so I wouldn't embarrass myself and get sick. Kael just laughed at me as I held out my hand for the leaf as soon as he brought me my plate. I saw Hemi give a nod of approval to Kael when he thought I wasn't looking. I would have tried to think of a good comeback for Hemi if I wasn't too busy shoving my mouth full of food.

Tomorrow we would reach Skyfell, and I slept soundly that night. I wasn't sure if it was because I had a full stomach or because a certain SwordBrother slept closer to my bedroll than normal.

~18~

Joss was a wreck. We were almost to Skyfell, and he couldn't sit still on Arrow, his horse. I couldn't blame him. It had been months since he had seen his family, and there would be one fewer person to greet him on his arrival, the reason for this trip, Tenya. It would be a joyous reunion cloaked in sadness.

I heard rushing water and the sound of a waterfall getting closer, and I felt my heart beat faster at the reminder of almost going over Kirakura Falls. As we traveled closer, I realized I didn't hear one waterfall; I heard the thunder of numerous waterfalls. And the air was filled with mist that clung to every strand of my hair, each branch and leaf. Birds of various colors flew from treetop to treetop singing a symphony of songs.

We finally came to a stop along a cliff that looked out into nothingness, just mists upon mists. I could see that the cliff stretched for miles in the shape of a half-moon, and that all around the various rivers spilled over the cliffs to create a meeting place of some of the most majestic waterfalls I'd ever seen. The mists created a continuous cloud right in the middle of the crest.

"Well, here we are," Joss said proudly, holding his hand out to the sky. "Isn't it great?"

I was confused; all I saw was cloudy mists, unless the Skyfell clan resided at the bottom of the cliffs. I leaned over and looked down the cliff to try to see the bottom below, but all I did was drench my face with more drops of water. Hemi appeared equally perplexed and looked around in wonder. Kael stood frozen, eyes darting back and forth, looking for danger.

"Joss, where? I don't see anything." I stared up into the giant trees, looking for any sign of life.

"Out there!" He pointed again, this time into the mists. I followed his finger and looked harder. I caught a hint of green, and then it was hidden by the mists.

"There's something out there." I pointed excitedly. "I saw it."

"It's Skyfell—I told you." Joss grinned at me, grabbing my hands in excitement. He released my hands to pull a whistle from his pack. Playing a fast trill of notes, he waited, and then the call of a bird answered. A beautiful white majestic bird flew from the trees and came to land on Joss' outstretched arm. The bird was at least two feet tall, with a rainbow of tail and a crown of feathers floating above his head. On the bird's claw was a small tube in which Joss inserted a small note. Joss threw the majestic beast into the air, and I watched as he flew straight into the mists. It wasn't long before I heard a loud zipping noise, and out of the mists flew what looked to be giant birdcage with people inside. Down out of the mists they flew at incredible speeds, and only slowed when the line it was connected to evened out.

The square cage slowed and came to a halt a few feet from where Joss stood. The solid lines for the cage were hidden in the trees that led out and up into the mists. Two men disembarked from the cage and came to greet us. One was the familiar form of Darren Hamden. He was dressed impeccably in colorful clothing, his smile spreading from ear to ear, along with the gold hoop earring and blue bead he always wore. Darren was the epitome of the rover lifestyle, loving one woman, Melani, but spending his days traveling and looking for adventure. He was also Joss' godfather. The other one with Darren was a young lad of about fourteen who was called Geff. He helped Joss unload his packs from his horse and then came over to get mine off Faraway.

"Wait a minute, what are you doing?" I stopped him from grabbing Faraway's reins. I startled the boy, and he looked scared.

"I'm taking the horses, miss. They are too heavy for the skycage." He nervously ran his hands down his pants and looked apologetically at me. "There are no horses where you are going; they don't take well to the heights."

"Relax, Thalia." Darren came over and threw his arm over my shoulder. "Geff is taking them down the hill to the bottom of the cliffs to Skydown; all of the horses are stabled down there. Skydown's a smaller village of people who live on the ground. Not everyone is suited for life in the sky." He chuckled at me.

I reluctantly looked at Faraway and then glanced at the cage, which looked barely big enough to hold four people. Darren was right; there was no way for Faraway to travel where I was going. I pressed my hands along Faraway's flanks and ran my fingers across his back. I felt if we were going to be parted, I wanted to let him know I was going to miss him.

He already knows. Faraway's soft nicker reached me. The boy's right—*I would not like to ride that box into the sky. I will be fine.*

Taking a deep breath, I took off Faraway's pack and let the boy lead my horse and tie his reins around Joss' saddle horn. The boy made a caravan of all four horses and grabbed

Arrow's reins, and began the long trek down a small hidden path in the side of the cliff.

"Come on, come on," Darren called. "We must get going." Hemi, Kael, and I followed Darren into the cage, and watched in fascination as he closed and locked the latch. There was barely enough room for the four of us to stand there comfortably.

"Joss, are you coming?" I called out to him nervously when I noticed he didn't enter the cage. Joss was over by a very large tree and was unwinding a rope that was carefully hidden within the branches.

"Yeah, I'll be right behind you. The dorabills can only pull at max four people. I'll follow behind with a skite."

I was at a loss as to what he was talking about. I had no clue what a dorabill or a skite was, but I wasn't left to ponder long when Darren pulled out another flute similar to Joss' and played a short melody. Whereas Joss' tune brought a beautiful white bird called a perot, Darren's song brought on a fearsome creature of giant proportions.

I heard the terrifying scream before I saw the large birdlike creature dive out of the mists, his wings tucked close to his body in what looked to be a suicide dive. At the last moment he spread his wings and stopped, hovering above our cage. I backed away from the bird in fright until my back hit the back of the cage. I was so scared I actually latched onto Kael's arm. Kael had pulled out his knife and was crouched, ready to attack the beast if necessary. Hemi just stared in wonder, never moving a muscle.

The bird, if you could call it a bird, was a deep red with blue plumes and a long, powerful beak. The talons alone marked him for the predator he was, along with his close-set eyes.

Darren laughed at us and reached into a bucket behind him on the floor, and pulled out what looked to be a rabbit carcass. Darren tossed the carcass out the side of the cage high into the air, and the bird dove after it and ate it in two bites. Screeching in what I could only presume was happiness, the dorabill flew back up to the top of the cage and grabbed onto a long, extended railing with his talons. The bird flapped his giant wings and began to pull us back up the line.

The jostling of the cage to the beat of the wings made me sit down in the corner and grasp onto the sides. The up-and-down motion was making me dizzy, and one look at Kael's strong face turning pale made me realize that I wasn't the only one with a fear of heights and falling. Darren grinned at me and told me to look over the edge.

"Are you CRAZY! I'm not doing that," I yelled at him over the beat of the dorabill's wings and the rush of the waterfalls.

Darren just laughed and pointed. "If you think this is bad, you could have taken the skite."

I stood up enough to look over my shoulder at what I presumed was a skite, and I about fainted. Joss was flying next to us on a crazy contraption built with poles and tarps. He was using the updrafts created by the waterfalls to fly what looked to be a toy that could fall apart any minute into the mists.

"Joss, don't!" I yelled as he waved and then caught an updraft and disappeared into the mists. That was it. I thought, *He's going to kill himself.* My heart raced with fear, and I forgot all about my fear of heights as my fear for Joss' life took precedence. But I didn't have to wait long to find out what happened to him, because the next moment we entered the densest part of the mist.

I thought we would be assailed with water that would surely bring down the dorabill and send all of us crashing to our dooms. In reality, we parted through a silvering veil, and the mist vanished. We came face to face with the most awe-inspiring view I had ever seen in my life; more beautiful than the city of Haven and the Citadel itself. I was looking upon a floating city suspended in midair. There were brightly colored houses, towers, and windmills, and flags flew freely in the air. I could see that along the bottom of the floating city were various plants, crops, and flowers growing in the crevices, and people were dangling above the mists, harvesting the plants using a variety of ropes and pulley systems.

A few waved at us as the dorabill flew higher and brought us level to the city. The line the cage was attached to led to a tall watchtower, and the bird flew straight to the tower and gently deposited us on the ground. Another man in the tower came out and gave the dorabill another dead animal for a treat. I grimaced as I heard the crunch of the bones. I could see the beautiful perot sitting on a perch by the watchtower. I much preferred the smaller, less intimidating perot to the powerful dorabill. When Darren opened the cage, I rushed out and firmly planted my feet on the solid ground, and Kael was right behind me.

Joss had already landed his skite and was hanging it up in the tower. He came over to me, his hands open wide, his face a triumphant grin of achievement. He was expecting me to congratulate him or admire his flying abilities. I did the opposite. I punched him.

"What were you thinking? You could have been killed!" I screeched in a very high-pitched voice. I wasn't expecting it myself, and I startled the dorabill, who shrieked in answer to my yelling. I jumped backward in response.

Joss pulled his hands up to defend himself against my onslaught, which had ceased as soon as the dorabill startled me. "Thalia, don't be mad. I've been flying a skite since I was eight.

You will find that many people of Skyfell prefer it as a mode of transportation instead of the skycage and the dorabill." At the mention of his name, the giant bird squawked again and cocked his head to the side, as if looking for another dead animal treat. I just gave the bird an ugly glare.

"You should have warned me about that." I pointed at the giant red bird, who was now also giving me a funny look back.

Joss laughed again. "And miss seeing the scared look on your face? Not a chance." When he settled down, he gave me a sad look and motioned for us to follow him. "Come on. It's time to meet my family."

Kael, Hemi, and I followed Joss through the floating city. Darren had disappeared among the mass of brightly dressed people. Hemi surprised me with his continuous slew of questions regarding the city and the Denai. I had forgotten that this was his first experience in a Denai city other than his one trip to Citadel.

"How does it stay up in the sky?" he asked as he looked over the stone fence that surrounded the city.

"It's what's under the city. It is a certain mineral that the earliest Denai, or, as we call them, the 'great ones,' stumbled on hundreds of years ago. They experimented with it and came across a huge deposit here at the bottom of the waterfalls. Using their gifts, they were able to pull the rock out of the ground and set it to floating in the air. I'm not sure exactly what the mineral is, but I can tell you that there isn't another deposit this big anywhere in Calandry." Joss was bursting with tidbits of information and continued to fill us in.

"The first Denai were strong enough to send whole objects and people from place to place instantaneously. So it wasn't anything for them to make a giant rock float in the air. Today there isn't a single Denai alive in Skyfell who is powerful enough to do what the first ones did. We've adapted our lifestyle since then, and many of us can only mimic what the old ones used to do. But we have since added and control the misty veil that hides our home from outsiders."

Joss words weighed upon my heart. He had saved me by grabbing me as I went over the waterfall and sending me back to the top, using his Denai power. But the effort left him drained and sick. It was too much for even a descendent of the great ones. That has been a problem throughout every clan in Calandry. The Denai were slowly becoming extinct. There were fewer and fewer people born each year with the Denai gifts.

I remembered what Adept Lorna had said about Joss and his first day at the Citadel. How Joss had great potential and could reach High Adept, as long as I discouraged his advances. I was a distraction to his studies. I felt a hint of shame that I was seeing Joss and possibly ruining his future. After all, I wasn't a pureblood.

"And that's how our clan got our name." Joss interrupted my melancholy thoughts, and I snapped back to attention to catch the last bit of information. "Those who weren't Denai thought that a piece of the sky fell from the heavens, and that's why it floats. So we've adapted the name: Skyfell."

The streets and houses were on many levels, built into the towering pieces of light rock and towers. We were walking down the street and stopped in front of a banner that waved softly in front of a flight of spiral steps. Joss cleared his throat nervously, and sadness shadowed his face. "Ahem, we're here."

I walked behind Joss as we followed the winding steps upward. Some parts of the stairs were open to the view of the city, and then we would turn and wind through a tower. Finally the steps ended inside an enormous round room with a mosaic domed glass ceiling. The room was spacious and airy, with wide windows that overlooked the city and the veil of mists which muted the thunderous waterfalls. There were stools and couches with brightly colored pillows on the floor and scattered throughout the whole room.

A silent girl came in with a tray of drinks and offered us refreshments. I took the drink and sniffed it thoughtfully before tasting the most heavenly concoction. The drink was served warm, with a hint of cocoa and milk and cinnamon. Hemi took a sip and then chugged the rest of the drink down greedily, milky foam covering his beard and upper lip. He held out his cup to the girl, who smiled softly and offered him a refill. Kael refused the drink and stood on the outskirts of the room in a relaxed position facing all the entrances and exits. I knew that even though he looked at ease, he was ready to do battle at a moment's notice.

With no one else in the room to greet us, I took the chance to observe the girl. She was about my age, with brown hair and hazel eyes. A small beauty mark was present above her lip. She looked exotic, like the drink she served.

"Mona," Joss asked quietly when she brought him a drink. "How's my mother?"

She looked away sadly before answering. "Not well, Joss. She was on the mend, and then your sister disappeared, and it seems she has taken it badly."

Joss nodded and then went to a window and waited. Mona picked up her tray and left as silently as she appeared. It was only a moment before a large blond-haired man came down the steps and entered the room.

"Joss! I'm glad you came home," the blond man said, and walked over to embrace Joss in a hug. The resemblance between the two was obvious; the man was a relative. "We are at our wits' end and are no closer to finding Tenya than we were a few weeks ago. Your mother has fallen into despair. Her illness isn't getting better, and this is only affecting her worse. I wish we had news to give her, any news at all."

Joss grasped the man's arms and shook his head. "I know. That's why I have come home, and I've brought help." Joss gestured to Kael, Hemi, and me. "This is Thalia, Hemi, and Kael. They have come to help locate Tenya. And this," Joss pointed to the blond man next to him, "this is my father, Nero Jesai. Lord of Skyfell."

~19~

I never knew Joss' full name and had never asked. He was Joss Jesai, the future Lord of Skyfell. When Darren introduced him to me, he was always known only as "Joss." I never thought anything of it because I was only known as Thalia until I rediscovered my family. There were many well-known families at the Citadel, and it was obviously the school's attempt to create equality by hiding some of the heritage of the students. I thought sarcastically of Syrani and her boastful bragging about her bloodlines and how well that worked.

After the Banished Kings War and the Denai reestablished Avellgard in Calandry with a Council instead of a king, a few human traditions still remained in the small clans: the human titles. Few were reluctant to give up their title of lord or baron, while other clans were more than willing to follow in the example of the Denai. Our clan chose to release all titles of a kingly hierarchy whatsoever to preserve our way of life. So we have a clan leader instead of a lord. Obviously Skyfell kept its titles.

What worried me the most was that made Joss' Denai bloodline even that much more important. He would need a powerful Denai heir to lead after him. All of a sudden, everything made sense; Joss' reluctance to speak about the changes that were happening to me. He would get uncomfortable whenever I brought up the experiments and my un-Denai-like powers. He would have to marry and lead Skyfell, and I would have to marry and lead the Valdyrstals. My heart dropped into the pit of my stomach like a cold stone.

My lips drew into a frozen, uncomfortable smile as I grasped Nero's hand in greeting. Kael refused to shake hands, just nodded. Nero froze when he came face to face with my giant clansmen Hemi. My people came in very large packages, well, except for me; I looked like a small child standing next to Hemi. Hemi was also intimidating-looking when he pulled off his sack of weapons that he carried everywhere with him. He was a walking arsenal.

"How are they going to help?" Nero asked, puzzled. "What can they find that the Denai haven't?"

"Because, Father, we believe that Tenya was kidnapped for a reason and may still be alive. There are others from all over Calandry that are being kidnapped." Joss conveniently left out the "tortured and experimented on" bit when confronting his father. "Thalia and Kael escaped from those who we believe took Tenya. They may know how she was taken and find clues that the other Denai missed."

Nero looked at us, incredulous. "So there is still hope. My daughter may escape just like these two. She may be able to make it home to us. This may just be the news that my wife needs to hear, to aid in her recovery."

Kael took this moment to speak up, and I almost wished he hadn't. "It is very unlikely that she would be able to escape without help. They keep most of the prisoners drugged. It would take a very strong Denai and a determined will to escape the Septori."

Nero's hopeful face dropped in discouragement. "She is neither. Our Tenya is sweet-natured and delicate like her mother, never coming into her gifts. You are right—she wouldn't be able to escape without help."

Kael strode right up to Nero and confronted him. "You had better pray that she becomes strong. Because where she is, the weak don't survive."

Nero paled and grasped for a chair behind him, and sat down heavily. He placed his face in his hands and took a few moments to collect his thoughts. As he looked up at us, I saw the love and desperation he had for his daughter.

He turned to Kael. "Please, please find her and save her. I will give you anything you wish. Just bring her back alive." In that moment the Lord of Skyfell looked broken and tired. "I don't think I could survive the loss of my wife and daughter."

"What's wrong with your wife?" I asked, as politely as I could. "Is she ill? Can your healers do nothing for her?"

"We are at a loss. There is nothing physically wrong with her body, but she is wasting away. We have tried healing her, and have even ordered a watch by her side around the clock to try to extend her life and find the answer, but nothing. She is young and still in the prime of her life. We don't know the reason for her illness." Nero shrugged dejectedly. "We don't know where else to turn."

The silence that befell created a general feeling of discomfort, and no one had any answers to give him. Finally, Nero stood and straightened his shoulders. "Come, I will show you to your rooms. Then I will leave you to yourselves so you can get acquainted with Skyfell and see if you can find out what happened to my daughter."

Nero led us down a corridor and then up another flight of stairs to the guest wing. The rooms were spread around another circular pattern, with the stairs in the middle of the hall. Each room had an expansive view of Skyfell. My room was right between Hemi's and Kael's, while Joss would be sleeping in his own suite on another floor. We were given an hour to freshen up, and then dinner would be served. I crawled onto the round bed lined with silk and looked around the light and breezy room. The wind blew on the silk curtains and created an eye-catching spectacle of color. I wondered if Faraway was enjoying the lower regions of the land-based Skydown. I opened my mind to him and got nothing. Sitting up in bed, I tried to reach him with my thoughts, but all I heard in my head was a fuzzy droning sound.

I jumped from my bed and flew out of my room, and pounded on Kael's door. He answered my frantic knock with his hand on his vest, keeping his knives within reach.

"Thalia, what's wrong?" he asked. "Are you okay? Are you hurt?" This was one of those rare moments when Kael actually seemed normal.

"I can't reach Faraway! I can't hear him or speak to him. Something is wrong." I felt lost, as if an important piece of my soul was missing; I had begun to rely on him so much lately that I felt numb without his connection.

"Come on!" We took off, running down the halls, and ran into Nero and Joss.

"Joss!" I yelled. "Something's wrong—I can't reach Faraway down below." Joss looked at my panicked face and let out a sigh of relief.

"Oh, I wondered about that." He actually seemed calm. "I wasn't sure if the mists would hinder your abilities to mindspeak. Many of our abilities are lessened because of the mists."

Nero walked over to me and tried to calm my fears. "No one can mindspeak outside the veil of mists. They act as a protective barrier. Just think of it as trying to have a conversation standing at the bottom of a waterfall—with all of the noise, it would be hard to hear the other person speaking.

It's the same with the veil, just amplified. In many ways our greatest protection is our liability, because it also lessens our ability to use our own gifts." He put his hand on my shoulder and led me to a giant window in the foyer; this side of the building overlooked the mists and the edge of the city. "If you are that worried, I can send someone to check for you."

Kael spoke. "Thalia, I'll go." I craned my neck to look at Kael in disbelief; had I heard right?

"Ha! No way, Sword Boy! You wouldn't be able to keep up," Joss taunted and I saw Kael's brow furrow in challenge at being called "Sword Boy." Even though Kael acted old and responsible, in reality he couldn't be but more than five years older than Joss.

"Keep up or I will bury you, puppy!" Kael was rising to the bait and willing to dish out his own insults. Joss was the only one who got under Kael's skin and made him act irrationally.

Kael had started to turn toward the door to exit when Joss hollered out. "Oi, this way." Joss stepped out of the giant window in the foyer and onto a terrace. I followed after him and had to pull myself back against the building in fear. There was nothing over the side of the terrace. I peeked over and all I saw was mists, and a whole lot of nothing. We were on the cliff side of the city, and Joss was reaching behind him to bring down another skite.

"You have got to be kidding me." I looked at Joss in surprise. "You aren't really going to jump off and fly down there with that?"

Joss grinned his adorable dimpled smile at me. "Of course. This is the fastest way to get to the Skydown. You want me to check on Faraway, right?" He pulled up a skite and handed one to Kael. He went over the harness with him and the instructions for steering. I could see by the clench of Kael's jaw that he was scared but too stubborn to let Joss outdo him.

I grabbed Kael's elbow and yanked him back inside the room. "What are you doing? You don't have to do this! Please don't do it?"

Kael looked at me in surprise, and I saw his blue eyes soften for a second before they hardened with determination. "You did say that you wished to never see me again. Why would you care what I do?"

I was at a momentary loss for words; he had caught me off guard. "I don't want to see you get hurt." I really didn't. The skite terrified me, even though I knew Joss knew what he was doing. But Kael had never operated one, and I was scared that he wouldn't survive the jump. Obviously my words were not what Kael wanted to hear. He abruptly pulled his arm from my grasp.

"You think I can't do it?" He turned his back on me, shoulders stiff and determined.

"What? No! I didn't say that." And I hadn't. Where was he coming up with this?

Kael whirled on me in anger. "I can do anything he can do," he spat.

"No, you can't! You've never flown one of those death machines. What if you make a mistake and die?" I was getting angry; I reached for his shirt and held on.

"Then the bond between us will be broken. You can be free to live your life without a pet SwordBrother following you around," he snarled in challenge. "You can then live your life with the Denai."

I dropped my hand limply to my side and stepped back. His words had hurt me; they were true, but they hurt all the same. This time I turned my back on him and waved him off. "Fine, go, jump and rid yourself of me. I see how it is—you prefer death to being bonded to me." I didn't mean it; I'd said it to hurt him back, if it was even possible to hurt him. I felt Kael draw closer to me, but then he stepped away as Joss jumped down from the ledge and came inside.

They were going to dive off one of the city launching points. The launching points were marked around the city by various colored flags that marked the distance from the ledge of the city to the ground. These were deemed safe distances to dive with a dorabill or a skite. The Jesai family had a launching point from their own veranda.

"You ready? I'll race you down." Joss was in his element; he wanted Kael to do it, and he wanted him to lose. Kael had been his sword teacher at the Citadel and was stronger and a better fighter. Joss had challenged Kael to try to impress me, but the plan had backfired. Now Joss was enacting a bit of revenge. I knew it, but did Kael?

"Let's go," Kael said stiffly, and they both turned and went out the window. I waited a minute before following. They were both harnessed into the skites and were standing on the ledge. Joss counted off, and they both jumped. I raced to the edge and looked over to see Joss' skite fly smoothly in a wide circle before disappearing into the mists. Kael's skite didn't glide like Joss'; it shook and dropped straight down into the mists, falling like a stone.

I clutched the veranda wall, my fingers digging into the warm stone. I heard myself scream Kael's name as my world spun.

~20~

He was dead. Kael was dead; I knew it. Warm hands pressed against my forehead and leaned me forward. Opening my eyes, I stared into the worried green eyes of Joss. No, wait; the eyes seemed older, as if they carried years of worry. It was Nero.

"Don't sit up too fast," Nero warned. "Take a deep breath."

"Is he okay? Did he make it?" I held Nero's arm in a death grip, refusing to let go until he told me that Kael was all right.

"I don't know. Would you like me to go after them?" He stood up, as if to get another skite.

"Yes! No! I don't know? I don't want to be left alone up here and not be able to know what's going on."

Nero's eyes hardened when he looked over the ledge. "I shouldn't have let him try it. We don't usually allow newcomers to try a skite without more practice. When you and Kael went inside, I tried to dissuade my son. Joss assured me that Kael could handle it."

"WHAT!" Now I was angry. Joss knew that this was dangerous and his father was against it, and he challenged Kael, knowing he wouldn't say no. I was so angry I could spit. But I was also nervous.

Nero ran out of the room, and I leaned over the ledge and yelled Kael's name, but the mists swallowed up my cry. Nero came back in with his wooden flute and played a familiar sound of notes. The hair on the back of my neck rose in anticipation as a loud screech filled the air, and another dorabill flew and landed on the veranda. This one was smaller than the last.

"Come, get on." Nero nimbly leapt onto the back of the giant bird and held his hand out to me. I tentatively gave him my hand, and with one quick pull I was sitting in front of him, grasping the horrible bird around the neck. Nero whistled, and I felt the bird lift off and dive down into the mists. I was too scared to scream as the jump took my breath away.

My eyes were squeezed shut, and I clenched my teeth and held on for dear life as the bird screeched again. I opened my eyes at the last minute to see the ground rushing toward us at intense speeds; just when I thought we would crash, the dorabill spread his wings, and our dive came to an abrupt halt as the bird leveled out. A few heartbeats later we landed, and I refused to let go of the terrifying bird, I was so scared.

Nero slid off and reached for me, and pried my fingers from around the dorabill's neck. My fingers were stiff from adrenaline, and I had problems getting them to cooperate. When I finally tried to slide off the bird, my legs refused to work, and I crashed to the ground in a heap.

Loud laughter reached my ears, and I looked up into the smiling laughing faces of none other than Kael and Joss. I was too shocked to see him alive and in one piece to even berate them for laughing.

"You made it? But I saw you fall!" I finally got my legs to move, and I stood up and put my hands on my hips.

"I did fall and was falling fast, but once I entered the mists, the updrafts from the waterfalls caught me and made it easier to glide down."

"You scared me. I thought you died," I yelled at him.

Kael just looked at me in the oddest way, and I could have sworn I saw his normal dark aura lighten. "I know. I heard you scream my name." His intense eyes met mine, and there was a moment of hidden question behind them. He looked at me longer than was necessary, and I felt my cheeks go red. A rush of uncertain feelings assailed me.

"No, I didn't," I defended myself poorly. "I just would rather have you not die today."

"Nice to know you care," he said.

"UGGHH, no, I don't!" I replied sarcastically. "Remember, you told me to." I was frustrated that he could tie me up in knots.

His demeanor quickly changed, and then the smiling face disappeared behind his stony SwordBrother face. I instantly regretted the words; even said in angry fun, they were strong and powerful words. Kael started to walk away but paused when Nero broke the silence.

Nero smirked. "She fainted."

Kael stopped and turned to look at me. His eyebrow rose questioningly.

"I did not. I…I…" I looked at Kael's blank face and saw a quick twitch of his upper lip as he held back a smirk. *He'd better not smile*, I thought. "Oh, bother." I turned and headed toward what I thought was the direction of the stables. It wasn't. Turning back toward the men again, I came face to face with Joss.

"And you! Don't get me started on what you did. You had no right to get him on that paper contraption. You are going to get an earful later." I jabbed my finger into his chest, and he grabbed it playfully.

"I knew he could handle it, and he did," he teased. He leaned into me and pressed his mouth to my ear. "I saw him fall, and I dropped quickly. Once I cleared out of the mists, I was able to control the wind to catch him. It took a lot out of me. But I wouldn't have let anything happen to him," Joss whispered.

I forgot that Joss's talent was air, and he could control the winds enough to save Kael. My heart instantly forgave him, because he was hiding that fact. He was giving Kael back some dignity.

I pressed my hand against his chest and gave Joss a warm stare. "You've been flying since you were eight, remember. And why in the world didn't you fly the big ol' rooster down like your father?"

Joss shrugged his shoulders playfully. "That particular dorabill, Cecili, only plays nice with my father. She can be a biter."

I could only roll my eyes at him.

We had to walk around the round lake created by the waterfalls and cross a wooden bridge before we hit the outskirts of Skydown. I could see that it was a smaller village, less flamboyant than Skyfell. There were various birds: perot, dorabills, and smaller, less intimidating monkey-like creatures. I could see a large field where hundreds of horses grazed peacefully.

A whisper touched my mind. *I can always cause a ruckus and make it less peaceful.*

FARAWAY! You're all right? I thought something might have happened to you. Where are you? I squinted my eyes against the sun and tried to find my white horse in the field amongst hundreds of others. It wasn't hard to spot him when he rose on his hindquarters in a majestic display of vanity. So it looked like we knew the limit of our bond was less than a mile.

I'm fine. *When I lost contact with you, all I could do was hope that the SwordBrother and Joss would protect you.*

Yeah, it's the veil of mists. It dampens the Denai gifts and apparently our mindspeech.

Good to know.

It seems I had stopped in my tracks when I was speaking to Faraway, and the rest of my group stopped and waited. When I was done communicating with Faraway, I turned around to head up the hill.

"What? All of that panic and worry, and you aren't even going to walk over there?" Kael stated incredulously.

"No need. He said he was fine and that we should get back to start trying to track the ones who took your sister. So I'm doing what he said." The rest followed after me, and when we got to the hill I opted to walk the path up the cliff and take the skycage over riding the big red bird bareback again; Joss and Kael accompanied me. My second trip in the skycage fared better than the first, but not by much.

After dinner Nero asked us how we thought we were going to find Tenya when no one else had had any luck.

I wasn't sure myself. I'd only come because Joss insisted I might be able to help find her, but I wasn't a skilled hunter or tracker. Secretly, I was relieved when Kael spoke up.

"How long has it been since she disappeared?" He leaned back in his chair casually and studied all of the dinner guests. Once again Kael had positioned himself with his back to the wall, facing all the exits. He scrutinized each person in turn, and I felt his eyes linger on me before moving on to the rest. Tonight's dinner included our small traveling party, Nero, Mona, Talbot, Xiven, Darren, and a few other friends.

Talbot was Mona's and Xiven's father, a short, balding mild-mannered man. Xiven was an older, masculine version of Mona. Neither looked like their father, so they must have gotten their exotic looks from their mother.

"It's been over six weeks now." Nero sighed and rubbed his eyes dejectedly. "I went to her room one morning, and her bed hadn't been slept in and nothing was taken."

"Why does that make you think she had been kidnapped?" Kael countered, his feelings hidden behind a steely face as he crossed his arms over his chest.

"Are you implying that he's lying? You low-level son of a pig. I wouldn't have brought you here if I'd known you were going to insult us." Joss' fist pounded the table, hard.

Kael didn't blink an eye. "You think I don't understand the female kind? I do. It's the quiet and innocent ones you have to watch out for. They are the ones most likely to run at the first chance of adventure or when something better comes along."

"You don't know her," Joss snarled.

"I probably know her kind better than you think. Let me guess—she didn't leave the house much, did she? A perfect example of an obedient daughter. Never asked for anything, always seemed content."

Joss' and Nero's mouths dropped slightly as they sat speechless.

Kael leaned forward and finished his tale, directing the rest of his tirade at Nero. "But over the last few weeks she started to change. She became more restless, absentminded, needing to run out at the last minute to buy something she'd forgotten. You probably found her daydreaming more than normal."

Nero closed his mouth and nodded sadly.

Kael's eyes lit with contempt. "They are the obvious signs you can't ignore. She was secretly seeing someone. Knowing you wouldn't approve, she more than likely ran away with him. There is nothing for us to do, no need for you to go out looking for a young lovesick woman."

"How do you know? How can you possibly know for sure?" Nero asked, his face a mask of brokenness.

"Because I had once chosen a young girl, Gwen, to be my lifemate. We went before the leaders and received their blessing to begin our courtship, and the closer we came to our Union day, the more hesitant she became." The shadow that I could sometimes see around Kael was back and becoming darker with his bitterness.

"These were the signs she showed before running off with another," Kael finished; a look of hatred swept his face as he glanced at me. I wasn't sure whether the look was directed at me or was for the girl in his story. I usually received many hateful looks from Kael.

Hemi, who had up until that point had been a quiet observer, eating and drinking without missing a beat, had started choking at Kael's announcement. Hemi sputtered and coughed until he received a hard pat on his back from Darren to clear his airways.

Nero cleared his throat and waved his hand in the air, conceding to Kael. "That may very well be the case in point. She was exhibiting all of those signs." Nero sighed loudly. "It hurts me dearly to say this, but I agree with you—all the signs point to her running away."

The silence that filled the dining room was so intense that it was almost unbearable. I was afraid to bite down on a celery stick for fear of drawing unwanted attention. But I definitely wanted to pull Kael aside and give him a piece of my mind. What was he thinking? How could he possibly believe she ran away? How could his viewpoint have changed within a few hours?

After dinner was finished, I was trying to catch Kael's eye when I was approached by Xiven and Mona.

"Are you close friends with the Jesai family?" I asked the exotic-looking siblings. Both were dressed in the colorful and flowing outfits that many of the people of Skyfell wore.

"We're like family," Xiven answered, and then bit his bottom lip as if he was debating on how much to tell me. "Our father is an old friend of Nero's.

"Our father, Talbot, is a merchant and spends more time away from home than home. When our mother passed way, Nero invited us to live here, so we wouldn't be alone when our father was traveling." Mona spoke up sadly. I felt my heart go out for her because I knew the feeling of losing a mother. I tried to uplift her spirits.

"That explains that delicious drink you gave us. Was that one of the spices that your father found? It was wonderful," I complimented Mona, and her face turned pink.

"Yes, it's called chai. I learned it from my mother. She loved to cook and would experiment with whatever Father would bring home," Mona replied.

"So are you a Denai?" Xiven asked. His brown hair flowed over his eyes in a rakish way.

"Um, sort of. I go to the same school as Joss, or at least I did," I replied casually.

"How are you only sort of a Denai?" Mona replied, her petite lips pursed in thought. "You either are or you're not." Her eyes were filled with doubt.

"I bet she is, and a strong one. Otherwise Joss wouldn't have brought her home," Xiven said, looking at me thoughtfully before finishing. "You know how particular Gloria is about marrying into strong Denai families." I didn't even get to respond before Mona turned toward me, her eyes wide.

"Is that why you've come? You're going to marry Joss?" Mona gasped.

"No! We've only known each other a few months. I'm not ready to be married," I replied, trying to keep the peace and not ruffle any of Mona's feathers. She seemed to be one that was easily excitable.

"Doesn't matter. I've seen the way he looks at you." She brought her hand up to her neck and played with a small gold charm she wore. "Just be forewarned. The Jesai family is very strict about purebloods, and you had better figure out what a 'sort of' Denai is, because Gloria, his mother, is the one you have to win approval from."

"What do you mean?" I asked. My mind whirled with questions. I didn't understand. Why was Joss not able to choose who he wanted to marry? But then, I felt I already knew the answer.

"The whole household revolves around Gloria, and with her being so ill, I can't see it in the near future for Joss to do anything to upset his mother. Especially since Tenya ran away."

Any hopes I might have about a future with Joss teetered on a small, precarious, and ill mother, whom I'd yet to meet. I was not lying when I said I wasn't ready to get married, but with no foreseeable future with Joss, should I break all ties with him now to save ourselves more heartbreak? I tried to keep the pleasant conversation going with the only other people in the room my own age, but I felt as if I had a rock in the bottom of my stomach. I moved to sit by myself on a lone chair and ponder the implications. Talbot came over and sat by me.

"Ah, I see you have met my children. They are very opinionated, just like their father." Talbot chuckled softly.

"They are very nice, and your daughter makes the most delicious chai I have ever tasted."

"That's because she is just like her mother." Talbot's smile grew wider, and his eyes had a faraway look to them. "Every day she becomes more and more like her, but she never came into her gifts, unlike her mother. Sometimes she can be hard to live with because she was the only one in our family to not develop the Denai power. Her brother's strengths keep growing, and it has been a difficult journey for her. So please overlook her bitterness and look at the girl underneath who desperately wants to fit in, to have friends." Talbot sighed and stood up, turning to me. "I hope that you can be that for her." Walking away, he went to fill his drink.

I took this chance to hunt down Kael, who was standing in a dark corner with an unapproachable scowl on his face. I had seen this look so often I didn't even blink an eye anymore. Storming over to Kael, I placed my hands on my hips and violently hissed at him, "You can't possibly think that she ran away. What happened to your promise to find her from just a few hours ago?"

Kael's hand reached out and covered my mouth, and before I could even blink an eye he had spirited me out onto the veranda. The night air was chilly, and there was only the light from inside to cast a faint glow on the stone steps. Kael pulled me far from the window and backed me into the wall, still covering my mouth with his hand. When his hand didn't immediately let go, I did the most childish thing I could think of. I licked it.

Startled, Kael pulled his hand back off my mouth and gave me a curious look before wiping his wet palm on his pants. "What in the world made you do that?" he whispered.

"Because I keep finding myself in the same situation, with your hand over my mouth," I answered.

"Have you ever thought that it is because you talk too much? Most men like their women quiet." Kael spoke quietly, his eyes alight like burning embers.

"Ha! Then I'm glad Joss isn't most men," I challenged, purposely trying to erase the emotion from his eyes. This new side of Kael was making it very hard for me to dislike him and was stirring up a plethora of mixed feelings. "He likes open honesty and doesn't hide things from me. I know the real Joss—unlike you. I don't know who you are. I don't know anything about you. I want to know the real Kael."

It worked. Kael's eyes turned dark with frustration; his breathing deepened, and I could see an inner battle erupt. "I'm not hiding things from you. It's just that there are things best left unspoken, for everyone." His hand reached up to lean against the wall, which brought him closer to me. "I'm trying to show you the real me. I'm not very good at it—it's not warrior-like."

"I see you. I just don't know if I believe it." I ducked under his arm to move away from him, giving him space. There were so many questions I wanted to ask him, but I chose the safer course, the ones that didn't include me. "How can you change your mind so fast? Earlier we were in agreement to help find Tenya, and now you're saying she ran away? How could you give up that fast?"

"I didn't give up. I don't believe she ran away." Kael turned to face me.

"Then why the lie?" I asked, confused. "Why besmirch a young girl's name with lies?"

"It was all a show. I convinced Nero and Joss that we needed to make everyone believe she ran away. That it would allow us to do some digging and hunting without raising the alarm to the Septori. Have you seen this place? There is no way an outsider would have been able to get in here and kidnap a girl and get out without help. A stranger wouldn't be able to control the dorabills or work the skycage without help. Nero said Tenya hardly ever left Skyfell, so that means the Septori were already on Skyfell or were working with someone here."

My mouth opened and closed like a fish; I was in awe at the obvious ease that Kael was able to come to this conclusion. This meant we were closer than I had first thought to finding the Septori.

"We needed to ease the suspicion of why we are here and plant the rumor of Tenya running away with a young man."

"Why the fake story about your lifemate running off with someone?"

Kael looked into the darkness, and the mists that looked like molten silver at night before looking at me again. "And what makes you think that my story was a lie?"

I barely stammered out an answer because I was so in shock. "It just didn't s-sound like something you, er, I-I didn't think that you could...I d-don't know." I pathetically shrugged my shoulders in final answer.

"You didn't think I was capable of love, did you?" Kael looked sadly at me. "Well, you are wrong...and right. I was at one time capable of it and in the same instance betrayed by it. So I will never let that happen again. I am no longer capable of loving, nor do I wish to be ever again." His strong jaw clenched in resentment. Quietly, we stayed like that before his earlier comment brought forth another question.

"So if we are not here to find Tenya, what are we supposed to be telling people we are here for?" I asked blankly, my brows furrowed in confusion. It was the middle of the school year for Joss, and I couldn't see an answer as to why we were here without raising suspicions.

Kael looked at me and his jaw clenched in anger; he'd opened his mouth to answer when a voice from behind answered for him.

"We are here to announce our intentions for marriage." Joss stepped out onto the veranda and came over to me, placing his hand gently on my arm.

"JESAI!" Kael growled Joss' last name like a curse. He was tense, like a loaded spring ready to go off.

"What are you talking about?" I looked back and forth from Joss' smiling face to the scowl on Kael's. "Is this some kind of joke, because it's not funny." I swallowed the lump that had formed in my throat and felt my mouth go dry.

"Kael and I spoke with my father and came to an agreement this afternoon on what we would do. We thought it would be the best cover story." Joss grinned at me.

"No, you thought it would be the best story. I hated it from the start," Kael grunted out.

"Okay, my father and I thought it would be the best reason for me to come home so soon: to announce our engagement. We will stay for the congratulatory feasts, and everyone from Skyfell will attend. It will be our chance to question everyone, and hopefully by then we will have a lead on where to go next." Joss seemed genuinely pleased by the plan.

"But we are just pretending, right? This is all just show?" My heart raced with panic and confusion.

"Thalia, this is all show, for now." Joss eye's twinkled with mischief. "But who knows what the future will hold?" He came over to me and gently pinched my chin with his fingers before pulling a blue aquamarine necklace out of his pocket. The necklace was beautiful and surrounded by an intricate silver knot. Joss walked behind me and undid the clasp before putting the necklace around my neck. I was now wearing two necklaces, Joss', and my father's ring, which fell below my neckline. "This is my engagement gift to you. It was my grandmother's. Proudly wear it."

I couldn't breathe; this was what every girl wanted, right? To be engaged to the most sought-after and handsome boy in Calandry. I really liked Joss and had deep feelings for him, and I could see a possible future, but there were so many unanswered questions, and I was overwhelmed with all of the pretending and lies. "No one will believe us." I desperately tried to get Joss to understand. "We are too young."

"No, we're not. You were about to give yourself away and marry the winner of a Kragh Aru a few weeks ago. That is what gave me the perfect idea for this plan. So you can blame yourself." Joss came over to me and looked deeply into my worried eyes. "Thalia, what's wrong? I thought you would be happy. Remember, it's just for show—we are doing this for my sister."

"It's just that a lot is happening really fast, and I'm feeling overwhelmed." I reached up to touch the aquamarine stone, which felt like a manacle around my neck. "What if all of the stress of pretending ruins our friendship?"

Joss reached for my hands and clasped them gently. "What if it doesn't? What if it brings us closer together? Will you do it for my sister? Will you pretend?"

The lump in my throat just got larger, and my eyes drifted for an instant to Kael. I instantly wished I hadn't looked at him. Kael was stiff as a board, face frozen, devoid of emotion. All I could do was nod to Joss, and I watched as Kael turned his back on me and walked back inside. Joss ignored Kael, and turned my face up to his and gave me a quick kiss. "You won't regret this."

Joss took my hand and led me back into the room, and nodded to his father.

Nero stood up and made an imposing figure, and he cleared his throat to make an announcement. "Friends, we've all been saddened by the choices my daughter Tenya has made, and we wish for her to come home soon. But at last we do have good news. My son Joss has chosen his future wife, Thalia." Loud clapping could be heard, and whistles from Darren Hamden, Xiven, and a few others. Kael stared at the floor, refusing to acknowledge the announcement. Hemi looked up at me in surprise, and I tried to make eye contact and nod to him that we would speak later. Mona was also one of the ones not clapping; she looked hurt and confused. Probably because not even an hour ago I had told her I had no desire to get married. I squeezed my eyes closed and tried hard to take a deep breath. When I opened them again, I felt that maybe, just maybe, I could continue with this farce, but I was going to need extra strength. The roar of congratulations, handshakes, laughter, and introductions continued throughout the evening, and when I finally had a chance to escape, I took it and retired to my room.

I couldn't believe everything that had happened in one day. It was a complete disaster, and I was a nervous wreck. In my soul I felt as if I was crumbling, falling apart. I opened my sight and tried to see what a real Denai would see. Nothing. I was taught at the Citadel that the Denai could use their sight to see all of the energies in the world in brilliant colors, and they could tap into them, control them and use them.

When I tried to use it, I never saw brilliant colors of gold or blues like Joss and the others did. All I ever saw was faint grays and blacks that would sometimes surround people like Kael, very depressing and somber. It was as if my sight was broken. The worst realization I had was when I could see a bright white actually pulsing in rhythm and coming from the center of each Denai. It was their life essence I was seeing, and I could actually steal it and use it for my own power. The thought of ever doing that to someone on purpose actually made me sick to my stomach. But I turned my sight inward to see if I could see any of the white glow that I saw in other Denai in me. There was nothing, just a faint pulsing blackness, which had started showing up when my nightmares began. Every night the blackness became darker and more substantial, and every night I would pray, to try to bind the darkness.

Curling up in my bed, I wrapped my arms around my knees and tried to sleep. I couldn't contact Faraway because of the mists and the distance, and once again I felt truly alone and scared. I grabbed a pillow and tried to snuggle my body around it, but it didn't work; I was too scared to sleep because of the nightmares, so I lay awake in bed until the sun came up.

~21~

omeone was pounding on my door. I could hear whispered voices in the hall and then rattling at my lock. At first I couldn't understand what the commotion was all about, until I realized that I had locked the door last night.

I had finally fallen asleep and wished I hadn't, for what little sleep I had was once again plagued by nightmares of being tortured and abused. I rubbed my eyes to feel that they were crusty from the salt of my tears. I must have been crying. The pounding on the door became louder, and I could hear Joss' voice calling my name, along with a softer feminine voice that must have belonged to Mona.

"I'm fine," I tried to croak out, but my voice didn't work. Clearing my throat, I tried a second time. "Joss, I'm awake, and I'm fine. So you can quit with the pounding."

His concerned voice reached me through the door. "Thalia, are you sure? You weren't answering."

"I'm sorry, I was just more tired than I had thought."

"Well, you've missed breakfast. Do you want something sent up? Also, I want to introduce you to my mother this afternoon."

At his announcement I flopped back in bed and dragged a pillow over my head in despair at the reminder of what we were trying to accomplish with our lie. When I didn't respond right away, Joss pounded on the door again.

"Thalia?" He pounded once more. My stomach did a familiar clenching at the reminder of food. For some reason nerves and food didn't mesh well with me. I sat up in bed and pulled the pillow off.

"No breakfast—I will be down shortly." I listened for the sound of retreating steps, and when I heard two pairs walk away, I crumpled back onto the bed and pulled the pillow back over my head. A split second later the pillow came flying off, and I looked into Kael's serious face.

"What are you doing in my room?" I hissed at him. I glanced around to see how in the world he had gotten in, and my eyes immediately went to the open window. Of course that was his specialty: climbing in windows.

"You locked the door and weren't answering, so I decided to take the roof and see if you were alive." He looked me over carefully, as if searching for signs of life.

"I'm fine. Obviously you heard me talking to Joss, so why don't you go back out the way you came in and leave me alone?" I gripped the pillow he held in his hands and yanked it back.

"No," he replied casually, and came and sat down on my bed. I immediately jumped out of my bed on the other side. "At least I didn't put my hand over your mouth," he teased.

"Kael, please leave," I whispered quietly.

"Not until I have a word with you." He looked out the window, as if to gather his thoughts before speaking. "You don't have to do this."

"Do what?" I asked.

"Pretend to be engaged to Joss. We can find another way." He turned to study my face, and he noted the dark circles under my eyes. "I can tell that you are bothered by it. You didn't sleep last night, did you? Another nightmare?"

"It's a little late now," I grumbled. "It's already been announced. And yes, more nightmares."

"I'll find them, Thalia. I'll find the Septori and the Raven and break this bond, and then the nightmares will stop." He looked at me, and I could see the determination written in his face. But his words, which should have reassured me, gave me pause, because once he did free us, he would be gone. And even though he irritated me and was short-tempered, I was getting used to him being around to depend on.

My shoulders dropped in sadness at the thought of him leaving me, but Kael took it to mean something else. I saw him stiffen and jump from the bed.

"You doubt me?" He was irate. "You don't think I can find them and—" This time it was I who walked over to him and put my hand over his mouth. Kael paused, his eyes widening.

"Don't you think you talk too much?" I quipped lightly at him, repeating the same words he had said to me last night. "Most girls like their men silent." I looked into his eyes, and saw the anger fade and his eyes lighten. "Kael," I whispered his name. "If anyone is able to find the Septori and free us, it would be you. I will never doubt that or your abilities. What you saw was my sadness at the thought of our bond being broken and you leaving me." Kael froze every muscle in his body, afraid to move, listening to what I had to say. "Because even though you've at one time thought killing me would break the bond, I know you won't. Instead, you have been my protector on numerous counts, and even though you try to annoy me to the high heavens. There are times I actually think of you as a friend, and the thought of you leaving makes me sad."

Kael reached up and grasped my hand and pulled it away from his mouth, but he didn't immediately let go. "Thalia,

I need to speak with you about something important." But before he could say another word, I heard a key turn in the lock. I spun around to tell Kael to leave, but he had already disappeared. The door opened, and Mona peeked inside, carrying a tray of her chai.

"I know you said no to breakfast, but I thought some bread and my special drink would help tide you over till lunch." Mona looked nice, wearing loose-fitting pants that fell just below the knee and a short-sleeved red and gold top. Her hair fell in a long braid over one shoulder. She placed the tray on my bed and sat on it with me while she handed me my drink. I hesitantly took the drink and was only going to take a sip, but as soon as the fragrant aroma reached my nose I took a greedy gulp.

"Mona, I have to apologize about last night. I had no idea that Joss was so serious about our relationship that he wanted to be married." I looked at her and saw her stiffen.

"Please, don't pretend. How could you not know what his intentions were, when he brought you here to meet his parents? It is obvious. Let's just pretend we never had that other conversation, shall we?" Mona gave me a wan smile and poured herself a cup of the drink, and sipped it daintily before going on. "Well, it will all depend now on Gloria. After you meet her, the engagement might not stand." Stiffly, she stood up and left the tray. "Believe me, you will want to eat lunch— you will need your strength."

I stared wide-eyed at Mona's departing back. I turned and looked out the window to see if Kael had overheard or would return, but he didn't reappear. Briefly I wondered what Mona meant and also what could Kael possibly have to talk about.

***

I thought I was mentally preparing myself to do battle with a venerable dragon. Instead I saw an angel incarnate, lying on a bed in a dimly lit room. She looked like a child in a giant-sized bed. The curtains had been opened, and a small table was located next to the bed with a familiar tray of drinks on it. Gloria was the epitome of her name. She was beautiful, angelic, with long blonde hair that spilled down her shoulders and back. Her eyes were closed when we went into her room, and her eyelids were so translucent I could see the blue veins. I thought that maybe she was dead, but I could barely see the rise and fall of her chest with her short breaths.

Nero went and kneeled by her bed and grasped her hand, pressing his lips to her knuckles. I saw Gloria's eyes flutter and then gently open. She gazed lovingly upon her husband, and he leaned in to kiss her forehead. Joss stepped forward and kissed his mother's brow as well. I watched as Gloria smiled and reached up to touch Joss' face. Too nervous to do anything, I hung back out of sight.

"How are you feeling, Mother?" Joss asked.

"Better, Joss, now that you're here." Gloria's voice was barely above a whisper, and I had to strain to hear her. I could tell that talking drained her. Joss reached out his hand and laid it upon his mother's chest, and I could see his concentration as he tried to use his power to heal his mother. But because we were inside the mists, it was harder to use. Sweat beaded across his forehead, and I was shocked at how hard it was for him. Joss was one of the strongest healers I knew. While using gifts takes its toll physically on the Denai, I'd never seen Joss get drained this fast. A faint glow surrounded Joss' hand, and I could see that Gloria regained some color in her cheeks.

"Joss, it's all right. You don't have to waste your energy on me. It's my fault for being so weak. If only I were a stronger

Denai, then maybe this wouldn't have happened." The little bit of power that Joss gave Gloria seemed to have brought back some of her old spirit.

"Mother, I have some wonderful news," Joss intoned quietly while he reached behind him for my hand. Grasping my cold and clammy palms, Joss pulled me close to Gloria's bedside so she could have a look at me. "I want you to meet Thalia. I have asked her to be my wife."

Gloria's eyes opened wide and flew to me in shock. Her grey eyes seemed to pierce my soul, as if she were looking for flaws. Her eyes traveled from my black hair to my blue eyes down to my feet. I was very glad that I had chosen my blue short-sleeve top and knee-length skirt. Gloria looked me over carefully before speaking. "What family is she from? Is she from a Denai family?"

"I am the daughter of Bearen, from the Valdyrstal clan." I spoke proudly, raising my chin up in the air a fraction of an inch.

"The Valdyrstals?" Gloria sucked in her breath as if she were holding it. "Joss, how could you? They are nothing more than barbarians, and they hate everything Denai. Your children won't carry our bloodline." Her small hand fluttered to her chest as if she was clutching her heart.

I clenched my teeth and bit my tongue to keep myself from spouting out at her. My family was not barbarians. And even though my clan hated the Denai, I didn't think it was very proper for her to insult my family with me standing right there. But then I had a minute to digest what she was saying, and it sounded very similar to my own father's complaints about Joss. So if Joss was able to sit through my own father's harsh words about him, I would do the same for Gloria. What I was pondering the most was Nero's and Joss' reasons for not telling Gloria the truth. Why did she have to be told the lie?

"Mother, I did meet Thalia at the Citadel." Joss tried to calm Gloria's fears.

"What? How? Everyone knows that clan doesn't have any Denai blood. What, was she a servant?" Gloria wasn't stupid, and I had to catch myself to keep from sputtering and laughing, because she had nailed it on the head.

"No, ma'am. I actually met Joss on the road before I ever attended as a student. I am unique and unlike any Valdyrstal before me." It was the closest I could come to the truth, without divulging my horrible past and scaring her about what her own daughter could be going through.

"Oh," was the only thing that Gloria said before turning her head once more to Nero. "Please, try to convince him to wait on this decision. Think of the grandchildren—I don't want any weak Denai in the family. Maybe if Tenya had been stronger she could have, she might have…" Gloria couldn't go on as she was overcome with grief over her missing daughter. Nero leaned forward and held her and nodded a silent message to Joss, who quietly grabbed my elbow and led me out of her room.

~22~

The days wore on, and even though I looked for him, I didn't see Kael. Joss said he was going to be scarce over the next few days since he was searching for leads on Tenya's disappearance. I wished that I could be doing something as well to help look. But I had no idea on where to even begin. Joss gave Hemi and me a tour through the city, but the more I saw, the more trapped I felt. We walked for miles and came to the edge of the city and the stone wall and another tower. I looked over the wall to see the levers and pulleys that the farmers used to grow the helios flowers and other plants and vegetables. Just leaning over the wall made me feel dizzy, and I had to step away and sit down on the ground. I was not a girl for heights, flying, or the skycages, so to me it felt like another prison. Skyfell was beautiful and ethereal, but it really was a gilded cage suspended in midair. I asked Joss to take me back to his home.

After another day the same as before with no news, I felt more restless inside. I was soon pacing the main room like a tiger in a cage. The more I paced, the more my anger grew at being useless. Hemi was sitting in an overstuffed chair with dainty pillows, and the huge clansman looked out of place while his eyes were half closed in sleep. I worried about stopping the Raven, finding Tenya, and Joss' sick mother. At every sound I heard, my eyes would fly to the stairs to see if Kael had returned with news of where to begin. I was wound tighter than a bowstring about to be loosed, and I had to find a release for my pent-up energy and nerves. I saw Hemi's eyes flick back and forth, watching me. An idea hit me.

I marched over to Hemi and held my hand out to him. "All right, hand one over," I demanded angrily.

"I do not know what you mean, Thalia. What am I to be handing over?" He spoke slowly, as if he had no idea what I was talking about, but his eyes knowingly twinkled in mischief. After all, I was my father's daughter.

"A weapon, you big lug. What do you think? And don't even pretend that you don't have one hiding on your body. Just because you don't have your giant pack and axe does not mean you aren't armed. Otherwise my father would never have sent you with me." By this time my foot was tapping impatiently, and Hemi's grin grew wide in merriment. He slowly reached inside his large leather vest and pulled out a small silver spoon and handed it to me.

"What is this? Hemi, what am I supposed to do with a spoon?" I stuttered at what he handed me. "Do you want me to feed my enemies? Why in the world are you carrying this in your vest?" My eyes widened in shock.

"I keep it to use for the cinnamon drink the girl brings me daily. I like to eat the topping with a spoon." Hemi turned red, and in an instant a picture of the giant bearded man scooping off the cream topping of the drink and eating it with a dainty spoon made me chuckle out loud. As I recalled, his first day drinking it, he ended up with the topping all over his beard.

"What do you want me to do with a spoon, Hemi? Be reasonable. Hand me over a weapon NOW, or I'm going to go find the biggest mallet and bash your head in." I wouldn't really and he knew it, but Hemi loved to tease me as if I was still a small child. Slowly, he stood up and walked into another room. After a few very long minutes, he returned with a wicked glint in his eye and two large broom handles. I could tell by the stray pieces of straw clinging to his pants that he had shucked the brooms like they were corn to make two makeshift staves.

"Hemi!" I admonished. "The Jesai family is going to be angry with you!" Hemi continued to walk over to me and handed me the broom.

"Nonsense. I gave one of the servants some money to run to the market and buy two new brooms. They should be back before anyone notices." He smiled at me.

"Why not give me the knife that I know you have hidden or a different weapon?" I challenged him as I weighed the broom in my hand experimentally before spinning it in the air.

"Because, my clan leader's daughter, I have to make sure that you don't get injured," he joked before moving a side table out of the way. "Even if you did almost win the Kragh Aru and fought in a battle at the pass, I still need to make sure you don't injure yourself," I glared at Hemi until he looked down at the floor and then back up at me, "or me." He made a motion with his hand around his neck. "I like my head where it is."

I made a playful swipe at Hemi's head, and he ducked. Even though I had started the exercise frustrated and needed the physical exertion to blow off steam, Hemi's well-thought-out playful banter helped alleviate most of my anger. I realized how much like my father I really was.

Hemi met each of my strikes but wouldn't return them full force. "Come on, Hemi, if you don't engage me in battle, how will I ever defend myself?" I shouted as I rolled on the ground around him and swept the staff at the back of his knees. Hemi missed while defending himself and fell backward over the staff. The wooden floor rumbled as his giant frame kissed the wood. I leaned over his prone form and taunted him as best as I could. "Come on, Hemi—don't let a girl walk all over you. Show me what you've got. Fight me like you would my father. That's an order."

Hemi looked at me wide-eyed from the floor and grinned at me. Like a flash he swung out his own stick and sent me flying to the ground behind him. Now both of us were on our backs, looking at the ceiling, and before I could even blink I saw his staff come flying down toward my head. Rolling to safety, I dodged the downward strike. Hemi was already on his feet, and this time he was taking me to task.

Jumping to my feet, I grasped the wooden broom handle between both hands. I was put on the defensive as Hemi used the broom like an axe, chopping away, using all of his strength. My fingers rang with each impact, and I heard the wood split in two from his last strike. Stunned, I looked at two halves of the broom in my hands and opened my eyes wide as he swung the broom straight at my head. I leaned backward and felt the wind from the swing brush my face.

My heart raced with adrenaline, and I crossed both sticks over my head to block a downward head strike. I tried to twist them and follow through by bringing Hemi's staff to the ground, and spun my body into his arm to break his hold. It worked.

Hemi smiled at me, his face beaming with pride. "This calls for some refreshments. I think I'm going to go find us some more of those nice drinks."

I laughed as Hemi lumbered down the stairs toward the kitchen.

"Nicely done, I'm impressed!" My face turned to the voice, and I saw Xiven leaning against a wall, his dark hair covering his eyes as he studied me. "Now, can you do it again against someone younger and faster?" Xiven picked up Hemi's staff, which had rolled over to his boot. He kicked it up in the air, caught it with one hand, and broke it over his knee into two even pieces in one fluid movement. I swallowed in nervousness.

"Um, I'm not that good—I just got lucky. I just needed to exercise, and now I'm done." I turned to put the pieces away.

"Come on, Thalia. I've finally found someone to spar with, and you won't even give me a chance. No one else will. Mona hates anything physical, and I've been bored. What do you say?" he pleaded. I looked over Xiven and saw a familiar look of anxiousness and something else. It was similar to how I'd felt earlier when I was about to explode.

"Fine, but just one round." I shook my braid over my shoulder and squared my feet, adjusting my hands around both sticks. Xiven was a ball of pent-up energy, and he danced around on the balls of his toes and did a few feints before engaging. He was fast, and I was constantly trying to keep him in sight. I would swing toward his arm, but then he was gone. I aimed for his head, but I was two seconds too late. I was hit in the back by Xiven and given a verbal taunt that I was slow.

I shook my head and tried to clear my sight to focus on him, but it seemed as if I were trying to fight through mud. Again I barely brought up my arm to block an overhead hit, but then his other arm shot out and jabbed me in the solar plexus. Gasping, I bent over and tried to regain my breath; I saw stars. Biting my lip to hold back my anger, I stood up and was knocked clean on my rear. Once again I was staring at a spinning ceiling. What was going on? How come I couldn't even touch him? Rolling over, I crouched, sticks up in a defensive stance, and this time I concentrated on Xiven.

Xiven was slightly strained. I could tell by the sweat beading on his forehead. And then it hit me; Xiven was cheating. I couldn't see the flow of Denai power he was using on me, but I could see the effects on his physical body. He was hampering my fighting. I instantly reached for Faraway but hit a wall. Those stupid mists were blocking me from using Faraway's strength. I had no way to counter any of his attacks; I was on my own.

Gritting my teeth, I focused my sight and tried to see what he was doing, but once again I was blind to the energy he was using. Xiven came forward and swung at my face, and I brought up the stick to block and countered. I tried to move offensively and keep him moving while I thought of a plan of attack. Pushing him around the room, I desperately tried to think of a way to hinder him.

But because of the veil, there was no power, no energy for me to grab except for what I saw pulsing deep within his body. I hesitated and felt sick at the thought. But Xiven swept at my arm with the broken end of the stick. I gasped as a long cut ran down my arm and blood started to pour out of it. I looked at Xiven's face and was disgusted by the look in his eyes. I thought I'd see sorrow or sympathy in his deep brown eyes, but instead I saw excitement. He enjoyed making me feel pain. Unable to control the rage, I mentally reached out and grabbed at the white pulsing light in the center of Xiven's body and watched as his eyes widened in shock. I took enough power to push Xiven hard away from me; he sailed backward and used his power to stop himself short from hitting the wall. The fuzziness in my mind and mental block I'd felt I was fighting through disappeared when I attacked him, proving that I was right.

"Finally, a worthy opponent. You're my perfect match." His eyes were black, and his chest was heaving from the physical exertion. He looked wild and feral; his grin was crazy, as if he were enjoying this too much.

I hesitated a moment too long as he rushed me, and when he punched me there was extra power behind it. This time I flew into the wall and dropped to my knees. Xiven's face was pale, and I knew he was struggling as much as I was to gain control of power. Because of the mists it was harder for him to use it, but I didn't know his limits.

"Xiven! Stop! This isn't right—we shouldn't be fighting like this!" I yelled at him, trying to keep my distance.

"Why not, Thalia? You are the only one that has even made this interesting for me. You need to prove you're a powerful Denai to Gloria, and this is one way to do it. Beat me, and I will personally vouch for you to marry Joss."

I tried to reason with him. "That's not the point."

But he interrupted me. "What was it that you did to me? I never even saw you use power."

"It's hard to explain." I needed to talk Xiven out of this fight, because the only way to defend myself against him would ultimately hurt him in the end.

"Doesn't matter, because you won't get to do it again." Xiven moved and rushed me, and I grabbed at his energy again and used it to push him to the side so he missed me with his charge. His face was becoming pale; he was tiring, and I could see the exertion of keeping Hemi immobile was wearing on him. I was feeling sick to my stomach from the use of power. It affected me worse than it did a normal Denai.

"Xiven, you have to stop, NOW! I don't want to hurt you." Xiven ignored my scream and gathered together all four broken broom handles in his hands, point sides down. They looked like stakes that floated menacingly above his hands. What had started as a physical exercise had turned into a duel between Denai. The only problem was, I couldn't fight fair. Xiven looked up at me, and what I saw terrified me. He was serious. Xiven was in this too far, and it was no longer a game.

It was war, and he wasn't going to lose. Just trying to access as much power as he did in such a short time was unsettling his mind. He was drunk on power and maybe a little mad. I could see it in his eyes.

I could feel the blood drain from my face as I saw all four stakes fly toward me. Desperately I tried to deflect them like I had been taught in the arena, but it didn't work. In a last-ditch effort I tried to drain everything I could from Xiven to make him pass out or give up, but it was too late. I barely was able to throw up a wall between the flying stakes and me. Three of them hit the barrier and disintegrated, and I watched in horror as Xiven paled and collapsed to his knees. I screamed his name and ran to him.

Xiven was limp like a child, and I grasped his head in my lap. He looked up at me, and he smiled weakly; blood trickled slowly out of the corner of his mouth. "Well played, Thalia. I had never met my match before. I've never seen anyone do what you did." He gazed adoringly at me. Hemi came and kneeled by both of us. I gave him a look that told him to be silent.

"Xiven, are you crazy? Why would you try to use so much power in Skyfell? You could have burnt yourself out, or worse, died." My gut clenched in pain at the thought of him dying because of me. I didn't want to tell him he was in this state because I'd stolen his life energy.

"I had to know," he whispered weakly, "if you were worthy."

I felt sick; I had no idea what he was talking about, but the use of all of that power was making me feel dizzy, and now that the adrenaline had worn off, pain was making it hard for me to speak.

"Thalia, I would be honored to be considered your friend." Xiven grinned at me, and I could see a little bit of color come back into his face. I was secretly relieved that the damage I had done to him wasn't permanent. My stomach was cramping again in pain, but I ignored it as I reached for Xiven's hand and noticed it was covered in blood. My eyes searched Xiven for other injuries but found none.

Xiven started to choke, and I looked at him. His eyes were filled with tears, and his lips were whispering a phrase over and over again. "I'm so sorry...I'm so sorry...I'm sorry."

I was having problems concentrating as I followed his gaze. Xiven wasn't bleeding...I was. I had blocked only three of the stakes. The fourth had embedded itself into my stomach, and the adrenaline and shock had kept me from feeling the pain. Xiven had seen the injury and had tried to heal it and couldn't, which was why he was apologizing. He couldn't because I had drained him of power; he was weakened from the mists, and I wasn't able to heal myself.

"OH!" I said, and felt the full force of the injury, as if my mind had been waiting for my consciousness to fully acknowledge it before assaulting me. All I could do was stare at the stake and the blood pouring out around it, and I felt a moment of relief as I realized my blood was still bright red.

~28~

"**S**on of Light, save us," Hemi howled. The drinks he had carried up the stairs fell from his hands, clattering and spilling their contents on the floor. He unceremoniously knocked Xiven's hands away and picked me up. Turning, he ran toward the stairs, yelling as loud as he could. "JESAI! Help!" Silence followed; no answering call came. The house was unusually quiet except for the sounds of Xiven apologizing. Joss must have left shortly after bringing me home. Otherwise he would have heard the fighting and would have come to investigate like Xiven did. Swearing under his breath, Hemi carefully hauled me down the winding steps and into the streets. Once there, he picked up his pace and ran, yelling for a healer, for anyone to come and help.

Despite the horrific display that Hemi portrayed—a giant man covered in furs, bruises, and my blood, carrying a small girl—someone was brave enough to approach him. A small copper-haired woman called out to Hemi, and he turned gratefully toward her as she motioned for him to follow her. The woman walked swiftly, and Hemi had no problem keeping up with her short legs. Skirts didn't hinder her because she wore a tan split dress with a brown apron and a leather tool belt around her waist. Turning abruptly down a side alley, she headed for a side door and entered what appeared to be a workshop. Beelining into a back room, the woman stopped before a short wall. Pulling a drab tapestry to the side, she revealed a copper-fitted door. Opening it, she motioned for Hemi to enter.

"Quickly—I can do nothing for her unless she is inside." Hemi stared into the darkness through the open door, and I felt his muscles tense. It was either fear or wariness, but the stoic warrior wasn't about to bring his leader's daughter into a trap.

"Oh, you big baby, it's fine, honestly." The little woman quickly grabbed a candle from a pocket in her belt and lit it. She went into the room first, where she knelt on the wooden floor and pulled a solid ring handle to open up another hidden door in the floor. A quick glance downward revealed a flight of stone steps leading into more pitch-black nothingness. When Hemi didn't budge, the petite copper-haired woman, who barely came up to his elbow, turned on him angrily. "Are you coming or not? I thought you were looking for a healer. If you are, then I have to get her properly shielded from the mists so I can use my power. If you don't care a lick about her welfare, then you are just wasting my time and can leave." Her brown eyes sparked with anger, and I could see that she had spirit.

By this time, I was becoming more lightheaded and dizzy, and I unconsciously clutched at Hemi's vest. As he looked down at me, his eyes widened in concern, and he practically jumped into the small room after the woman. She stepped down the stone stairs first with the candle and led the way. Hemi followed close behind.

"Wait. I have to shut the door." She pressed against the wall, and walked back up the stairs and closed the copper door with a thud, encasing us in darkness except for the glow of her small candle. Sliding back in front, she led the way down another flight of stairs. The light caused our shadows to stretch and dance across the walls, mimicking our movement.

My eyes were getting heavy, and I watched as the walls of the stairwell turned from dirt into the blackest stone, similar to obsidian. The whole passageway was chiseled out of the rock. This must be the mineral that kept the city floating in the air, and we were traveling deep into the heart of it, I thought.

"Quickly." The woman opened another door. This time Hemi didn't hesitate but plunged himself deep into the darkness. The woman followed behind and lit a few more candles. "Put her on the table," she ordered. Hemi obliged, and I froze in terror as I felt my body lowered onto a familiar cold steel table.

"NO!" I cried out. Feeling faint and weak, I reached for Hemi's arm and saw him covered with my blood.

More lights were lit to reveal a small workroom with shelves, beakers, tubes, and various odors. Metal instruments and measuring devices lined the table.

"Hold her down," the woman commanded, and stepped into my line of vision. Her brows were furrowed, and her lips were lined in determination. She leaned forward to grasp the piece of the stake that was miraculously still embedded in my stomach and was the only thing keeping me from bleeding out. But when she leaned forward, the light revealed an ominous instrument on the wall that her body had previously shielded from me. I screamed in terror at the exact same time she pulled the stake from my stomach. My screams were swallowed by pain as she pressed her hands into my wound to staunch the flow of blood. Desperately I tried to move my arms, but Hemi was pinning me down onto the table, watching the woman and not paying attention to me. My mouth gaped open from the pain, and I stuttered and shook, unable to speak as I gazed in horror at the wall. At the metal apparatus that glinted ominously in the candle light. At the familiar form of the iron butterfly.

"That's better. Keep holding her down. For some reason she is trying get off the table, and I can't for the life of me fathom why." The small woman wiped her forehead with the back of her hand in exhaustion. She looked me over with concern and then smiled in triumph as she examined my now nonexistent wound. "You know many laughed at Ol' Fanny when I told them about my idea of trying to heal people deep underground within an earthen shield. They thought I was crazy. But I showed them." She chuckled softly and slapped her thigh. She let out a long, tired sigh before sitting down on the nearest stool.

By this time, my terror had abated as soon as I realized that the woman wasn't trying to murder me but was in fact helping me. But I still wasn't comfortable lying on the table and was trying to wriggle out from under Hemi's firm grasp. Hemi wasn't budging, so I turned my head and bit his hand. He yelped and pulled back from me, and I rolled over and off the table, landing in a heap on the floor. Scooting backward on my hands and feet like a crab, I put as much distance as I could between the device and myself.

"Why do you have that?" I asked her angrily, pointing at the iron butterfly. "Why is that here?"

Fanny looked up in the direction I was pointing and studied the iron contraption before answering me in disbelief. "You mean the lightning catcher?"

"The machine that looks like a butterfly. Yes," I replied snidely. "And what do you mean, a lightning catcher? Why do you have it here?"

Fanny furrowed her brow in confusion and looked at me. "I don't understand why you would be interested in it. It was created to harvest lightning during storms as another way of creating an energy source for those that live in the thunder regions. But why do you even care?"

"Because I've seen it before, but it wasn't used in the way you described. It was used for experiments on children." I watched Fanny closely to see her reaction, looking for telltale signs that she was lying. She was shocked.

"I'm sorry, you must be mistaken." Fanny looked visibly shaken and upset.

"I'm not mistaken." My voice shook with anger. "I know the thing that tortured me night after night, and that is it." I pointed again at the machine, my voice rising in volume. "You are wrong!" I challenged her ruthlessly as I found the courage to stand up. Reaching out blindly, I found that Hemi had come to stand by me. He was even now pulling me behind him so he could guard me from this new threat, a threat that a moment ago had saved my life.

Fanny turned deathly white, and her hands trembled as she grasped the fabric of her shirt over her heart. "That can't be. What you're saying is impossible."

"Why?" I asked. Even standing behind Hemi, the sight of the iron butterfly still made me tremble in fear, but I had to know the answer. "Why would it be impossible?"

"Because the inventor of this machine only built the one, and it was never created with the intention to harm others," she answered. Her eyes dropped to the floor in quiet submission.

"How do you know?" My heart was beating so hard in my chest, I felt as if it were going to explode. This could be the answer to everything. "Who was the one who built it? Do you have their name?"

"Yes." Fanny looked up from the floor, and her brown eyes were filled with quiet, unshed tears. "I invented it."

"I don't understand. How can that be?" My knees became weak, and I clutched Hemi's arm, digging my fingernails into his muscular bicep. Hemi, bless him, didn't even flinch at the pain I was undeniably causing him in my distress.

Fanny answered me but made sure she kept distance between us, as Hemi still loomed over her menacingly. "I'm an inventor. It's what I do. What I live for. I try to better the world through my inventions."

My anger was rising to an almost equal level as my fear, which was intense. "THAT THING you created in no way betters the world. Why would you invent it to begin with?"

Fanny looked exhausted and slumped on a stool as she slowly explained. "I was approached by a man who lives in Thunder Valley about creating an invention that harvests the lightning from within the valley. The valley's rocks and ground hold a constant charge, which draws unusual amounts of lightning storms and thunder. If I could create a machine that could draw the charges and lightning strikes from the sky to the machine, then it would make it safe for the area to be settled by people year-round instead of just the fall and winter. And at the same time the people would be able to use the lightning as a renewable energy source to power the village. I was to create the plans for one for the gentleman, and create a small version to be used as a test subject. What you see behind me is the test version I created." Fanny motioned behind her.

Pulling Hemi with me, we approached, and I took a closer look at the device and saw that it was indeed smaller, and there were slight differences in her machine from the one used to torture me. It was missing the bands with the needles that pressed into the pressure points and along the arms of the victim. My fingers unconsciously traced the slight scars on the underside of my arm. My body shivered uncontrollably as I recalled Raven discussing using the machine to activate something in my blood. Tears burned at the corner of my eyes as I grabbed a hammer from a table and began to beat at the contraption. I released all of my pent-up anger, hurt, fear, and frustration on it.

With each metallic ring that echoed from the hammer strike, the guilt over not being able to save Cammie melted away. Tym's death, his brother Sal, Kael, Tenya; I let the hammer be the therapy my mind needed in order to heal completely from the past. Finally exhausted, I realized I wasn't doing much damage other than denting it. I picked up a pickaxe and tried prying it apart. Fanny watched me silently, eyes wide in confusion. She never spoke or tried to stop me.

Hemi let me vent my frustration but after a few minutes decided to help me. The giant clansman reached up with his massive hands to yank at what I called the wings and Fanny had told us was the lightning catcher. As I brought it down from the wall, it rang with a dull thud as it landed on the earthen floor. He gripped the metal bands on the wings and began to pull with all of his strength against the rivets holding it together. Hemi grunted and sweat started to form on his forehead as the bands creaked and resisted his strength. Finally they snapped apart and rattled to the floor in a heap. Reaching for another piece, he started to do the same. Somewhere deep inside I knew I wasn't leaving until I had torn the machine apart.

A shadow to my left made me turn in surprise. I saw Fanny with her apron donned and a determined look on her face. She grabbed a tool and started prying at the rivets, helping us to dismantle her own invention. We worked for what seemed like days but really could only have been an hour in silence. When the iron butterfly/lightning catcher was completely disassembled and no longer resembled anything other than a pile of garbage, Fanny finally found her breath to speak up.

"You do realize that what we took apart wasn't the one that tortured you, right?" Her eyes showed only compassion as she held out her hand to take the hammer I had dropped on the floor and began put it away.

"Yes, I know," I replied meekly, wiping my sweat-covered hands on my pants. "The one used on me was different, bigger." I explained the differences and the way in which the larger one had been altered to hold a person in the middle and lock them into it, with pressure bands that pierced the arms. Fanny looked sick to her stomach.

"I usually hate destroying my inventions, but this one obviously should never have been created." Fanny walked over to a cupboard and pulled out some ointment and strips of bandages and waited patiently in front of Hemi. When he didn't move, she tapped her foot angrily and demanded. "Hands."

Hemi looked startled and held two cut and bloody hands palm up to her. Fanny cleaned the wounds and applied a salve to them before wrapping them in bandages.

"Why don't you do that thing you do and heal them?" Hemi asked, surprised.

"Because I only use my gifts for emergencies. Not for little cuts that can heal on their own and acts of stupidity like yours," Fanny shot back with a hint of a smile at the corner of her mouth.

Hemi stared back at the woman, and growled an ungrateful response under his breath about women knowing their place and belonging in the kitchen baking pies instead of building torture machines. Fanny's response was to tie the bandage tighter around his palm until Hemi flinched in pain. Her eyes twinkled in challenge.

Even though I would have loved to watch the rest of the interchange between them, I needed to find out more information from her. "Fanny, do you remember who asked you to build the machine for you?"

Fanny turned to me and pondered my question for a moment. "No, I don't. I'm sure I have his name written down with his order somewhere in my home. I can find it for you. It was commissioned almost two years ago, and he wasn't happy with the final product during its test run."

"Did it work?" Hemi asked.

"Of course, it worked perfectly," Fanny harrumphed haughtily. "It did everything it was supposed to. He kept finding fault with it and in the end refused to pay, saying that he wouldn't invest in a lightning catcher made by a woman until he had inspected the blueprints for mechanical faults. Needless to say, that night my blueprints disappeared, and so did the man." Fanny sighed in frustration. "He spoke with an accent, and I'm sure any name he gave me was probably false. If he had plans to do something illegal with my invention, he probably covered his tracks. But either way I'm sure with some digging I can find his name. I can swing by your home as soon as I find it."

We reluctantly agreed and told Fanny where we were staying. She showed us out of her shielded chamber and took us back down the streets we had come down earlier, and pointed us in the direction of the Jasai family home. Mixed emotions rolled off me in waves as one moment I was excited that we had stumbled across the creator of the Iron Butterfly, or lightning catcher, but the next moment I was disappointed that we hadn't found out who the leader of the Septori was. I was traveling at a fast and determined pace and had accidentally walked past the stairwell to Joss' home. Hemi had already gone up the steps when I was immediately pinned from behind and pulled into an alley.

Strong fingers painfully dug into my arms, and heated breath went down my neck. I tried to struggle, but a furious voice spat at me, "DON'T." Immediately my body froze as I recognized Kael's angry voice. Not wishing to anger him more, I did as he said. He pulled me down another street and up a set of smaller stone steps until we were on a small balcony overlooking the drop-off. Silently, I followed him and recognized that we were still on the Jesai property. When we were alone, he spun on me. "Where were you?" he growled, eyes flashing dangerously.

"I was injured and Hemi took me to find help. As you can see, I am fine now." I twirled sarcastically with my hands up in the air, showing off to him that I was uninjured. Kael grabbed my wrist to keep me from spinning and looked me over carefully from head to toe. His eyes that never missed anything stared at the bloody hole in my shirt. Kael moved his hand over my stomach to where I was previously injured and moved the cloth aside to assess the damage. Obviously there was none.

"No! Where were you?" he asked again. His chest was heaving, and I could see that he hadn't caught his breath from whatever previous activity he had been doing. "One moment I could feel our bond strong and as annoying as ever. Then the next moment it disappeared, vanished. I couldn't feel you anymore." Kael's blue eyes searched mine, and I could see the worry and panic that he for once was unable to hide from me. The SwordBrother exterior was gone and replaced by a normal, unsure young man. My eyes softened in response, and I reached up to cup his face.

"I'm fine," I tried to reassure him. "Hemi found someone to heal me. We entered a shielded chamber deep within the city so she could heal me without being hindered by the mists." I was about to say more, but Kael still held a death grip on my wrist, and in one smooth motion he pulled me into him and wrapped his arms around me and buried his face in my hair.

Shocked, I stood absolutely still and felt the wild beating of his heart and the deep breaths he was taking to try to calm down. Sure signs, I thought, of suffering the aftereffects of being out of the boundaries of our bond. Gently I placed my cheek against his chest and rested my hand against his beating heart, taking in his familiar scent. It was the same scent that had chased away my nightmares at the way station. A wall that I had built up against Kael crumbled in that moment, and I felt a stirring of attraction. I turned my face up to look along Kael's strong jaw, and he pulled back to stare deeply into my eyes.

We stood like that for a moment and then Kael, realizing what he was doing, stumbled back from me awkwardly. It was one of the few times in which I had known Kael that he had appeared ungraceful. I pressed my lips together to try to hide a smile.

This time it was my turn to look over Kael. "Are you all right? Did you suffer this time from the bond?"

Kael straightened his shoulders and shook his head at me in the negative. "No, there was no pain. It was worse, far worse. A complete and utter sense of loss and hopelessness overcame me." He stepped back and leaned against the balustrade, grabbing his head in frustration. "I felt as if my world had suddenly come to an end, and that I had failed. The feeling was so intense, I felt as if a giant hole had opened up and swallowed me, and all I felt was numbness, nothing. No hope." Kael looked up from the ground, and I saw fear, true fear, deep inside. He looked at me, eyes pleading. "It stripped me of all of my SwordBrother senses. I'm nothing without my senses. I rushed to the house to look for you, but you weren't there. No one knew where you went."

"Xiven knew what happened," I answered thoughtfully. "He wasn't injured as much as I was, but maybe he went in search of a healer, too?"

Kael shook his head. "Xiven has run away. His room was in shambles, and his clothes are missing."

"Why would he do that?" I stuttered.

"Because he tried to kill you?"

"No, I don't believe that. It was an accident—we were sparring and he got carried away. What I can't figure out was how he was able to access so much power here within the mists." I chewed on my lip to ponder the thought before my eyes opened and I blurted out the information I had discovered about Fanny and her inventions. Kael listened wide-eyed and angry throughout the whole conversation.

"So she thinks she has the name of the man who ordered this machine?" Kael started to pace. "How do you know that she is telling the truth? She could be lying to you to throw you off the scent and then escape while we are here discussing this." He turned to me and grabbed my arm, pulling me down the stairs after him. "Show me where this house is—I will make her talk. If she knows anything, she will tell me." Kael was taking the steps two at a time, and I stumbled when we reached the street level again. Violently, I shook my arm out of his grasp.

"NO!" I stood firm, feet planted.

"What do you mean, 'no'?" Kael turned and looked at me in confusion. "This could be the answer we were looking for in finding Tenya!"

"No, not like this." Deep down I trusted Fanny; she spoke truth. I could tell that when she found out the man had twisted and misused her plans for the invention, it hurt her deeply. I wasn't about to punish her more by having Kael torture her into telling us information she didn't know. "I believe her, Kael. I trust that she will find out everything she can and help us if she is truly able."

"You are crazy if you think she is going to help you. You can't trust strangers." Kael was angry, and, truthfully, I couldn't blame him.

"I trusted you, Kael! You were a stranger, and you helped me escape the Raven's prison. So does that mean I shouldn't have trusted you, either?"

Kael froze, and he looked down at the ground. The wind from the various windmills in Skyfell blew his hair wildly in all directions and also blew away his whispered words so that they were barely audible. "No, you shouldn't have."

I turned my back on Kael and started to walk up the stairway that led to the Jesais' home. Spinning once more on Kael, I shot out, "She saved me. She could have let me die or kept me prisoner deep underground, but she didn't. She saved my life. I will give her the benefit of the doubt."

Kael looked up from the bottom of the stairway to stare into my eyes. "I hope you're right, Thalia. Joss' sister's life depends on it."

A cold chill spread through my bones, and a flicker of doubt flooded my body. Shaking my head, I pushed all negative emotions and feelings away and found my inner strength. "I know I'm right. Fanny will come through."

Just then a flurry of activity came from the streets as Joss, Mona, Nero, and a large amount of servants came up, carrying crates of bread, fruits, and other odds and ends. We had to move out of the way quickly or be trampled by the caravan of goods.

"Joss!" I called out, and he turned to me. "What's going on?"

Joss grinned his dazzling boyish smile at me. "Don't tell me that you've forgotten already?" His carefree manner and the

~24~

I felt as if I had been punched in the stomach. Where had the time gone? Somewhere deep inside I had secretly hoped to be farther along in our search and possibly have even found his sister by now so that we could drop the whole charade of being engaged and go back to the way things were. But a week had passed, and here we were on the day that I had been dreading.

Grabbing Joss' sleeve, I pulled him aside. "Joss, are you seriously still thinking of going through with this? We are supposed to be faking so we can find your sister."

The mask of joy fell from Joss' face, and a sterner, more serious one replaced it. "Thalia, we are, don't doubt that. But if you could see what this is doing to my parents, you would understand. They need this. They need a moment, no matter how brief, to forget their grief and find happiness. Even if it is a lie."

Joss' face looked pained, and that was when I realized how much of his hurt he was hiding from me, his family, everyone. He was doing it to spare his family pain by pretending to be the same old carefree Joss that they knew and loved.

"Joss, I don't th—"

"Can you do this for my parents, for me?" The silent ache I saw deep inside him silenced any forthcoming arguments, and all I could do was nod in agreement. He reached out and cupped my cheek, placing a quick kiss on my forehead. "That's my girl."

What was wrong with me? I must be the only girl my age not dreaming about finding a lifemate and starting a family. Maybe everything that had happened to me in the last year had made me more wary of happy endings and true love. Learning my mother was murdered when I was a child, being kidnapped the same day that Fenri asked to be my lifemate, and being tortured and almost killed on numerous occasions could definitely skew a young girl's heart and mind.

Sighing in defeat, I grabbed a crate of fruit and followed Joss up the stairs. It was only when I saw that I was carrying passion fruit that I felt a pang of remorse that I never got to say goodbye to Avina and Berry, or tell them why I had left to follow my father. Concentrating on them must have somehow conjured them, because when I entered the Jesai family's main hall, I heard two screams fill the air. Shocked, I dropped the crate and watched as the passion fruit rolled across the floor to stop right in front of Avina's boot.

"Thalia!" she screamed and ran to hug me.

"What? How?"

"Joss sent a messenger to the castle to get us," Berry said, coming to give me a hug as well once Avina had disentangled herself from me. "Although he never told us why."

"Yes, Thalia, is everything all right?" Avina stopped flittering about the room and paused.

"Why, umm, yes, I mean, no." I stumbled over the right words to say. But Joss came to my rescue and wrapped his arms around me, placing his chin on my head.

"Why, of course it is. We couldn't have an engagement celebration without Thalia's friends here, now, could we?"

More screams filled the rooms as they both jumped up and down in excitement, congratulating me.

"You're going to let me make the dress for the ceremony, right?" Berry trilled joyously.

Avina and Berry chattered together, and not much could be understood between the two as their excited, buzzy babble faded into the background. I saw Mona on her hands and knees, picking up the passion fruit I had spilled. Her back was to me, but it was stiff in anger. Apologetically, I quickly dropped to the floor and started to help pick up the mess I had created. Gently, I touched her shoulder to hand her my fruit to put in her basket. But she stood up abruptly and turned on me, and I saw hate burning there.

"Don't touch me!" she snarled and whirled out of the room, her dark braid swinging after her.

Mona must know about what happened to her brother, or she is jealous about the celebration tonight. I scanned the room for Joss and saw him and Hemi deep in conversation, and I could see the pale look on Joss' face. Hemi must have just told him about the events of this morning. Joss' worried glance toward me that dropped to my torn shirt confirmed it.

"Girls, we have much to discuss, but I think it would be better if we went to my room first," I said. The whole way up the stairs they couldn't stop talking. They found everything fascinating.

"Can you believe the giant bird that flew the skycage up to the city? I positively thought it was going to eat me for dinner. I have never been more scared in my life," Berry gushed once we had entered my room.

What had started as a joyous reunion turned solemn as I explained the long chain of events that had led me to Skyfell and to lying about being engaged to Joss. It took hours, and the afternoon sun became twilight.

"Oh, Thalia, we didn't know," Avina said, sympathizing with me.

"Not many do, but I think we are close to finding the Septori and what happened to Tenya. I don't know how, but I feel it in my bones."

A knock came at my door. Avina rushed to answer it and came back with a sour expression on her face.

"Who's the girl with the dark hair and eyes, the pretty one?"

"Mona?"

"Yeah, what bit her in the butt?"

I laughed out loud. "What are you talking about?"

"She came to the door all high and mighty and demanded that you be ready for the dinner that starts in an hour."

"Oh, my goodness! I completely forgot to get ready." Jumping off my bed, I rushed to my closet and changed out of my dirty clothes and did the best I could with the pitcher of water to clean the dirt off my face.

"Relax," Berry chimed in. "We're here to help you. Plus, I brought a surprise for you."

Berry's surprise turned out to be a pale blue short dress trimmed in silver. Avina worked wonders on my hair, and I entered the main hall with confidence and grace. My entrance caused quite a few heads to turn to me in surprise and a few positive nods my way. The main room had been turned into a joyous reception hall filled with colorful silk streamers that danced across the ceiling and blew gracefully in the wind. Silver bells and chimes were attached to them and added a simple melody to the night air. All of the seating, pillows, and chairs had been removed to create standing room only. Torches lit the wall and along the veranda, creating a soft ambiance.

Many hands reached out to congratulate me, all of them belonging to strangers. I swallowed my nervousness at being touched and smiled politely at them, weaving my way through the room as I looked for a familiar face. Where was Joss? Kael? Nero? There must have been over fifty people on this level alone.

A cold hand grabbed my elbow, and I turned in surprise to see Talbot, Mona and Xiven's father. I breathed in sigh of relief at the sight of someone familiar.

"I don't know if I congratulated you last week when Joss first made your announcement."

"No, I don't think you did."

"Well, I would like to extend that now."

"Thank you, that's very kind."

"By the way, have you seen my son?"

"Xiven?"

Talbot threw his head back and laughed. "Why, of course, Xiven. Who else would I be speaking about? I have no other sons."

Thinking quickly, I tried to tell him the truth without divulging everything I knew. I didn't want to be the one to tell him his son had run away. "Umm, not since this morning?"

"Really?" he drawled out slowly. Talbot's eyes narrowed thoughtfully and studied me closely. "And what was he doing this morning when you last saw him?"

"I was exercising with Hemi, and Xiven challenged me to a sparring match. We both ended up pretty beat up in the end." It was the truth, but I didn't elaborate more.

Talbot's firm mouth twitched. "Who won?"

"What?" I asked, confused.

Talbot ran his thumb down his jawline thoughtfully, his dark eyes boring into mine. The gesture made me feel slightly sick to my stomach. "I asked you, who won?"

"Oh, uh..." He had caught me off guard, and all I was able to squeak out was, "Tie." I turned my back on him and tried to disappear into the crowd of strangers. But Talbot's arm snaked out and grabbed me again. Pressing painfully, he leaned into me and whispered in my ear.

"We both know that's a lie." With a shake he released my arm and walked away. Talbot left me with a feeling of unease, and I tried to shake it off.

Mona was walking around with a tray of the chai, and I had just reached for one to calm my nerves when Kael's hand shot out and grabbed my wrist, stopping my hand midair. Mona's tray rocked as my hand collided with it. She desperately tried to settle her tray and was only at the last minute able to keep it from dropping to the floor.

The liquid in each of the cups sloshed over the rims and made little pools around each cup. Her eyes flashed a warning, and she opened her mouth to say something to me, but her eyes flicked over my shoulder and whatever she saw made her bite her tongue. I was almost positive that what was going to come out of her mouth was an insult.

"I'm sorry. I was clumsy." Mona lowered her eyes and offered me the tray to have my pick of a drink. Again I reached for one, but Kael's grip on my arm tightened in warning. Pulling my hand back, I nodded to Mona. "Maybe later." Her eyes shot venom at Kael, and she walked away. Turning around, I tried to see who or what she'd seen in the crowd but was unable to.

"Kael, what's going on?" I pulled my wrist out of his and rubbed it to get the flow of blood back into it. My fingers had started to go numb.

"Don't drink any chai. Not tonight," he whispered into my ear.

"Why?"

"I'm not sure, but will you promise to not drink any?"

"Only if you come and tell me later what's going on."

Kael drew back from me with a nod and almost instantly faded into the background, something he was extremely talented at.

Nero came into the room and invited all of the guests to the observatory for dinner. Joss appeared at my side almost instantly and took my cold shaky hand in his, giving it a reassuring squeeze.

"Where have you been?" I hissed out between clenched teeth, while trying to smile politely to another guest. "I've been left here to the wolves."

"Sorry, I was taking care of some last-minute details. But I'm here now, and I promise to not leave your side the rest of the night." He rubbed his thumb against my hand and tucked it in the crook of his arm.

Joss looked ravishing. He looked every inch the leader's son. His jacket was dark blue with gold, and he wore a gold vest and cream-colored pants. I felt drab in comparison, but he must have seen my face because he leaned over and whispered,

"You look beautiful."

My cheeks flushed. "Thanks."

Joss led us to the observatory, a room that I hadn't known existed before now. This was unquestionably the largest room in the house; the floor was white marble, and there was a high-domed glass ceiling. Rows of tables had been laid out, displaying a vast array of food. I saw that someone was already seated at the table Joss was leading me to. She was pale with blonde hair—Gloria.

So this was Joss' last-minute business. He had gone to assist his mother in coming to the celebration dinner. I gave Gloria a small smile, and she looked at me as if through a veil of nothingness, her eyes unfocused and blank. A moment later the veil lifted, and she started, as if seeing me for the first time. She paused in confusion before returning a hesitant smile. Her attempt at amity was miles above the obvious disdain she had previously displayed toward Joss and me as a couple.

The seating arrangement put Gloria on my right along with Mona, who watched over Joss' mom protectively. Joss and Nero were seated on my left, and across from us were Talbot, Darren, and an empty seat, which weighed heavily upon my conscience, as it was obviously reserved for an absent Xiven. Berry and Avina were seated farther down our table.

I craned my neck the room for Hemi and Kael. Joss, sensing my distress, nodded to the pair, who stood off in the shadows, watching silently. Hemi, who was clearly trying to blend into the background, stood out awkwardly, as if he was trying to hide his large hulking frame behind a small pillar. An uncontrollable chuckle escaped my lips and drew the direct gaze of Talbot, whose eyes turned hard as he studied me under the candlelight. Dropping my eyes, I looked at my clasped hands in my lap until I felt his gaze move elsewhere.

Keeping my eyes downcast, I tried to search the same area where I'd spotted Hemi for Kael. Kael blended easily, and my eyes skimmed over him twice before noticing him leaning casually against a window. The look Kael was aiming at our table unsettled me; it was a mixture of resentment and suspicion. My mouth went dry with nervousness as I toyed with the possibilities of who he resented at our table. Was it me, because I refused to tell him where to find Fanny? Was it Joss? I tried to concentrate on reading Kael more closely, but he had gotten a tighter rein on his feelings, and I couldn't discern any darkness around him.

My nervousness made my stomach roll in protest at the smell of food in front of me, and I desperately wished for the leaf that Kael carried to settle my stomach. When Nero made his celebration speech and everyone began eating, I made the motions of eating by cutting my food and moving it around on my plate to make it look like I had eaten.

Reluctantly my eyes found themselves drawn to the empty chair where Xiven should be sitting. If I had only been able to refuse sparring with him earlier. Guilt weighed heavily upon me as I replayed the day in my mind and desperately wished I had found another outlet for my temper. If I had, though, neither of us would have been injured. Then he wouldn't have felt the need to run away. But I also would never have met Fanny, who could possibly lead me to the man who had ordered the Iron Butterfly. Could this man be the leader of the Septori? Could he be the Raven? The questions ate away at me.

Gloria noticed my odd behavior. "Is there something wrong with the food? I find the beef to be quite delicious." She took a small bite and chewed slowly as if savoring every bite.

My stomach cramped uncomfortably and started to burn. I bit my bottom lip until the pain made it disappear and licked my lips nervously before answering her. "No, everything's delicious—it's just my nerves are getting the better of me." I took a bite of the beef, chewed, and smiled, giving her my best attempt at looking like I enjoyed what I was eating.

She nodded encouragingly at me. "Yes, see, it is good, isn't it? You know, you are quite pretty. I think you would make a good match for Joss. Give us fine-looking grandkids. Yes, yes, you would." Her voice drifted off dreamily.

Taking advantage of the moment, I turned away and did my best to make myself swallow the meat. A slight pressure began to build in my side, and I identified the poke of a hand. Recognizing the presence immediately and without drawing attention or turning around, I slipped my right hand nonchalantly under my left elbow as strong fingers pushed a few dried leaves into it. I waited a few heartbeats before opening my hand to recognize the same leaf Kael had given me while on the road. Slowly I lifted each leaf to my mouth and chewed it until the pain in my stomach went away.

I stared at the window, which was now empty, and waited until I saw his form take up his spot again. Kael had taken care of me; he was still watching over me as he promised my father and had noticed that I was in distress. This small act of kindness proved that he wasn't angry with me. When I felt sure he was looking in my direction, I slowly mouthed the words "thank you." Kael nodded once in answer. I felt heat rush to my cheeks.

The conversation at our table traveled from the weather to dorabill racing to crops. Gloria spoke very little and seemed to forget I was at the table. But when she did speak to me, it seemed as if she had forgotten her animosity toward me. It wasn't until a tray of chai drinks was brought to our table that I once again remembered Kael's warning. Mona filled Gloria's cup to the brim, and the pale-haired beauty drank it down greedily as if it was the essence of heaven in a cup.

Mona's hands rested lightly on Gloria's arm, as if giving her a reassuring pat. A cup was placed enticingly in front of my plate, and I slowly pushed it out of reach. Gloria watched me; her back stiffened and she turned on me, eyes blazing.

"Do you think you are too good to drink with us? This was specially made for your party tonight. The least you could do is to honor our guests with a toast."

What had I done? Why the sudden change in tone and demeanor within a few minutes? I thought fast. "Oh, yes, a drink sounds lovely, but my hands are shaking so badly with nerves that I'm scared to even take a sip for fear of spilling on myself and embarrassing you or your family in public." The words came rushing out in an awkward attempt to appease

Gloria. It seemed to do the trick, as I saw her eyes take on a glazed look, and she seemed to calm down again.

"Yes, that is smart. You mustn't embarrass us. No, never." Gloria looked off into the crowd and seemed to get lost in thought.

Breathing a sigh of relief, I looked over at Joss to see if he had observed any of that last exchange with his mother, but he was leaning toward his father and was in a deep conversation.

Oh, no! I thought to myself. I had forgotten to tell Joss not to drink anything, either. Grabbing his cup, I lifted it to feel that it was already emptied. Whatever had gotten Kael on edge, he obviously wasn't concerned enough to share his suspicions with Joss.

Mona had gotten up and brushed past Gloria to stand behind Joss and personally refill his cup. Her hand brushed his arm as she placed the drink very carefully on the table. Mona's eyes met mine over Joss' head in a challenge, and then she left the room. Joss had barely given Mona a glance during this whole silent scene, but no sooner had she left than he started to reach for his cup again. I had no choice.

Reaching out quickly, I beat him to it and knocked his cup over in an awkward attempt at pretending to hand it to him. The brown-gold liquid spilled out of the cup and all over Joss' pants. He jumped up, covered with the chai, and gave me an exasperated look, which pierced my heart.

I had disappointed him. He didn't understand. How could I tell him in front of all of these people about Kael's warning? Would he believe me? Joss looked at me sadly and touched my head before promising to return as soon as he changed.

The whole room had stopped to stare at the young girl who had spilled a drink on their lord's son and had embarrassed him. My cheeks burned in embarrassment. Berry shot me a worried look, and Avina looked horrified. I felt tears burn in my eyes. Nero just looked at me and tried to tell me it was fine. That he'd had drinks spilled on him numerous times at dinner. His try at consoling me only made me feel worse. What I was most surprised at was Gloria's reaction.

When no one was looking at me, she leaned into me and whispered in my ear, "Leave. You are not wanted here."

"I'm not going to leave," I shot back quietly. "I have no reason to."

"Even if I told you that he is only doing all of this to make Mona jealous?"

I looked at Gloria to see if she was serious, to see how much she could possibly know. Joss and his father had decided to not tell her about our pretend engagement, so what was she talking about?

A small knowing smile played around her lips as she went on. "He talks to me, you know, when he thinks I'm sleeping. I listen, and I hear him pour out his unrequited feelings for her. He's tried to court her, but she's refused. He brought you home to try to make her jealous and change her mind, which I think she has. You'll see."

"No, you're wrong." My heart felt like it was in a vise, and doubt, that ugly thing called doubt, began to creep in. Our relationship was still new, and we really hadn't known each other that long. But my insecurities made it all seem perfectly plausible. Why would Joss be interested in someone like me when he could marry someone as beautiful as Mona?

"Am I?" she challenged me. "If that's so, then where is Joss right now? Hmmm? You see, he doesn't really care about you."

"He went to change, that's all. He's coming right back." He had to. I couldn't stand to be here one more minute defending him to his mother. My first impression of her had been wrong. She wasn't a beautiful angel; she really was a vengeful dragon.

"I know that all of you are lying, pretending. I'm a mother, and I know my children. I know when they try to deceive me." Gloria's eyes burned angrily, and she shuddered in anger at me. "I don't like liars, and they are not welcome in my home." It was unbelievable how much venom she could spew forth in such a cultured voice. But each word found its target deep within me.

My hands shook from hurt and the deep insecurities she was flushing out, but the doubt was becoming most prominent. It was as if she could read my mind.

"Poor, poor Thalia. Can't you see? You are even lying to yourself." Gloria reached her hand out and touched my skin, and I felt an onslaught of mixed emotions, though muted. "It's Mona—it has always been Mona. It would be better if you left now, quietly, while no one is the wiser."

I couldn't take it. Pushing out my chair, I slowly stood up. Talbot's eyes shot to my face and watched me quietly. Raising my chin up high, I walked out of the observatory and down the hall, taking the first set of stairs that I came to. At first I wandered aimlessly, trying to fight back any fear and doubt I had as I replayed the conversation with Gloria over in my head. When I had thoroughly cooled down and felt composed, I decided it was time to go back to the dinner. By now Joss would have changed and could even be waiting for me. But with all of the different levels in the tower, I was lost as to which floor I was on. I decided to open a random set of double doors to determine where I was.

Opening the first set of doors I came to, I found I was in the library. I was about to close the door when I saw two people locked in a tender embrace by a window. Small feminine hands could be seen locked around strong male shoulders.

Once again embarrassed, I tried to avert my eyes and quietly close the door, but something about their silhouettes looked familiar. Pushing the door open wider, I let it slam against the doorjamb on purpose, hoping that one of them would look up. They both did, and I felt my heart hit the floor.

It was Joss and Mona.

~25~

ide-eyed and confused, I turned and rushed out the door.
I was not sure what I had seen; I decided that, with the way I
was feeling, I wasn't ready for a confrontation. Was I running
away? Probably. But why wasn't I turning around to confront
Mona and fight for Joss? Maybe it was because, deep down, I
knew that Gloria's words had struck a chord with me, and I
was still feeling the reverberations from our conversation.
Maybe Joss had chosen a long time ago, and this was all just a
farce. If so, then why did my chest hurt so much? Why did he
bring me here? Was it all a lie just so I would come and bring
Kael and look for his sister?

Angry tears blurred my vision and I found myself back
on the same floor as the observatory. The sound of music and
laughter echoed into the dark hallway where I stood alone.
Pressing my forehead into the wall, I tried to calm myself
down. But it was no use; I couldn't go back in. I couldn't
pretend to be happy and carefree. I didn't belong here. I hated
living up in the air on Skyfell, and all I wanted to do was
escape. And that's when I realized that Mona was right. Gloria
had won. I was going to leave.

Ripping off the necklace that Joss had given me, I placed
it on the windowsill in the hallway outside the Observatory. I
was taking the coward's way out and was going to sneak out in

the middle of the night. I would leave Joss and Nero a note to explain my disappearance. After all, I never wanted this. It was premature. I never wanted to pretend to be engaged to Joss for fear of ruining our relationship. I was right. It had.

I made it to my room without making any wrong turns. I grabbed my small bag and threw the few items of clothing I had in it, not wasting time on folding them. Very carefully, I laid out the dress that Berry had brought for me on the bed in hopes that she would take care of it for me. Now for the hard part: leaving the Jesai residence without being seen.

With the celebration taking place on another level, it was easier than I had anticipated. I only had to stop and duck around a corner once before I made it down the steps and back onto the street. Walking in what I hoped was the right direction, I followed the road to the end of town. It was only when I saw the tall tower in the distance with the sky cages that I faltered in my decision. Where was I going to go?

Lanterns along the street led the way, and I approached the tower to see the beautiful white perot on its perch, who trilled softly when I came near. I had stopped to admire the bird when a louder screech sounded. I stepped back and fell on my rear. How could I have forgotten that the dorabill also had a perch outside the tower? The dorabill screeched again and flapped his wings, and the rustle of a chain drew my attention to his foot. A long chain was attached around his leg and led to a metal hook in the tower.

"Who's there?" a gruff voice called into the night. A light came on in the tower, and a middle-aged man stepped out into the street, wearing a nightshirt. I hadn't realized the difficulty in trying to leave Skyfell at such a late hour and the attention it would bring.

"Just me, sir," I called back unthreateningly. I held up my hands to show that I was not hostile. "I was hoping to take a skycage down."

"Well, hasn't anyone told you?" he answered, rubbing his hands over his whiskered face.

"Told me what, sir?"

"We don't run the skycages at night."

"Well, why not?"

"We just don't."

"Well, what if it was an emergency and I had to get to Skydown?"

"Then you would risk your own neck and take a skite. It's too dangerous for the operators of the skycages to run night shifts. Plus, it's harder for the dorabills. They aren't nocturnal, ya know."

"But I can't operate a skite," I said dejectedly.

"Well, then, missy, it's best you wait until morning. You'll see. I'm sure whatever problem you are running from will have worked itself out by then."

"What makes you so sure that I'm running from something?" I challenged him.

"Pretty little thing like you, with a little bag in the middle of the night. Yeah, you're running. Just wait—with morning comes a new day." With a shooing motion the skycage operator yawned and returned to his tower. A few minutes later the light inside was extinguished.

The white perot cocked his head and looked at me questioningly. The large red dorabill shuffled from sided to side as if it were sulking. I glared angrily at the bird and hissed under my breath. "Tattletale," for it was the dorabill who had alerted the skycage operator to my presence. I'm sure that was exactly what they were trained to do, and it only made me dislike the bird more. The bird puffed out his chest to make himself look bigger and settled down again, still giving me a woeful look.

Walking away from the tower, I made my way along the wall that surrounded the city. What was I to do now? I definitely couldn't fly a skite, so I was stuck waiting for sunrise. Trying to make the best of the terrible situation that I had gotten myself into, I hunkered down into the lee between two buildings that were close to the wall. I was still within walking distance of the tower. At first light, I would be at the tower waiting for the first skycage out of here. Then I would find Faraway, and then what? I guess I hadn't planned further than that. Placing my forehead on my knees, I wrapped my arms around my legs and tried to think through all of my options.

Was I going to abandon everyone? Leave without telling Hemi and Kael? I was wrong for leaving, and I knew it. Just when I'd decided to be strong and confront my fears instead of running, when I'd decided to accept who I was and Joss' choice, I was attacked painfully from the inside out.

"AAAAHHH!" I cried, and grabbed my stomach. It burned, and I felt as if I were being ripped apart. Falling to my side, I curled in a ball and rocked myself, hoping the pain would depart as quickly as it had come. Sweat dripped from my face, and I bit my lip in hopes of stopping the pain. It worsened, and I screamed into the night, digging my fingernails into the ground. My breath was ragged and sent little puffs of dust into the air. Turning onto my knees, I tried to get up, but I was crippled with pain. My hair had fallen out of its beautiful coif and dangled in the dirt, hiding my tears as they dripped onto the ground.

I cried out again, and this time I heard an even louder scream. Only it wasn't mine; it was higher-pitched, but it echoed my cries. Every time I screamed I heard a louder one, until loud voices could be heard in the distance, along with a commotion. Shortly after, a great shadow loomed over me, and the answering calls of my screams stopped. I heard the rustle of a chain and felt something powerful nudge me in the side. I toppled over and saw the giant red head of the tower's dorabill inches from my face. Painfully, I tried to crawl away from the bird, but I watched as the bird's great talons kept stepping in front of me, blocking my escape.

The manacle around the dorabill's leg sported a foot of broken chain, and I could see fresh blood from where the bird had struggled to break free. He had heard my screams and probably mistook me for a dying animal and fresh dinner. I was probably a more tempting piece of meat than a rabbit.

I heard a whimper escape my throat, and I thought how pathetic I was, unable to gather the strength to put up a fight. The dorabill cocked its head and darted quickly forward toward my stomach as if it were going to attack. I threw my hands over my neck and tried to curl into a ball to protect my soft spots. Who was I kidding? I was all soft spots. The bird stopped inches away and turned his head back and forth before leaning back away and screeching loudly into the night. More voices could be heard, and I saw torches coming, lighting the night. The dorabill stepped back from me as men came around the corner.

The tower's operator was the first one I recognized, still in his nightclothes but wearing boots and holding what looked to be a giant club and a bucket of rabbit. Other townsmen gathered around and froze when they saw me on the ground, huddled in fear and pain. They looked confused and shocked. They were probably here looking to find someone who'd stolen a dorabill, not an injured young girl.

"Well, the least you could have done is wait till morning," the skycage operator fumed. "I didn't think you had it in you to try to steal a dorabill!"

"I…I…d-d-didn't," I gritted out between clenched teeth as another painful cramp came on, and I curled up and groaned loudly.

"Larn, she's hurt!" came a female voice.

"Well, I can see that now!" the operator, whose name was Larn, shot back. Larn stepped forward and dropped the club and bucket on the ground. The dorabill shot out his giant neck and overturned the bucket to get at the pieces of rabbit, and ate his fill in two crunchy bites. Larn leaned down and touched my forehead, which was hot to the touch. "Golly, she's burning up!"

The female spoke up again. "Who is she?"

"She's staying with the Jesai family. I've seen her with their son." This time another unidentified man spoke up.

"Quickly, we must get her back."

I was lifted into the air and carried swiftly down the street. The mob of people that started with us died down as they stopped following us and one by one entered their homes.

"No!" I tried to shake my head. I didn't want to go back, and the pain in my stomach was dying down into smaller, controllable cramps. "I'm fine. Please let me down." But it wasn't Larn who was carrying me, it was someone else.

A voice shot out from the darkness. "I'll take her from here."

The man carrying me stopped and waited for the speaker to come into the light. I felt myself cringe as I recognized the balding head and robe of Talbot.

"Oh, Talbot, it's you. Do you know her?" the man carrying me asked. He must have known Talbot and known that he was a close friend of the family.

"Yes, she is the guest of honor at the party, and she ran off. I'll take her around the back so no one will be the wiser."

The stranger carrying me shook his head and carefully set me down feet first onto the ground. Weakened, I leaned against the closest building for support.

The stranger spoke. "All right! Just make sure she seen to right away. She's apparently sick and running a high fever."

"Wait," I called out. But the stranger, having done his good deed for the middle of the night, turned and ran back home.

I clutched the wall and glared at Talbot as he came near me. "Is it true?" he asked.

"Is what true?"

"Are you running a fever?" He stepped closer to me and raised his hand as if to feel the temperature of my skin.

Turning my head I avoided his touch. "Not anymore," I lied.

"Do you have cramping in the stomach? Does it feel like you're on fire?" he asked quietly, surveying me with his dark eyes. A chill went up my spine as I stared at him, trying to place that cold calculating stare.

"Sometimes."

"Hmmmm, Thalia, Thalia, Thalia," he chanted, walking around me while still keeping me pinned between the wall and himself. "What am I going to do with you? You were the only one worth keeping. At first I thought you wouldn't survive, but you're stronger than that. You've surprised me. And now you are proving me wrong again. Even as we speak, you are trying to resist." He stopped pacing and leaned toward me. "But you can't."

Fear shot up my back, and I froze at his words. My heart began to race, and I could hear its frantic thud loudly in my ears. The dark eyes were suddenly familiar; only, I had seen them watching me from behind a silver mask. Here was Raven in the flesh. I felt myself go weak with terror at facing my greatest nightmare.

"You are coming with me." Talbot grabbed my wrist and commanded me to follow him. Out of fear, I followed for a few steps, and then I resisted. He pulled on my arm again, but I was tired and weak, so I dropped like dead weight to the ground and pulled away from him. "All she was supposed to do was make you drink," he snarled angrily at me. "You didn't drink anything, did you?"

I smiled weakly at him in triumph.

"Stupid girl," he spat out. Whether he was talking about me or Gloria, I wasn't sure. "I'll show you," he threatened, and grabbed me around the throat. I felt a jolt of power slice through me, and I went limp. Talbot grinned evilly, and sweat dripped off his bald head. He was tired, weaker now, but so was I.

The jolt paralyzed me, and Talbot grabbed me under the arms and started dragging me down an alley, murmuring curses under his breath. "Stupid female couldn't even follow one instruction. How in the world you figured out about the drink, I don't know, but it would have made it much easier if you hadn't."

He fumbled with his jacket and pulled out a small packet. He dumped a few seeds on the ground as he reached for another and tried to shove it in my mouth. I bit at his fingers and felt the bitter familiar taste of the drug used to paralyze me in prison and which Bvork had used to incapacitate me in a solid, concentrated seed form.

Talbot forced one into my mouth. I pushed out the seed and bit down with my teeth to keep him from forcing another one in. But I was already feeling the effects of it being in my mouth, and a numb feeling started to take a hold of my senses.

"I hate wasting the nulle seed. They are so few and rare. It's why I prefer to shave it down and use it in drinks. It stretches farther," he chuckled.

My eyes started to get heavy, and I felt him grow larger in my sight.

"When used in the right dosage, it's also a great mind control—did you know? Mona, of course, didn't have the gift of persuasion until we stole it from a poor little Denai. It's sad that Mona was only able to retain that one ability."

I had no choice. I was losing this battle, so I decided to give in to it, let him think that I had swallowed the whole seed. Pretending to go limp in Talbot's arms, I let him drag me down the street, waiting for the perfect opportunity to surprise him. Plus, I needed to see where he was going to take me.

"You probably wonder whose Denai gifts we gave you. But ah, ah, ah, that would be no fun. I'm interested to see what you retain and which ones are still developing. You are a conundrum. I've counted four Denai gifts running through you, and it seems that another one is going to appear soon. I know, I always know. Headaches, stomachaches, fevers. It will be so much fun to re-create our studies. Mona has asked if, when we are done with you, she could have your gifts. You'd think the girl would be satisfied, but no, not that one."

"Stop!" a voice yelled out of the darkness.

Talbot froze and dropped me on the ground but stood over me, keeping his hands free, eyes darting back and forth, looking into all the shadows for the speaker.

"YOU!" the voice yelled again. "How dare you!" I took this moment of distraction to roll into Talbot's legs and knock him off his feet. His moment of surprise didn't last long, as he scrambled to his feet, but I was already scrambling away toward the now familiar voice of Fanny.

Fanny stepped into the street, carrying a torch, which lit her copper curls to look like a ball of fire. "How dare you take my invention and turn it into a means to inflict pain?" She shook with anger, and I tried to stand next to her and take the torch from her shaking hands. Fanny shook me off and stepped forward to confront Talbot. "You stole my designs and perverted my creation."

"No, I didn't. I made a few changes, and it has been immensely useful to me. It is helping us make the world a better place."

"I highly doubt that," she growled, clenching a hammer in her hands that she'd pulled from her work belt.

"Oh, but it has. Even now, after all of these months, it is still affecting her, changing her, making her stronger."

"What have you done to me?" I had found my voice, and for once I could get my answers. "What did you do to Kael?" I screamed at him.

"Why, I've started the wheels of fate in motion. I've released your true form. You can feel it, can't you, trying to get out? It's going to break free. There's no stopping it now. I injected the serum, and the machine has activated it." Talbot spoke, but took a step backward away from me.

"That's not an answer."

"That's all that the answer you're going to get."

"Why me?" I yelled at him.

Talbot didn't answer but looked at me, eyes squinting joyfully, knowing that he held the answers I was so desperate for.

"Why not?" he intoned, taking another step away from us as Fanny and I took a step closer to him.

"Where's Tenya? Where is Joss' sister? What have you done with her?" The questions poured out as I realized he was starting to play a game and was refusing to answer my questions. I desperately needed him to answer these ones, if any.

"Oh, she is far from here. Don't worry. She is safe in the hands of my faithful Septori, experiencing their humble hospitality." Talbot spoke with his hands dramatically; he cocked his head to the side as if he were listening for something. "But I fear my welcome here has come to an end. It's such a pity that you chased away Xiven. I'm very eager to personally see how strong you've become. But that will be another day." The noise Talbot was listening for became louder and drew closer.

Unsure of what Talbot's next move would be, I tried to prevent him leaving by draining him of his life energy. If I could drain him and make him pass out, then he couldn't escape. But it wasn't there; there wasn't any power or life force for me to steal. How could it be? Was he somehow shielded from me?

"I'm tired of playing games with you, like a cat and mouse. This time you will come to me, and I will show you what your greater purpose is. I shall be waiting for you, Thalia." Talbot bowed deeply before us and waved farewell. "Till then." He turned and walked into the shadows.

"Stop him!" I yelled to Fanny. "Use your powers."

She turned to me with defeat on her face. "I can't. I only have powers of healing, nothing more."

I took off at a run but found that I could only stumble along painfully after him into the darkness. "Kael!" I yelled loudly. "Kael, help! Where are you, you stupid SwordBrother? Kael!"

A shadow jumped from one of the balconies of the Jesai home and landed in front of me, grasping my shoulders to steady me. "Thalia, what's the matter?"

Swinging with all my might at him, I pushed Kael roughly into the wall, not bothering to notice the bloody and ripped shirt he already sported. "Where have you been? Where were you when I needed you?" I cried desperately, my hands shaking as I grabbed his shirt. "Go after Talbot. It's Talbot. Talbot is Raven, and he is getting away."

Kael looked at me, his face a blank mask. A deadly blank mask. He only spoke one word. "Where?"

"He went that way." I pointed into the darkness, and Kael flew after him. His hands reaching for the throwing knives he kept hidden within his vest. Kael's footsteps were silent as he chased after him, and I wondered to myself how long it had taken him to learn to run so silently.

A soft hand touched my shoulder, and I turned quickly to see Fanny. Standing this close to her, I realized how petite she was. She was even a few inches shorter than I.

"I'm sorry, Thalia. You must hate me. I've disappointed you twice now." Fanny looked devastated. Her head dropped in shame, and she dropped her hammer into the dirt and fell to her knees. "I couldn't stop him. I'm not strong outside my workshop shield. Plus, there wasn't anything I could have done."

I dropped to my knees next to her and put my arm around her. "No, Fanny, don't blame yourself. I'm not disappointed. It was wrong of me to ask you to do something I couldn't. I just assumed you had other gifts besides healing. It was my fault." I wrapped my arms around her and comforted the older woman.

"I was coming to tell you that I found the information you asked me about. I didn't think you wanted to wait until morning, so I was going to leave a message at your home. I was on my way when I heard his voice. I would recognize that voice anywhere, although he wasn't speaking with an accent. I hung back in the shadows to be sure, and when I saw him, I knew it was him."

"What did you find out?" I asked.

"Well, I was right about the fake name." She ruffled in her apron pocket and pulled out a much worn, yellowed piece of paper. "The order was placed by a Balto Varen from Thunder Valley. That man was definitely him, except that when he spoke with me he wore a wig and spoke with an accent." Fanny stood up, and I walked with her as we headed to the closest entrance to the Jesai home. We parted ways, and I told her to come by if she remembered any more information for me. Heading up the stairs to the main room door, I opened it to find that the place was quiet, empty.

Was I gone so long that everyone had departed and gone to sleep? That's when it hit me. I had forgotten about Mona. She was a traitor, in league with her father. I flew up the stairs as fast—or should I say as slowly—as my wobbly legs would let me and burst through the observatory door. What I saw left me speechless. The room was destroyed.

~26~

Furniture was broken, tables overturned, with food spilled all over the floor. What looked like either blood or wine was splashed across the marble walls. People were lying in heaps on the floor. I saw Berry's body lying protectively over Avina.

Crying in fear, I stumbled through the room and knelt down to them, touching their skin. It was warm. In fact, it was too warm. And that's when I saw Berry's eyes, wide with fear, blink at me.

She was alive! I moved Berry's hair aside and saw that Avina was alive and well, too. They were only paralyzed. Avina tried to speak through frozen lips.

"Shhh, shhh. It's going to be all right." I tried to comfort them. "It will wear off in a while, and then you will be good as new. I promise." I knew all too well the emotions they must be feeling. First it would be fear and helplessness, followed later by anger.

Standing up, I surveyed the rest of the room and the damage. I checked every guest in the room, and all of them were no worse for wear. A few bumps and bruises, a couple of cuts and scrapes, as some guests were unlucky enough to fall on glass. But everyone was in the same condition: paralyzed, but alive. Had Mona done this? What had happened after I had left?

Hemi, Joss, Nero, Gloria, Darren, and Mona were unaccounted for. I tried to reassure everyone who was still in the room that I would be back in a moment and began a hunt for the missing Jesai family. It wasn't until I had checked in Gloria's room that I found them. They were mostly unharmed.

What surprised me the most was that Mona was gagged and tied up in a corner of the room. She had been tossed there like a bag of rotten potatoes. Joss had a fat lip, and Nero sported a bruised cheek. Both of them were sitting on either side of Gloria's bed, clasping her hands. Darren stood guard over Mona and kept giving her disgusted looks. As soon as Hemi saw me, he rushed over and picked me up, giving me a large hug. He then crushed my wrist within his large hand and held on for dear life, as if he were afraid I would disappear again on him.

"What happened?" I asked. My voice sounded loud in the near silent room.

Joss glanced at me but looked away from me in shame, refusing to make eye contact. Nero's shoulders were shaking as if he was crying.

It was Darren who finally answered me. "We aren't really sure what happened. One minute we were happy and celebrating, and then the next we were all fighting amongst ourselves like dogs. I can barely remember who started it. But I think it was meant as a distraction. Only I don't know how it happened or why." Darren gave a seething look at Mona before looking over to Gloria again.

"It's the drink. The more you drink, the more she is able to control you," I said. Mona's head snapped up, and her eyes glared angrily at me. "I ran into her father, Joss, and he said as much."

Joss didn't even look at me, but hung his head in shame and buried his face in his hands.

"Joss." I said his name, trying to get him to look at me. "Joss, please look at me." He didn't move and I was getting frustrated. "Joss, Talbot is the Raven. Talbot has your sister." When my words sank in, Joss turned and flew from the bed in a single motion to face me.

"Are you serious?" Now that Joss faced me, I could see that he had been crying.

"Yes. Talbot is the Raven, and he said he has your sister. He ran away, and Kael is looking for him."

This time it was Nero who spoke up. "Why? Why her?" Nero was in shock and clasped the hands of his wife. I wasn't sure whether he was talking about his daughter or his wife.

"Nero, what happened to Gloria?"

"When we started fighting amongst ourselves, there were only a few not affected. They tried to stop us. Kael knew something we didn't and went straight for Mona. She tried to defend herself against him. If what you say is true and she can control others, I think she lost her hold on them, and everyone just fell to the ground. Kael subdued her, as you can see." He motioned to the tied-up Mona, who at the mention of Kael's name screamed in rage against her gag.

Darren nudged the raging Mona with his foot, and she tried to kick him. When she had stopped fighting, Nero looked at me again with a look of utter helplessness. "It wasn't until after Mona was tied up that Gloria started to have a seizure. She hasn't spoken or moved since. She's fading away fast and is resisting our efforts to heal her."

I let Nero's words sink in, and I tried to think of something to do, anything. Should I run and find Fanny? Would that even help? My gaze rested on the cup that was on a table next to Gloria's bed. She had been drinking the concoction made by Mona a couple of times a day for months or even years. By now Gloria was nothing more than a drug-addicted puppet.

Closing my eyes and opening them again, I looked deep into Gloria and sought the glow: her life energy. It was strong and blazing bright, but shadows surrounded it, squeezing, trapping, trying to subdue the light. I picked at a thread of shadow and followed it with my consciousness, and it didn't surprise me one bit when the thread of shadow led to Mona.

"It's Mona. She's still controlling her. She's been doing it for months, making Gloria believe that she's ill when in fact she's not. She's trying to trick Gloria's body into thinking it is dying." It all made sense. If Mona was under attack by Kael, then she knew she was in a fight for her life, and she would do everything she could to keep the upper hand. And in the palm of her hand was Gloria's life. She couldn't control everyone, so she released them to take hold of her weakest-willed puppet, a puppet she'd been controlling for months. It was her only bargaining tool, and that was why she hadn't killed Gloria yet.

I relayed my thoughts to Joss and Nero, and both of them turned angrily on Mona. Her eyes lit up in triumph when they realized that she was the one holding the power. Nero stormed over to her and shook her shoulders, demanding her to release his wife. When Nero shook her, I saw her torn dress move an inch to reveal something dark underneath.

"Stop!" I touched Nero's shoulder and he stepped away from her, turning his back on her in anger.

"How could you do this to us? We took you in—you were like family!" Nero's shoulders quivered in anger. Mona's eyes flicked between Nero and Joss and then to the floor.

Kneeling before Mona, I reached toward her shoulder and torn dress. She hissed and tried to kick at my hand. I jumped back because she startled me. "Darren, hold her, please." Darren did as I asked, holding her from behind, but looked as if he would rather do anything else than touch her.

Stepping close to Darren, I looked sadly upon Mona's torn dress. It had been beautiful at one time but would be headed for the trash bin. What had caught my eye wasn't the dress but rather the large tear that started by her collarbone and ended by her shoulder blade. Pulling Mona's long braid aside, I lifted the flap of silk to reveal a familiar brand on the back of her neck: two slash marks surrounded by a circle, the hidden mark of the Septori. I dropped Mona's braid back down on her back as if it had burned me and stepped away.

Here was all the proof we needed against her; she was a member of the Septori. "Joss, she's one of them."

"Make her stop," he yelled angrily. "Make her release my mother."

His heated words made me pause in wonder. Only a few hours before, I had seen the two of them in a warm embrace, kissing. The betrayal and turmoil of emotions had sent me running. Was I mistaken in what I saw; had I judged Joss too soon? Here he was acting completely different.

"I don't know how," I whispered back.

The look Joss gave me was one of complete helplessness. How could we get her to release control of Gloria without harming her? I was at my limit; my skin was still burning to the touch, and I was emotionally and physically exhausted. The run-in with Talbot had drained me and stirred up a plethora of mixed emotions, ones that felt like chains were being slowly drawn around me.

"Please, Thalia," Joss begged. "If anyone can, it's you." The words spoken in complete honesty were meant to encourage me, but instead it felt like a weight had been added to the chains around me and was now dragging me into an abyss of hopelessness.

I nodded to Darren, and he pulled off her gag so we could speak to her.

"Mona, please release Gloria," I pleaded softly. "I know you must secretly care about her. Otherwise you would have let her die weeks ago." It was a gamble. I had seen Mona hovering protectively over Gloria. So I was gambling on the fact that, since Mona had lost her mother, she might have secretly seen Gloria as a substitute mother figure.

Mona's eyes started to tear up, and I should have stopped speaking then, but I didn't. "If your father forced you in any way to do his bidding, we understand. You don't have to be part of the Septori. You can leave them and help us. We'll help you."

"You have no idea what you are talking about." Mona started to laugh hysterically. "No one forced me to do anything—I chose to become a member of the Septori. You have no idea the rush that absolute power gives." Mona glared at the Jesai family and spit in their direction. "You said you gave us a home. You probably thought you were extending that invitation out of the goodness of your heart. Well, I have a word for you. You didn't. I made you think you did. You didn't know us or Talbot, but a few hours, and I made you think you had known us for years." Mona started laughing joyfully, kicking her feet in exultation.

Nero's face paled, and his hands started to shake. "No, that can't be. I remember…."

"NO! You only think you remember. I altered your memories, and it will take years for you to filter through them and find the truth. That's what being a member of the Septori allowed me to do. I controlled and ruled the leaders of the Skyfell family within the misty veil. And once I had proven myself, then I would be allowed an even greater task." Mona looked crazy, blind with greed and power.

"Is that why Xiven was so strong within the veils?" I asked. "Is he Septori, too?"

"Xiven was here to make sure I did my job—that is all. He was assigned because we looked alike. He was my watchdog and look how good of one he turned out to be. He's probably long gone by now, off licking his wounds." Mona's lip curled in distaste. "Thanks to you."

My mind whirled as I tried to process all the information that was coming at me. Mona was put here to control the leaders of Skyfell. She was able to easily with the concentrated chai they all drank greedily until Joss had left to train in Haven. How could she control the future leader if he was gone?

"You would have gotten away with it, too, until Joss left. That's why you kidnapped Joss' sister. It was so he would come back."

Mona nodded. "Catch on quick, don't you? I got in trouble when he left. I actually think Gloria knew something was up and orchestrated him leaving for school when I left for a few days and the drugs started to leave her system. When I returned, he was gone. But that's all right. I know how to bide my time. He was promised to me as a reward, once I had proven myself to Talbot.

"When Joss finally came home, I was shocked to find out that he'd brought home a lost puppy and even more shocked when he announced his intentions to become your lifemate. I would have killed you, Thalia, believe me, I would have, but Talbot recognized you and made me wait and watch you." Mona shifted her feet uncomfortably and looked me over from head to toe, as if realizing something for the first time. "You're one of them, aren't you?"

"One of what?" Saying the words made them feel like gravel in my throat.

"His experiments."

Since Mona obviously didn't know off-hand, she wasn't as important to the Septori as she thought. She wasn't apprised of all of their doings, or her father's. But the way she was speaking about Talbot led me to believe that he wasn't even her father, just a ruse to allow him into the Jesais' home. Her attitude sparked something deep inside, a cache of hidden determination and will. The stubbornness that helped keep me alive in the prison began to rise to the surface.

"Apparently one of the better ones," I challenged, pretending pride. Obviously Mona wanted power, and I stood for what she secretly wanted. Mona's eyes grew dark with jealousy. I decided to push her further with a lie. "And you're one of his!"

"What do you mean?" Uncertainty filled her eyes.

"Do you honestly think he never spoke of you, of his disappointment in you? I spent many hours in his presence, and I've overheard many things spoken when they thought I was unconscious." I stood up straight and put my own look of contempt on my face. "How you are one of the failed ones." It was another gamble, but I saw that it had a ring of truth to it, because Mona's face turned ashen white, and she slumped lower to the ground dejectedly.

"You lie," she whispered unconvincingly, as if she were trying to persuade herself.

"Even in the alley a few hours ago, he spoke of your incompetence. Of your inability to make a young girl drink a drugged beverage." Finally piecing together the facts, I was starting to make sense of everything. After all, knowledge was power.

"You're wrong. I will prove myself to him. I will." With a final scream of desperation, Mona pulled on the thread of power, and I saw Gloria on the bed gasp for breath and struggle.

"Stop her!" Joss and Nero yelled.

Without thinking, I, too, grabbed a thread of life, Mona's, and squeezed. Mona struggled and refused to release her hold on Gloria, but she was no longer trying to kill her. Panting, she fell to the floor, trembling, but the thread linking her to Gloria was still there.

"What should we do?" Nero said as he had grabbed his wife and brushed her blonde hair with his hands in an attempt to comfort her, though she was still unconscious. "How can we break her control over her? I don't know if she can survive another attack like that. It's not something I can heal. She made Gloria stop breathing."

Hemi spoke up gruffly for the first time. "Kill her. If you can't do it, I will." To him it was a simple choice, and not one that he would ever lose sleep over.

"What? No! We need her to find my sister," Joss argued.

"Then get rid of her," Hemi snapped.

"Where can we bring her that she won't be able to hurt anyone else?"

"I know where." And I did.

I gave instructions to Hemi and Darren, and they re-gagged Mona and walked her out. They were taking her to Fanny's to place her deep within the underground shield, but first they were going to drug Mona using the same techniques she used on us. She would be drugged and unable to reach any power within the shield, but the shield would also block her from reaching those outside it.

A few minutes later I saw the dark thread of power that was linked to Gloria vanish instantly, a sign that they had entered Fanny's underground workroom. Gloria's color returned, and her breathing became more even. Now all we had to do was wait for the drug to work its way out of her system and out of the systems of the others in the main room.

Slowly, one by one, they regained control, and every one of the guests affected wanted answers to what had happened. I promised Berry and Avina answers later, and I left Joss and Nero to explain what they felt was appropriate to share with the affronted guests.

Blindly, I made my way to my bedroom and crawled into bed, and felt my eyes, heavy with fatigue, close as the first rays of morning sunshine entered my room. I was falling deep into sleep when a stray thought floated into my head before disappearing with the morning rays. Kael hadn't returned.

~27~

"Well, he has to be somewhere," I yelled, cutting Joss short. It had been hours since I had last seen Kael.

"Thalia, he'll come back. He's probably following Talbot, er, uh, the Raven back to his stronghold. He's a SwordBrother. He will be fine."

"No, he won't. Joss, he needs me."

Joss' beautiful face scowled in disagreement. We hadn't had the chance to talk alone about what had happened between him and Mona or the fact that we could officially drop the charade of our engagement.

"I highly doubt that he needs you," Joss grumbled.

"No, he does. It's something they did to him, to us. It's really complicated. But believe me when I say that if we can't find him soon, he could die."

Joss' head jerked up in surprise. "And when were you going to tell me about this?" he asked accusingly.

"Hopefully never." It was the truth. We had hoped to find a cure or fix for the bond. "But if you won't help me find him, then I will go on my own." I grabbed my pack and set off down the stairs to start my own search party for Kael. Joss grabbed my arm and turned me to look at him.

"Does he mean that much to you that you would go back onto the streets where Talbot and Xiven are running free and try to find him? When you could end up captured or even killed?" Joss searched deeply into my hurt blue eyes.

I stared at Joss and raised my chin in defiance, showing him that I wasn't afraid. "He would do the same for me." I shook off Joss' arm and ran down the steps onto the street. Louder thuds behind me attested to the fact that Joss was following me.

We took to the north tower and checked with the skycage operator to see if anyone matching Kael or Talbot's description had left any time last night or early morning. He hadn't. Joss led me at a fast pace as we followed a less worn path and cut through the city, using back alleys to reach the skitesmith.

Skyfell's skitesmith was very much like Haven's blacksmith. Since there weren't any horses or tack on Skyfell, his main line of work was repairing the city's skycages and skites.

Bartus looked to be in his eighties, with wiry limbs, long scraggly white hair on his head. Bottle-lens spectacles covered his eyes, giving him a bug-like appearance.

"Why, Joss. Bless my soul. To what do I owe the pleasure of your visit?" Bartus chuckled while standing to give Joss a warm hug. He was so thin that I thought for sure he would break if a strong wind blew in.

"I'm sad to say this isn't a pleasure visit, Bartus. We are looking for a friend who went missing late last night." Joss was about to say more when I cleared my throat and held up two fingers. "Well, actually, one young man and an older went missing, and I'm wondering if they made it off Skyfell without using the skycages."

Bartus stared at Joss as if he were reading his lips and then shook his head in silent understanding. "Well, now, I didn't hear anything, but one of the skites I was to repair for the Quints family went missing sometime last night. The tarp's stitching needed repair, so I feel sorry for the poor fool who took it for a joyride. Most people are smart and know not to mess with them if they are hanging outside my shop, because those are the ones waiting to be fixed."

Visions of Kael falling through the misty veils the first time flew through my head, and I felt myself go weak. I grasped Joss' arm to steady me. The first time Kael had been saved by Joss, since he controlled the wind to catch him.

"Joss, I think I'm going to be sick," I whispered and ran outside Bartus' skitesmith shop.

A few moments later Joss followed me and came to give me a reassuring hug. "It will be okay. We know that someone left Skyfell with a broken skite. Now we can send out search parties along Skydown and the riverbeds."

"Joss, if the skite malfunctioned, what are the odds of someone surviving the fall?"

"Not good. Only a Denai could possibly survive the fall, which is why we offer the skycages."

I covered my mouth and concentrated on deep breathing so I wouldn't dwell on the possibility that Kael could very well be dead.

We ran as fast as we could back to Joss' home and told Nero what we had learned. Gloria had recovered and was sitting up in bed, her eyes wet with tears. Berry and Avina were keeping her company, telling her stories of living in the Citadel. I saw that Berry's hands were filled with what looked to be the makings of a lovely dress for Joss' mother. They were doing their best to keep her spirits uplifted and to keep at bay the probable guilt that was assailing her.

Nero told us to take the dorabills, and search the riverbeds and the ravine along the skite launching points. Joss nodded and ran to the veranda, and pulled out his flute. He played a short tune, and I saw a red speck fly through the mists and grow in circumference until Nero's Cecili landed in front of us. The same Cecili that Joss had said was a "biter."

"Get on," Joss commanded.

Too nervous to disobey, I scrambled behind him and held on tight as the dorabill alit into the air with the mad pumping of her powerful wings. It was a short flight, as I saw that Joss was aiming for the southern skycage tower. We landed in a cloud of dust, and Joss hopped off to run in and notify the operator of a need for a search party. A bell began to ring out from the tower, and within moments people began to gather together to help with the search.

It was a different operator who came out of the tower, and he pulled a map out of his pocket and circled the different areas underneath Skyfell that we were to search. From the operator's cool demeanor, I guessed this wasn't the first time someone had gone missing or fallen and a search and rescue mission had been ordered. In our case, we had little hope of it being a success; it was more of a recovery mission.

Joss and I crawled onto Cecili, and we dove off the launching point by the tower after three other dorabills and their riders. The jump was very much like my first dive with Joss' father—scary. This time I was able to open my eyes as we dove through the silvery mists. Once we cleared the mists, I saw exactly how far down the earth was from the city. The distance was incredible, and nothing could survive the fall. All this made me wonder why people were crazy enough to live in Skyfell to begin with. Skydown was becoming much more desirable property by the minute.

I watched as Joss, with subtle touches and by leaning his own weight, directed Cecili. She was one of the larger dorabills, and I was able watch her wings in awe as she rode the currents so effortlessly. Joss turned Cecili, and we spiraled lower and took to flying along the riverbank that we were assigned to.

Back and forth we flew, and I scanned the river itself, its banks, and the surrounding foliage, looking for the black of Kael's clothing. Nothing. I tried calling his name, but the wind just whipped it back at me and I found it hard to breathe. I saw another dorabill in the distance, scouring the ravine.

I had about given up hope when a whisper touched my mind, and I almost jumped. It had been so long since I'd felt his touch, I almost cried with happiness.

Faraway? Oh, I've missed you.

I've missed you too, my lady.

Faraway, we can't find Kael.

Have you searched for him?

What do you mean, have I searched for him? I've been looking for him all morning.

Faraway chuckled at me as if I were a child that needed chiding. *Have you searched for him since you've cleared the mists?*

"What? Oh!" And that's when I realized what my omniscient horse meant. Clearing my mind, I stretched out my consciousness and realized how easily the power flowed to me once I was out of the mists. It was as if a powerful ocean was flowing back to its bed. The power came so willingly that my senses were almost overwhelmed. Never before had it been like this; I was usually borrowing energy from Faraway, but, once I was out of the mists, it seemed to come from the very earth itself.

Closing my eyes, I searched the banks and river with my mind. Only this time with my mind searching for him, I was able to cover more ground than three dorabills together could fly.

No, Thalia. Don't search with your mind, Faraway corrected. *Search with your heart.*

How, Faraway?

In my mind, my fears began to take control, and I sounded like a little girl who was lost.

Think of Kael, remember Kael, and your heart will find him.

Taking a deep breath, I released my fears and concentrated on Kael, the stony demeanor that he always showed people. I thought of him in his favorite unapproachable position, leaning against a wall, with arms crossed. Of his incomparable fighting skills and how he was unmatched in battle. How honor was everything to him. I tried to remember every SwordBrother detail about him, and I got nothing.

No, Thalia. Not Kael the SwordBrother, Kael the man.

It was then that I let the floodgates open. I thought of Kael, and all the feelings I had tried to keep hidden burst forth. Kael, who comforted me and held me through the storm, keeping my nightmares at bay. Kael holding his hand playfully over my mouth; Kael watching over me, making sure I was eating and sneaking me bits of mint leaf. I thought of the way Kael embraced me outside the Jesai home, and how worried he was for my safety. How he fought off a pack of wild dogs to save me, and how he liked to tease me to get me mad. Kael, who was my protector and friend.

Everything I remembered made me miss him more, and tears poured down my face, though they dried almost instantly because of the wind. I had almost given up when I felt a pull on my spirit so light I almost ignored it. When it came again, I snapped my attention in the direction of the pull and sought with my sight. We were flying under Skyfell, and shadows covered the ground and made it hard to see. Then I felt it again, and it was above me. Looking up, all I saw was darkness on the underside of the city.

"Joss, fly higher," I yelled into his ear, and pointed up. With a quick command from Joss, Cecili started to climb higher, and I vision-searched again until I saw movement, barely discernible against the outcroppings of the city.

It looked like one of the farmers who harvested the plants that grew on the underside of the city, but then I realized this person had no harness attached.

"Joss, there!" I screamed and pointed, and he flew. It was another thirty seconds before we reached a point where we could see with the human eye what I had seen by vision-searching. Flying closer, we saw that a man was gripping various rock outcroppings and was slowly, very slowly, trying to climb up the side of the city.

"It's Kael—he's alive!" I cried in relief. Somehow Kael was, by sheer strength alone, holding his body weight and scaling the city. But he was exhausted; he had probably been out here all night, holding on to the rocks to survive. If he slipped or let go, it was certain death. Only a SwordBrother would have the stamina or the stubbornness to attempt what Kael was doing.

"Hold on, Kael," Joss yelled, and flew Cecili up and under him.

Kael looked at us in shock and he tried to smile, but I could see that the effort was costing him. He was scraped up, bloody, bruised, and tired.

"Joss, can Cecili hold all three of us?"

"Not for long, she can't! But we can't leave him there. He could fall if I go for help." But Joss did what he could and flew up practically underneath Kael. Cecili bobbed up and down, and I reached up to touch Kael's back.

"Kael, we are right under you. Give me your hand." I tried to steady him so he could release the ledge and grab onto us, but Kael's hands were frozen, his muscles so strained that he had problems moving. He looked stiff and mechanical releasing the wall and giving me his arm.

"Come on, Kael, I've got you," I said in the calmest voice I could as he turned and viewed the distance between him and the giant bird. No matter how close we flew, he was still going to have to jump. There was no way to fly closer without injuring her. Kael looked at me, and I felt as if I were drowning in his eyes. There was so much emotion deep inside them, and I felt as if I could read his mind. But then the rock Kael was holding on to came loose from the cliff, and I could see his eyes widen in surprise as he lost his grip.

"Jump, Kael. Jump!" Joss yelled. And Kael did, despite his sore and stiff muscles. He jumped toward the dorabill and landed on his stomach behind me across the bird's back. There was a struggle as Kael reached for something to hold on to but found nothing, and then he started to slide down the side of the dorabill.

I screamed his name and lunged for Kael, grasping his arm as his hands grabbed onto mine. The jerk of his weight pulled me down, and I started to slide off the dorabill. "Kael!" I grunted as the tears I was crying earlier fell down my chin to land on his face. "Hold on! Don't let go."

Joss tried to reach behind him to grab onto Kael, but he couldn't do it and fly Cecili. "Just get us down," I screamed, and Cecili started to descend. But it knocked us around, and I was getting pulled farther and farther sideways. I couldn't hold him. We were both going to fall. I was going to lose Kael, and he knew it. I saw the realization in his eyes.

"Thalia," Kael called softly. "Let me go."

"No!" I snarled back at him, the way he had snarled at me plenty of times before. "I don't want to lose you."

"You have to, or we're both going to fall."

"I'm not letting go." But just then Cecili hit an updraft, and we jerked and I screamed as I fell farther. Joss grabbed my belt to hold me as much as he could in my seat.

"Thalia. If you care for me at all, you will let me go."

"That doesn't make any sense."

"I couldn't live with myself if I were the cause of your death," Kael argued, and before I could reply, he wrenched his hands from my grasp and let go.

~28~

"Kael, no!" I screamed, and it was just like before when he fell. "JOSS! HELP HIM!"

Joss reached out his hand, and I saw him glow with power. All of a sudden the speck of black that was Kael's falling figure disappeared through the mists. Cecili screamed and flew sideways as Joss, drained and sick from using so much power, collapsed forward, startling the dorabill. Joss was unconscious.

Grabbing Joss and holding him in his seat, I leaned forward around him and tried to grab Cecili's neck. She was panicking, with the floppy dead weight on her back and the inconsistent directions I was giving her. I didn't know how to guide her.

"Whoa, girl. Steady, girl," I called, as if I were talking to a horse. When that didn't work, I tried to force a mind connection like I had done with Faraway and the wolf. It worked, and I was instantly dizzy as everything came into focus. I tried to show her mind what I wanted. Cecili's flying steadied, and we were still descending at a very fast rate. She let out a screech right before we landed, and she stumbled but recovered.

Joss and I fell from her back in a heap on the ground. I rolled Joss over to check on him. He was breathing, and his color was healthy. Other than being physically exhausted, he was fine.

Jumping up, I scanned the surrounding area, and saw the dark clothing of Kael farther up the riverbank. Running toward him, I fell to my knees and touched his face and his chest to see if he was still breathing. He was. Joss had saved him.

"Kael, are you all right?" Kael's dark hair was wet from the mists, and his knuckles and hands were bleeding. His shirt and vest were ripped, and numerous knives were missing from his belt. Kael had yet to open his eyes. Slowly Kael's stormy eyes opened, and they were the most beautiful sight I had ever seen.

"Am I dead?" he asked, looking at me in confusion. "Are we dead?" He dropped his head back down into the grass and groaned. "We are. Stubborn girl. Why didn't you let go of me? Why did you have to die, too?" Kael turned away from me and looked as if he were in pain.

"Kael, you're not dead. We're not dead. Joss saved you."

"Yeah, right. Why would that young puppy want to save me?" He groaned as he tried to move again. But I placed my hand over his mouth to stop him from talking.

"Just take pleasure in the fact that you're alive. It doesn't matter in the least how." I smiled at him.

Kael studied me, and I could see fire burning in his eyes. Before I could ask him if he was all right, he grabbed my hand, covering his mouth. He reached up with the other to grasp my neck and did something completely unexpected. He pulled me toward him and kissed me. It wasn't a peck on the lips, either, but a real full-fledged, spine-tingling kiss. I was shocked. At first I resisted, until I felt the need and the desperation he was pouring into the kiss, and then I gave in.

My heart fluttered and pounded loudly, my blood rushed, and I felt an almost electric current rush through the kiss. It was intoxicating. Here, Kael was telling me how he felt and not hiding it behind puzzles and stoic faces.

When I finally came to my senses, I pulled away from the kiss. Kael's eyes were filled with passion.

A cough alerted me to the presence of an audience, and I scooted back to see an angry Joss, blond hair blowing, standing over us with the rest of the search team.

My cheeks burned red in embarrassment, and Joss just glared at Kael, who slowly, painfully stood up and glared right back in challenge.

"I save your life, and this is the thanks I get," Joss growled, and pushed Kael in the chest hard.

Kael just grinned. "No, this is the thanks she gets for saving me. I didn't know that you were feeling left out," Kael said, goading Joss, looking for a fight.

"You know that we are intended. How could you do this?" Joss stepped toward me, and Kael gripped my elbow, pulling me behind him possessively.

"No, I know that you were pretending. Remember? I never heard you actually ask for her, just demanded, more like it." Kael stepped toward Joss threateningly.

"Stop it, both of you," I yelled. Joss and Kael both looked at me, and I saw the hurt in Joss' eyes and the possessiveness in Kael's, which confused me. "This is not the time or the place."

When I couldn't think of anything else to say, I turned my back and walked away. I didn't want to have this conversation in front of an audience. The rest of the search party had landed and had drawn the attention of the villagers of Skydown. People were popping up all around us to stare and gawk.

I knew that was coming, Faraway said, his soft laughter tickling my senses as he sent a picture of Kael and me kissing back at me.

Oh, no, you didn't, I mentally argued back.

It's inevitable.

It's inexcusable.

It's entertaining?

It's what? I choked.

Faraway snorted. *This isn't over between them and will make for a very entertaining trip back to Haven.*

Wait, how do you know we are going to Haven?

Where else are you going to take the girl?

I had almost forgotten that Faraway listened in on the thoughts of other Denai if they didn't properly shield. I had a very nosy horse.

You're right. Since Talbot got away, that is our best bet in getting answers about where Tenya is. Adept Lorna can read her mind for lies, and they will know what to do with her.

Suddenly I felt old, tired, and sore, since I had fallen quite awkwardly from the dorabill to the ground. But we were still a few miles away from the cliffs and the path up to the skycage lift. And for once, I really didn't feel like walking. But I also didn't feel like flying on the dorabill again.

Slowing my pace, I tried to listen in on the heated argument between Kael and Joss.

"So you fell and let him get away?" Joss snorted.

"I did not fall. I followed him and saw him harness himself into a skite and then jump off the northern launch point. I grabbed a skite that was outside someone's home and attempted to go after him."

"I figured as much when we spoke with Bartus and he said he was missing a broken skite. I thought you must have stolen it," Joss said, putting emphasis on the word *stolen*.

"Borrowed," Kael interrupted. "But now I owe that family a new one, because I crashed it into the side of the cliff. I could tell something was wrong with it as soon as I jumped, but I saw the Raven disappearing into the mists, and I had to go after him. It wasn't until I tried to steer that I realized my mistake."

"Ha! The SwordBrother just admitted to making a mistake. Write this down—no one will ever believe me," Joss chuckled and jokingly punched one of the men next him. Kael just held his tongue.

A curious listener, one who turned out to be the other skycage operator, asked, "You're a SwordBrother? How did you survive and not fall to your death?" He was obviously in awe of the SwordBrother, despite Joss' ribbing.

Kael glanced at the man only briefly before he searched for me in the crowd and caught my backward glance. "I was nearing my limit and needed to turn back instead of go forward. So I tried to maneuver the skite back toward Skyfell."

"But that was suicide. You should have tried to ride the wind out and attempt to land. Then you would have—" A different listener from the gathering crowd had spoken up and immediately quit speaking when he saw Kael's dark look.

"It was falling like a rock. The wings were damaged, so I tried to aim it toward Skyfell. Luckily the skite crashed into a crop of tanglewood vines, and I was able to grab on before it fell to the ground."

A larger man who was chewing on what looked to be a piece of straw spoke up; from his dress he was definitely a farmer from Skydown. "Ahoy, those tanglewoods be the strongest vines in the world. They can only be harvested from underneath our city. You were lucky, lad, very lucky."

"Well, they saved my life, and I was able to anchor myself quite comfortably with them and wait out the night. But with morning I had yet to see anyone, so I had to get to a higher spot where someone could see me. So I started climbing."

By now I had stopped walking completely and watched the crowd of people from Skydown and Skyfell gather around Kael in awe and barrage him with questions.

Kael looked uncomfortable with all of the attention he was getting. The crowds of people that surrounded him and pressed in to touch his arms, his clothes, made him nervous, and I could see him sweat. All of it was harmless, but to a trained bodyguard and assassin who was used to looking for hidden knives and attack at every turn, this was his worst nightmare. Something he couldn't defend against, innocent and curious bystanders. I could only imagine that right now he wished they were a mob of angry attackers. He knew how to ward off those.

Joss looked angry. He was the one who had saved Kael, and yet Kael was getting all of the attention.

"Come on." Joss grabbed my arm and blew on his flute to call Cecili. The dorabill, who had been scratching in a hillside looking for rabbits, much like a chicken would look for bugs, looked up and flew over to Joss. Grabbing my arm, he swung me up behind him and took off into the air with Cecili.

"What about Kael?" I asked, worried that we had left him there in a mob of people. I wasn't worried about Kael but about the bystanders, who could get injured.

"He'll be fine. He's a SwordBrother. He can handle himself." That was the only thing Joss said the entire flight to his home.

~29~

Ⅰt was good to be riding Faraway again. I really missed him, and being away from him felt like I was missing a part of myself. Talking to Faraway made me feel less crazy. He was able to pull me out of the spiral of negative feelings and doubts that I could send myself down sometimes. And the trip from Skyfell to Haven was everything that my horse had promised it would be and then some.

We hadn't stayed long in the Jesai home once Joss had brought us back. A day and a half later, we were on the road to Haven. Kael had finally made it back as well, but he looked like a cat that had all of its fur rubbed the wrong way. He was definitely on edge and kept staring daggers at Joss. A meeting was soon called. After an hour of discussion, it was decided that the best thing to do was take Mona to the Adepts to have them interrogate her, and then take an army to flush out the rest of the Septori and their leader.

Gloria spoke up from her chair in the main room. "I would feel much better if you took more people with you." Now that she was no longer under Mona's influence, she had regained her strength and was sitting in the same overstuffed chair with pillows that Hemi had designated as his favorite.

She kept apologizing to me every chance she could for the way she had treated me.

"You have to understand, I wasn't me. I wasn't really saying those things. I think you are adorable and would be honored to have you in our family." Since our last encounter, I had done my very best to avoid her at all costs. Well, except for this family meeting.

Nero was the one to counter Gloria's worrying. "We've discussed this, darling." He walked over to Gloria and gently put his hands on her shoulders. She raised her hand to grasp Nero's.

"It's just that I'm so worried for them. I don't want anything to happen to my boy." She looked over at Joss, and he rolled his eyes. "You don't understand how hard it was for me to know what she was doing to me and not be able to stop it. There were times where I blacked out and had no memories. But other times I didn't, and it was horrible." Her eyes widened in fear. "What if she is able to do it again to you?"

"I do understand. I know what it's like, and so does Kael. I think we will be extra careful because of it." In reality, I didn't want to be anywhere near Mona, and this whole idea of transporting her made me sick to my stomach.

Kael stepped forward and held up a pouch containing the seeds found in Mona's room. "This is the seed that, when shaved and boiled, in small doses can be infused in drinks and teas to initiate mind control. Also, it can be concentrated and used to create paralysis. I will be the one administering this to Mona to keep her docile while we travel."

A few more weak arguments came forward from Gloria, but they were quickly set aside as a knock came on the door and Darren entered.

"We are ready," he announced to the room, giving Nero a nod and bowing to Gloria.

It had been decided that Berry and Avina would stay and leave a week after we did in case any of the Septori were following us. Neither one of them was happy about it. After a few fits from Avina, Nero finally offered to teach her to fly a skite during her and Berry's stay. That sealed the deal.

Darren would come with us as far as Haven and then return home to his Melani. Fanny surprised us the most with her argument to come with us.

"It is my invention that did this, and I feel that I need to speak with the Queen and the Adepts to defend what I had done. I don't want there to be any repercussions on my family. Also, I may be able to answer their questions better if I am there in person. And you will need another female to take care of your prisoner."

"We are going to be traveling fast. Can you be ready to go in an hour?" Kael looked over at Fanny, and I originally thought he was going to deny her request like Berry and Avina's. But he must have seen her stubbornness and determination.

"I'm ready to go now. I'm already packed. My bag is at the bottom of the stairs," Fanny answered smartly, her copper hair bouncing as she motioned with her head down the stairs. "If you had told me no, I was going to follow you anyway."

Kael nodded impressed. "You'll do."

What also impressed Kael was when Hemi and Fanny brought Mona to the Jesais'. Fanny had fashioned handcuffs lined with leather and various lengths of chain.

"That won't hold a Denai," Darren had scoffed.

Fanny raised her eyebrows in challenge. "Care to try them on? They can mute a Denai power more than the misty veils." Darren and everyone in the room dropped their mouths in disbelief.

"I've never heard of anything like that," Nero muttered.

"Nonsense, the knowledge has been around for hundreds of years, but many people forgot how to forge them.

It's a special technique passed down through my family. I will not be sharing this one, thank you very much. But I thought it would help us."

That had finalized our traveling party of Darren, Hemi, Fanny, Mona, Kael, Joss, and me. Joss had not spoken to me, other than to ask if I was ready to leave, since the awkward kiss with Kael. I hadn't sought him out, either, to discuss what had happened between him and Mona.

It was never the right time or place, but the road to Haven left us plenty of awkward silences to fill.

I tended to ride next to Darren as much as possible, but that meant I was right in the middle of the pack. Kael refused to allow me to ride rear guard in case of attack, but he also didn't want me near Mona.

Hemi and Fanny were designated as Mona's personal guard. Hemi volunteered because the obvious threat to me came from Mona, so he wanted to keep a personal eye on her. I also couldn't help but wonder if my fearsome clansman was starting to get sweet on Fanny. The strong, silent warrior would tend to get even more quiet and awkward whenever the strong-willed, copper-haired woman came near him.

I couldn't help smiling as Hemi blushed bright red, as red as his beard, when she leaned close and whispered something to him.

"Now, that's the first smile I've seen on your face in three days." Darren chuckled as he turned his head to study me. "You've been quiet."

"I've been thinking," I intoned.

"Careful, that could be dangerous to your health," Darren said out of the side of his mouth, eyes twinkling.

I couldn't help but laugh. That was why I loved Darren, his easygoing manner and quick wit.

"No, I'm not kidding," he chuckled as he nodded toward Kael and Joss riding front guard, both of them with backs straight as they rode. Neither one was willing to pick up with small talk. "I know what you are thinking about, and upsetting those two could be hazardous to all of our health."

Tongue in cheek, I agreed with a silent nod. He was right. We were all walking a very narrow tightrope, and no one wanted to upset anything. But we would have to talk, and soon.

"The sooner you speak with them, the better, Little Fish. None of us wants to drown in the tidal waves of the storm that's brewing." Darren had slipped back into calling me the nickname that Joss and he had given me when we'd first met. They had fished me out of a river and saved my life after my escape from the Septori.

"Darren, can I tell you something that I haven't told anyone yet?"

"You can tell me anything. I know how to keep a secret." He made a motion of putting a lock in his mouth and throwing away the key.

"I don't think Talbot was the Raven."

"What do you mean? He admitted it, didn't he?"

"I know, I think he was there. No, I know he was there in the room. It's just..." I was finding it so hard to explain the terrible feeling I was having in the pit of my stomach. "The more I think about it, the more I'm convinced he was there, but he's not the Raven."

"You're joking, right?"

I shook my head. "I'm remembering more and more as time passes and I'm having these dreams. Talbot is too short to be the Raven. Or at least, he was too short some of the time."

"Thalia, girl, you're not making any sense."

"No, I'm making perfect sense. Every night, the Raven wore a silver hook-nosed mask, and he always had other fellow

Septori in the room who were hidden by hoods. Sometimes his voice was high, other times it was raspy. Sometimes he was taller, while other times he felt short, but never as short as Talbot. I don't know—maybe I'm crazy."

"You are not crazy, and I think you should spit out what is plaguing you."

"It's something my uncle had said about a master and apprentice. Also how Talbot used the words 'us' and 'we.' I think there are multiple Septori posing as the Raven. I think they are duplicating these experiments in various places and traveling between them. We've already encountered quite a few Septori, but now we have to kill the heads."

"That is quite a secret."

I sighed, feeling better. "Thanks for listening."

"When are you going to tell the others?" He nodded toward Kael and Joss.

"Soon. As soon as I'm absolutely certain. But what I am certain of is that we've probably already met the Raven, whoever he or she is, and Talbot is taking the fall for his master."

"Let's just pray that the Adepts can help."

"Yes," I said slowly chewing on the inside of my cheek in thought. "The Adepts."

We had accomplished a lot in a few short days. We had saved Gloria and captured Mona. She would hopefully, with the help of a truth serum, tell us how to find the rest of the Septori and the Raven. Granted, we hadn't found Joss' sister yet, but I knew we would. I could feel it in my bones. I knew she had to be alive, and I knew that I would be the one to find her.

But first we had to take Mona to Adept Lorna, and then I would hunt her down and find the Raven—all of them. It was time, and I wasn't going to be afraid anymore. I was definitely not the same person I had been a year ago, or even two years ago. Now, I was a powerful Denai with a vengeance.

The search for the Septori was only beginning. Even now I could tell I was still changing: the fevers, lack of appetite, headaches, etc. Talbot confirmed it. I was evolving into a stronger monster. The Septori had made me into what I was today. And now it was time for me to hunt down my makers and kill them. The master and apprentice.

Chanda Hahn takes her experience as a children's pastor, children's librarian and bookseller to write compelling and popular fiction for teens. She was born in Seattle, WA, grew up in Nebraska and currently resides in Portland, Oregon with her husband and their twin children; Aiden and Ashley. Visit Chanda Hahn's website to learn more about her forthcoming books.

www.chandahahn.com

Also by Chanda Hahn

The Iron Butterfly
The Steele Wolf

Unfortunate Fairy Tale Series
UnEnchanted
Fairest
Fable

Special Thanks

I want to say a special thanks to everyone who took part in the process of helping me with the Steele Wolf, whether you were a reader, editor, encourager, or critic. Thanks to Philip Hahn, Steve Hahn, Jane Hawkey, Alison Brace and Richlie Fikes. I have the best team ever.

5/15

11846830R00161

Made in the USA
San Bernardino, CA
01 June 2014